DIRTY
MONEY

A Chase Adams FBI Thriller

Book 5

Patrick Logan

Books by Patrick Logan

Detective Damien Drake

Book 1: Butterfly Kisses

Book 2: Cause of Death

Book 3: Download Murder

Book 4: Skeleton King

Book 5: Human Traffic

Book 6: Drug Lord: Part One

Book 7: Drug Lord: Part Two

Dr. Beckett Campbell, ME

Book 0: Bitter End

Book 1: Organ Donor

Book 2: Injecting Faith

Book 3: Surgical Precision

The Haunted Series

Book 1: Shallow Graves

Book 2: The Seventh Ward

Book 3: Seaforth Prison

Book 4: Scarsdale Crematorium

Book 5: Sacred Heard Orphanage

Book 6: Shores of the Marrow

Book 7: Sacrifice

Prologue

SIX MONTHS AGO

"Look at this asshole," Senator Tom DeBrusk said, his eyes locked on the giant billboard overhanging Massachusetts Avenue. "Fucking hell... goddamn talking head... how do you think this douchebag William Woodley can afford a sign like this?"

"I don't know, sir," the driver answered.

"Well, I know. *Fifteen trillion dollars in debt and you're putting your faith in the government to run our businesses?* Well, part of that debt is from financing your sign, you TMZ wannabe."

The billboard containing William Woodley's giant, hairless face, threatened to sour Tom's mood, but he wouldn't let it. Besides the fact that it was probably designed just to piss him off, today was a good day. A *great* day.

And nothing would change that.

"Pull over," he instructed. When the driver didn't immediately do as he asked, he leaned forward and tapped the man on the shoulder. "Simon, pull over here, please."

"Excuse me, sir?"

Tom turned his attention to the window and leveled a finger at the Dunkin' Donuts that they were just passing.

"Need a coffee. Can't stand the sludge they pass off as coffee in the Capitol. Shit, the president's taste in coffee is almost as bad as his taste in ties."

"Sir, the vote on the Senate floor is scheduled in less than an hour," Simon said, but even as he spoke, he pulled the black Lincoln over to the side of the road.

"They'll wait. Trust me on this one, they'll wait. This is my moment of glory, Simon. I'm going to enjoy this."

"Yes, sir," Simon said, reaching for his door. "One cream, one sugar?" he asked.

Tom shook his head.

"Sit tight, I'll get it," Tom said, "You want anything?"

Simon shook his head.

"No, sir. Thank you, sir."

Tom knew that Simon wanted to get him his coffee, but this was *his* day. He was gonna get some sun on his face, maybe even grab a cruller to go with his coffee. A *honey* cruller.

As he tucked the dark blue binder under his arm and stepped from the car, he wondered if there were any other types of crullers.

Chocolate cruller? Powder cruller? Jam cruller?

That would be good… a cruller filled with jam.

He was so lost in thought, considering different types of crullers, that he nearly tripped over a woman pushing a stroller.

"Sorry, ma'am," he offered with a smile. His apology was met with a sneer.

Top of the mornin' to you too, m'lady.

Tom reached for the door to the Dunkin' Donuts when a sound from behind him drew his attention.

It was a buzzing sound, a persistent whir that reminded him of an electric lawnmower. Confused, he noted that Simon had stepped from the car and was also looking around.

"Simon? You hear—"

And then he saw it: hovering roughly fifteen or twenty feet above his car was a drone. It was roughly the size of a paperback—a thick paperback of the George R.R. Martin doorstop variety—with four blades that held it suspended in midair.

Tom tilted his head as he stared at the spinning blades. Something in the back of his mind told him that he should get inside, that nearly all of Washington, DC, was a no-fly zone, but he was intrigued, hypnotized even.

"Sir?" he heard Simon say.

There's a camera on the drone, Tom realized. As if the machine had read his thoughts, the gimbal holding the camera spun and focused directly on his face.

This was no amateur drone operator who'd accidentally stumbled upon a US senator on what was to be his greatest day as a politician. No, this was deliberate, planned.

"Shit," Tom grumbled, scrambling to pull the door to Dunkin' Donuts wide.

He never heard the shots. In fact, he didn't even hear the boiling of air as the high-speed rifle rounds accelerated toward him.

Something struck the binder under his arm, and he looked down at it, a confused expression on his face.

There was a smoldering silver-dollar-sized hole in the center of The Great Seal. Tom pulled the binder away from his body and was shocked to see a similar sized hole in his suit jacket.

"What the—"

Something struck him in the chest, knocking him backward. He tried to stay on his feet, but it was suddenly difficult to breathe. Tom DeBrusk's grip on the door failed and he slid to the ground. With blood spilling from the two wounds, he slumped into a seated position with his legs out in front of him.

The last thing Senator Tom DeBrusk heard was that strange whirring sound. The last thing Senator Tom DeBrusk saw was the drone ascending to the heavens.

PART I – Broken

SIX MONTHS AGO

Chapter 1

"SHE DOWN THERE, HOLE number two."

Jeremy Stitts took a drag of his cigarette and surveyed the quarry. It had long since been abandoned, and now served as a surrogate garbage dump for the local residents.

Which made it the perfect place for Chase Adams to go and die.

Rock Quarry Two was about a hundred yards to his left, marked with a sun-weathered sign that was only just legible. Stitts swallowed hard and turned to the dope fiend who was looking up at him with bloodshot eyes.

"You sure?"

The man nodded vigorously, and he ran his tongue across his festering lips. He held a filthy hand out to Stitts.

"I'm sure. They be saying she's been here for two days, at least."

Stitts glanced down at the man's filthy palm, making no effort to hide his disgust.

Two days? The last two days had been miserable; it had rained nonstop and twice the temperatures had dipped to below forty degrees.

He couldn't imagine someone being out in the quarry overnight, let alone for two days.

It wasn't just possible that the fiend was lying to him, but likely. After all, every one of his other inquiries had led to dead ends.

Still, he had to keep looking.

Shaking his head, Stitts pulled the cigarette from his lips and then brought the fingers of his opposite hand to his mouth and whistled shrilly.

"Over here! Quarry number two!"

The three men and one woman who were congregating around a Tesla Model X, looked over at him, identical expressions of concern on their faces. Like Stitts, they too were tired; tired of wild goose chases and tips that led nowhere.

But, also like Stitts, they were unwilling to give up.

One of the men, a man with a goatee and short blond hair, knocked on the car window. A fourth man, this one sporting an expensive-looking suit, stepped out.

And then they started in Stitts's direction, moving at a clipped pace.

Stitts waved again and then he turned in the direction of quarry number two.

"Hey, man, you going to—"

Stitts cast a glance over his shoulder and saw that not only had the fiend extended his grubby hand, but he was now rubbing his thumb and forefinger together.

Stitts scowled and the fiend's expression suddenly changed, his eyes going wide.

"Hey man, you promised, you said if—"

Stitts reached back and shoved the man in the chest. Beneath the soiled sweatshirt, the addict was rail thin and he stumbled backward, only by some sheer miracle managing not to fall on his ass.

"I promised not to throw you in jail. Now get the fuck outta here before I change my mind."

The addict's eyes narrowed, but when Stitts took another step forward, he just shook his head and turned away, mumbling something about pigs.

Moments later, the man in the lead, who had bleach-blond hair and was carrying a medical bag in one hand, made it to Stitts.

"What's Hunter S. Thompson's problem?" the man asked.

"A handout," Stitts grumbled, turning back to quarry number two. "They always want a handout. Says that she's in number two, but I doubt it. Probably just thought he could drag me out here and rob me. Probably never even seen her before."

He took another drag of his cigarette.

"You go… just in case."

The man with the blond hair nodded.

He understood.

If Chase *was* in the quarry, and she was indeed dead, he didn't think he could see her. After everything that had happened, everything they'd been through together, he didn't know if he would ever get over seeing her like that.

"Fuck," he grumbled, flicking the cigarette butt.

"You stay here," the man said. "I'll check it out."

Stitts nodded and watched him leave. A moment later, a hand came down on his shoulder. He didn't turn.

"S-s-special A-a-a-agent Stitts, are you o-okay?"

Stitts didn't reply. He couldn't. In fact, breathing had suddenly become difficult.

For the better part of three months, Stitts had devoted nearly every waking hour to searching for Chase. For half of that time, he'd worked alone, but there'd been just too many crack dens and trap houses to search. Too many addicts hiding in alleyways, too many dope fiends squatting in abandoned buildings.

In the end, he'd needed help. Chase thought she was alone in this world, and Stitts didn't blame her; after what had happened to her all those years ago, and what happened when she finally found her sister again, it was too heavy a burden for one person to bear.

But that's where she was wrong.

Chase wasn't alone. For one, she had him. But that wasn't all; she'd made an impact on others as well.

Stitts sighed and looked over at Floyd Montgomery. His usually goofy expression had hardened into something more serious.

He didn't think he'd ever seen the man look like this before.

"I'll be fine," Stitts said as he reached for another cigarette.

The others had arrived now, and Stitts looked at all of them as he lit his smoke.

The first was Louisa, the person who had perhaps the most in common with Chase, having been kidnapped by the same men who'd taken her and her sister. Both had run.

Both struggled with addiction.

The man in the fancy suit was Stu Barnes. The wealthy millionaire that Chase had managed to convince to give her two million dollars after only meeting him twice.

And then there was Screech. Screech, who Stitts had a better relationship with than his curmudgeonly partner, a man who'd also undergone significant changes since their time in New York. Screech had gone from a low-level tech analyst to someone who had witnessed things that, well, quite frankly, no man who spends most of his days behind a computer had any business seeing.

Dead sex slaves, mass poisonings, prison breaks, and gangland murder.

Yeah, Chase touched a lot of people in her life. She meant something to them, too.

And she meant a lot to him, of course.

There was only one man who was missing from their crew, one who'd worked closely with Chase for —

"She's alive!" someone shouted from behind Stitts. "Help! *Help!* She's alive! Goddamnit, Chase is in here and she's *alive!*"

Stitts spun so quickly that the cigarette fell from his lips. And then he was off and running toward Rock Quarry Number 2 and Dr. Beckett Campbell's voice.

Chapter 2

FLASH

Stitts's face, coming close to hers, their lips meeting, his tongue probing.

Flash

Blood. Blood on her hands, blood on her wrists and forearms.Blood soaking the front of her white dress.
Her knuckles raw, sliced, her palms shredded.

Flash

Georgina's face, round and cherubic, looking up at her with watery eyes.
"Don't leave me, Chase. Please, don't leave me."

Flash

A fdirty needle, the syringe filled with a yellow, murky substance. The rim around the insertion point, raw and red. A shaking hand—*Is it mine? Is that my hand?*—a thumb with a filthy nail pushing the plunger. A tremor, then relief.

Flash

"You're going to be okay," said a disembodied voice, coming from the ether. A flicker, then brown eyes, a shaved head, a wispy goatee. A young man, someone she should recognize, but doesn't. "Hang in there, Chase."

Flash

Handsome, older. A perfectly manicured white beard. A bespoke suit. Her hand shoots out and she fumbles with the man's belt. She tries to get inside his pants, tries to grab a hold of him, but he pulls back and fades into the darkness.

Flash

Incredible pain. Eyeballs that feel as if they are going to explode. An itching so intense that she wants to take a cheese grater to her skin, to tear it all off so that she could get at the creatures beneath. The millions of tiny insects—ticks, fleas, spiders, millipedes—that are feasting on her from the inside. Grinding her teeth so hard that a fine powder coats her tongue.Seizing. Her back arching, her toes curling. A moment of sheer ecstasy.And then more pain.

Flash

"Shock her, shock her! She's going into cardiac arrest. Give her a jolt!"
A beep. A blur. Another tremor.

Flash

"You were never there, Chase. You got away. You ran."
A lightning bolt inside her brain. The taste of burnt rubber in her mouth.
"You got away. That's what happened, Chase. They took your sister, but you got away."

Flash

A man with a bomb strapped to his chest, his thumb on the dead man trigger. A woman carrying matchsticks and duct tape in one hand, a beer bottle tucked into the belt of her pants. A man with his forehead caved in, but somehow still grinning. He's clutching a cast-iron pan in one hand and it's sizzling. The smell of burning meat in the air.

A man in blue overalls, huge aviator sunglasses covering most of his face. Crooked, yellow, nicotine-stained teeth.

Flash

Felix.

Flash

Her husband Brad.

Flash

Drake.

Flash

Stitts.

Flash

Georgina…

Chapter 3

"YOU ALMOST DIED, CHASE," Stitts said. "In fact, you were... shit, never mind. We're not gonna do this like last time. Last time didn't work. And I won't sit around and watch you kill yourself."

Chase snarled and stared up at the man. Stitts looked nearly as haggard as she felt; he had huge dark circles around his eyes and his lips were chapped something fierce. He also fidgeted like a fiend—only she was fairly certain that his drug wasn't heroin like hers, but nicotine.

"I never asked you to watch me. I don't need you to—"

Stitts surprised her by reaching out and grabbing her shoulder tightly.

She tried to squirm away, but the hospital bed on which she lay was too small and the best she could do was deepen her scowl.

"You *do* need me, Chase. You need me, and I need you. And there are others out there, others that need you, too, Chase. Others who don't want to see you dead."

Chase closed her eyes and took a deep breath. Stitts relaxed his grip on her shoulder.

Her memories since fleeing her apartment in Virginia were foggy at best.

She recalled returning to the trap house that Louisa had nearly overdosed in, and she remembered shooting up.

But everything after that was a blur.

At some point, Chase thought she saw people she knew, the faces of people that she'd come across over the years, but that could have just as easily been a drug-induced dream.

Or nightmare.

She shuddered.

"This self-destructive streak has to end, Chase," Stitts said in a quiet voice. She opened her eyes. There was a deep sadness in her partner's face. A brooding pain that ran deep.

As there should be, she thought. *He lied to me. He's been lying to me since the moment he met me in New York City. He lied to me, and he can't be trusted.*

"This *isn't* going to be like before; this *isn't* a simple outpatient procedure. You're going to stay here, Chase. You're going to stay here until you get better. And you're going to do everything and anything that Dr. Matteo tells you to do. He wants you to walk on water? You're going to do it. He wants to call you Ma'am and be your protector? You're going to let him. He wants you to go to NA meetings for the rest of your life? You'll be there."

Chase's scowl returned.

Who is this man standing before me? It most definitely isn't the handsome, introspective man who profiled for the FBI. This guy... this guy is an asshole.

A grade A asshole.

"Or what, Stitts?" she responded reflexively. "You gonna call my mommy? My pops? Get me in trouble? Put me in time-out?"

All of a sudden, Stitts's hardened expression softened and he looked away.

There he is. That's Stitts. That's the man I remember. Not the other one, the greasy, leathery Cheerio of an asshole.

"What? You already called my daddy? Is he on his way?"

She was prodding him, deliberately trying to get a response, but Stitts wasn't biting. Either he had more resolve than she remembered, or —

All of the scorn suddenly left her voice, and Chase reached out and touched his arm.

"What, Stitts? What is it?"

A deep, body-wracking sigh, and then he finally looked at her.

"The doctor said not to tell you, but I won't lie to you again, Chase. I made a promise to myself, that I'd never lie to you again. What I did—"

Chase dug her nails into the man's forearm.

"Get to the fucking point, Stitts. What doesn't the doc want you to tell me?"

Stitts took another deep breath.

"Your dad... your dad's dead, Chase."

Chase's eyes bulged.

"He's... what?"

She'd heard what he said, of course. Only, she couldn't believe it.

Chase pictured her father in her mind, not the way he was now—overweight with gray and thinning hair—but the way he'd been back *then*. Ruggedly handsome, devoutly religious, but a man who liked his beer.

It had been some time since she'd seen him. In fact, after Chase had gone her own way in Seattle, her contact with both her father and mother had been sporadic at best.

She knew that every time they heard her voice, they were reminded of Georgina. And it stung them; it stung them deeply.

So, she'd shut them out, just like she shut out everyone.

Tears unexpectedly welled, and Chase looked away from Stitts. She stared into the distance, her eyes not registering the myriad of medical equipment that surrounded her or the tubes that seemed to protrude from every one of her orifices.

"He can't be dead," Chase whispered. Tears flowed down her cheeks.

"I'm sorry, Chase. I'm really sorry."

She turned her eyes back to his and saw that he too was crying.

"Was it his heart?" she asked softly.

Stitts looked down and stared at his nicotine-stained fingers.

When he didn't answer, Chase asked him again, more aggressively this time.

"You said you never—"

Stitts's eyes suddenly shot up.

"It wasn't his heart, Chase. Your father... he... your dad committed suicide."

Chapter 4

"I HAVE TO GET out of here," Chase said angrily. "I need to get out of here, now!"

"Chase, you—"

Chase's face suddenly turned red and she felt her blood start to boil. She tried to sit up but was too weak.

"I need to go to the funeral... I need to see my mother... I need to—"

With every ounce of strength she had left, Chase rolled onto her side and tried once more to force herself into a seated position. She failed again, but this time it wasn't because of a lack of energy, but due to the chain that ran from her wrist to the metal frame of the hospital bed.

"What the fuck, Stitts?"

"Chase, your father died six months ago."

Chase was in the process of trying to slide the metal cuff all the way down to the end where there was a break in the guardrail when Stitts said this.

"What?" she gasped, turning slowly back to Stitts. Her head was starting to spin, and she could feel the all too familiar itching sensation again.

"Six months? Six *months*?"

Stitts nodded and then, with a subtle gesture that Chase only just picked up on, motioned with his right hand in the direction of the door.

"When we found you, you were barely alive, Chase. And since then, it's been an up-and-down battle trying to keep you that way. You've been here for almost four months, passing in and out of consciousness. You don't remember talking to me during this time?"

Chase's eyes narrowed.

She had newfound skepticism for everything that Stitts said, especially given her surroundings. It seemed to her that all the things she had once considered as solid as a rock, were more like waves in a pond. Look down one moment, and you're likely to see a trough. A second later, however, and the trough had become something completely different: a hillock.

And that's what her mind and memories had become; instead of permanent invaginations in her gray matter, her brain was just a series of troughs and hillocks. Things were malleable, things changed, things that she had once considered concrete were now transient.

Exhausted, Chase collapsed onto the bed and closed her eyes. Sweat had broken out on her forehead and her entire body suddenly felt clammy.

Six months, six fucking months? Dad died six months ago?

She heard the sound of a door opening, but her eyes remained closed.

"I missed the funeral," she whispered. "Shit... my mom. How's my mom?"

There was a pause and, even though Chase's eyes were still closed, she imagined Stitts's face contorting.

"She's in a home, Chase. She's been... she's been sick for a while. And after everything that happened... she couldn't handle it anymore. Dementia, they say."

Chase shook her head.

It wasn't fair. None of it was fair. It was no secret that her and her mother's relationship had become strained when Georgina never made it home. Her mother hadn't overtly blamed Chase, but the insinuation was always there. As was the guilt.

Chase imagined her mother who once had long, tanned legs that sent men into a frenzy. Now they were pasty and covered in a network of varicose veins, her thickened ankles jammed into the stirrups of a wheelchair.

She'd seen people with broken minds before, of course. She'd seen them in the trap houses when she was undercover, when Tyler Tisdale was still running the show.

Drugs couldn't warp your mind, not on their own. But they excelled at taking a warped mind and pushing it over the edge.

Chase wondered briefly what her mother's drug of choice was, but she didn't have to think that hard. It was a toxic combination of guilt and self-loathing.

There was a tug on her left hand and Chase opened her eyes. At first blush, she thought that the doctor who was fiddling with her IV was Dr. Patterson from all those years ago.

But it wasn't him. The man was probably dead now.

The man injected something into the port on her IV bag without saying a word. It was almost as if he wasn't even there.

Chase tugged her wrist once more and the metal handcuff clanged off the bed frame.

"How long do I have to stay here, Stitts?" she asked.

FBI Special Agent Jeremy Stitts sighed heavily and got to his feet.

"Until you get well, Chase. You're not leaving here until you're well."

Chapter 5

STITTS STEPPED OUT OF Chase's hospital room and then rubbed his eyes. He knew that she was staring at him through the glass as the sedative took hold, but he fought the urge to look back at her.

The right thing to do used to be so cut and dry with him. Now, Stitts found himself second-guessing nearly every decision he made. TBI Director Conway might have been convinced that Stitts had done the right thing by telling Chase the truth about what had happened to her thirty years ago, but he had more doubts than nicotine coursing through his veins.

With a heavy sigh, he started down the hallway. A large orderly who stood just out of sight of Chase's room, arms crossed over his substantial chest, nodded as Stitts passed.

Stitts nodded back.

One thing was for certain; Chase wasn't going anywhere this time.

He was nearly at the front doors when Floyd approached him, a desperate expression on his young face.

"Sh-sh-she g-g-gonna be okay?"

Again, Stitts hesitated. He *wanted* to say yes, to say, yeah, Chase'll be fine, she'll recover, she'll be up on her feet in no time, but he wasn't sure. And he was tired of lying.

Instead, Stitts just shrugged.

Floyd stared at him for a moment but didn't say anything. Two other men suddenly appeared at his side and, for a fleeting moment, Stitts thought they looked a little like a degenerate Boy Band.

"Is she stable?" Screech asked.

Stitts nodded.

"Yeah, she's been sedated again. I think… I think she's starting to come around, though. Remembering things."

"Can we visit?" the man in the suit asked.

Stitts shook his head.

"No, Stu, I don't think so." His eyes darted to Floyd, and then to Screech. "In fact, I honestly don't think there's much more any of you can do here. To be honest, while I want to say that she's incredibly grateful for all you guys have done, all you've sacrificed on her behalf, I don't know if she feels that way. What I do know, is that the doctor thinks that she should be eased back into the present. Seeing all of you guys…"

Stitts held his hands out at his sides and let the sentence trail off.

Floyd exchanged a nervous glance with his bandmates before addressing Stitts.

"I'm going to stay," he said. "I won't see her, though. Not unless you say it's okay."

The fact that Floyd didn't stutter surprised Stitts and he found himself nodding. He figured that this might be okay; he was, after all, the least likely to bring up bad memories. So far as Stitts knew, Chase hadn't hurt Floyd the way she'd hurt the others.

Not yet, at least.

Fearing that the others would fall in line, Stitts took a proactive approach.

"When she's better, I'll tell her what you guys did."

Stu took the hint and nodded.

"I have business I need to attend to back in the desert," he said as he shook Stitts's hand. "If you need anything — including anything with the Bureau, let me know."

"Thank you. And I will."

Screech spoke up next.

"And I have one hell of a mess to clean up in New York. A clusterfuck," he said. Stitts had a sneaking suspicion that this had to do with Drake's absence, and the lame excuse that his partner had offered up for him, but he didn't have the time or the energy to get into it. Stitts knew that Drake had his own problems, not the least of which was the bullshit lie that he'd spun about needing some of Chase's possessions a couple months back.

Her hair, her blood.

After another round of thank yous, Screech hurried after Stu.

"I can take you wherever you want to go," Floyd said when they were finally alone. Stitts was about to politely decline, but then reconsidered; after all, this was what the man did.

He was a driver, and while Stitts couldn't pay him, Chase could. He was about to take him up on the offer, when another man approached, a serious expression on his face.

"Stitts, can I talk to you for a second?" the man asked, running his hand through his blond hair.

Stitts looked over at the doctor and nodded. Then he turned back to Floyd.

"Give me a second, Floyd, then I'll take that ride," then to Beckett, he said, "What? What is it?"

Dr. Beckett Campbell frowned.

"I think we need to speak to Chase's doctor. In private."

Chapter 6

BECKETT LED STITTS INTO a private room. Waiting inside was one of the doctors who had spent considerable time with Chase since her half-dead body was dragged in. He'd saved her life on multiple occasions, including when her heart had stopped from endocarditis.

"Dr. Calderon," Stitts said with a nod. The doctor nodded back but offered nothing in terms of response. This silence made Stitts uneasy.

"What is it? What's going on?"

"We found some anomalies—"

Stitts didn't even hear the rest of the man's sentence.

"No," he moaned.

After everything… after everything she's been through, this is it, he thought miserably. *This is the end. They're gonna tell me that Chase has multiple system organ failures and that she's going to die.*

Beckett reached out and gripped Stitts's shoulder and then shot a scornful glare at Dr. Calderon.

"What Dr. No-Bedside-Manner means to say is that we've found something on her MRI. But it's not fatal, Stitts. Nothing like that. Dr. House, why don't you switch on the monitors instead of giving him a fucking heart attack?"

"What?" Stitts said, confused. "What'd you find on her MRI scan? Beckett, what the fuck is going on?"

His hands were shaking again, and he instinctively reached into his pocket and fondled his pack of cigarettes.

"One sec, it's easier to explain when looking at the scans."

A black and white image of a brain appeared on-screen.

"You can see here, in the amygdala, heightened—" Dr. Calderon began, but Beckett cut him off once more.

"Parlez-vous Anglais?"

"Pardon."

"Just fucking speak English, man, this isn't a neuroimaging conference, for Christ's sake."

"All right, all right. Sorry. So, you know that we gave Chase an MRI when first she came here, right? Well, we actually gave her several during her time here in the hospital to monitor how the parts of her brain that were damaged from her drug use and dehydration were recovering."

Stitts nodded and the doctor continued.

"Well, at first we didn't notice anything dramatic, but then... this."

Dr. Calderon pulled up another image of Chase's brain, this time in a quasi-3D format that Stitts recognized.

He'd seen dozens of these scans on his mother's brain before she'd died.

"So, this is from the first MRI, when Chase first arrived and was barely conscious." He tapped the screen and the program zoomed into an area just behind the forehead. "You can immediately notice that her subcortex—" he cast a furtive glance at Beckett before backtracking— "the, uhh, the area that is more ancient, uhh, from, uh, uh, evolution—fuck—the part responsible for the subconscious, for reactions and feelings and things like that. The less ordered structures."

Stitts made a face.

"What about it?"

"It's bigger than I think I've ever seen before. It's... well, it's, uh, strange, to say the least."

"Show the other one," Beckett instructed.

Dr. Calderon, who seemed more intimidated by Beckett than by the FBI agent standing at his left, quickly minimized the image and called up another one.

It took a moment for Stitts to make sense of the image. It was grainy, of a much lower quality than the previous one.

"Now, back when this scan was taken, the MRI technology was far more primitive. We don't have the same level of detail and Chase's brain was less developed."

"This was taken immediately after she was abducted," Stitts offered. "Before her… *treatment*."

Dr. Calderon swallowed hard and nodded.

"Exactly. As you can see, the area that was enlarged on the recent MRI is normal here. Now, it's entirely possible that these changes were unrelated to what happened to her back then, and they are simply a result of genetics, but it could also be—"

"From the shock treatment," Beckett said. "I've seen something like this before on MRIs from patients in mental institutions that underwent shock treatment. Usually, the enlargements are not so confined, but in Chase's case…"

Stitts turned to the man with the tattoos and blond hair and gaped. He wasn't sure what surprised him more; the fact that Beckett somehow knew about her treatments, or that he was comparing her to a mental patient.

"How do you—how did you find out?"

Beckett shook his head.

"Don't worry about it. But here's the weird thing; Dr. House, show him the most recent MRI."

Dr. Calderon frowned; clearly, he was not in favor of being referred to as an enigmatic and ornery fictional TV character.

But that was the thing about Dr. Beckett Campbell; he didn't give a shit who you were, he was going to be himself no matter what. No slick suits or smooth talking for this man.

And Stitts admired him for it.

"This here is a special type of MRI, one that shows the active parts of the brain. This was given just a few days ago when Chase was almost fully lucid."

The doctor clicked the screen and a short video started to play. In it, Stitts observed what looked like fireworks exploding in the area the doctor had called the subcortex. After this ended, however, there looked to be a direct line of red light that moved backward, toward what looked like a gland near the base of the spine.

"What's that? Where did the activity go?" Stitts asked, leaning forward.

"That's the hippocampus," Dr. Calderon replied. "It serves many functions, one of the primary being episodic memory."

Stitts blinked. They'd lost him.

"Sure, but what does it mean?" he asked, trying hard not to sound frustrated. His head was starting to hurt and he desperately needed a cigarette.

"Well, to be honest, we're not sure. I think—"

Beckett rolled his eyes.

"Look, we can't say for sure, because there's no precedent for this. But it looks to me like not only is the subconscious part of Chase's brain bigger, but it's connected to her memory system. Let me put it this way: we know more about the ocean than we do the human brain. And we know nothing of the deep sea. But here's the thing, Stitts. We ran this test several times, but we only got this sort of response when *I* entered the room. Now, Dr. Narc over there said I wasn't supposed to go in, but you know, I'm not much for rules. Anyway, this event—" Beckett aimed his finger at the hippocampus that was still lit up, "coincides exactly with when I touched her hand. I thought I was fucking nuts, correction, I am fucking nuts, but I thought I was *more* nuts. So, I repeated this experiment three times. Each time, the result was the same. It's like… I dunno, it's like somehow when she got fucking zapped all those years ago the wiring in her brain changed. Her subconscious grew larger and linked to her memory system."

Stitts swallowed hard.

Are you gonna do that voodoo thing again, Chase? Step into the mind of the victims.

The urge to smoke was almost overwhelming now.

Her skill, if you could call it that, had always been their little secret. Something that Stitts had always just assumed was linked to her ability to pick up subconscious cues that others glossed over.

But now, now that there appeared to be a scientific basis for—

"Has Chase ever said anything to you about this? I mean, I have no idea what it must be like to have these parts of your brain linked, but has she mentioned… I dunno, that when she touches someone she feels like she shares the memories?"

Stitts licked his lips and blinked rapidly.

He didn't know what to say.

"Shit, I'm just spitballing here, Stitts. I have—"

All of a sudden, sweat broke out on his forehead.

"Stitts? You okay?" Beckett asked, his face overcome with concern.

"Water," Stitts croaked, reaching for the back of a chair to support his weight. "I need some water."

Chapter 7

DREAMS ARE JUST MEMORIES that haven't happened yet.

At least, that's what Chase thought as the drugs that had been injected into her IV bag took over.

Her emotions, which had previously been heightened, suddenly became numb, and she was finally able to analyze some of the facts relating to her loved ones.

She'd found Georgina, but her sister didn't recognize her. She had a niece, but her sister had taken her when she'd run.

Her father had committed suicide.

Her mother was in a home.

One of the few men in the entire world that she thought she could trust, Special Agent Jeremy Stitts, had lied to her.

These thoughts came to her not in a deluge of emotion that she was accustomed to, nor did they incite a base reaction.

Dr. Matteo had told Stitts that she dealt with her problems in one of three ways: she used, she fucked, or she threw herself into her work.

The first had cost her years of her life, literally and figuratively. Chase had injected herself with every poison she'd come across, using the same drugs that she put people behind bars for selling.

She'd fucked; Chase had slept with so many people in order to get her fix, that she'd long since lost count. She had sex with a serial killer who was hell-bent on murdering her. Chase had sex with a suspect and she tried to have sex with numerous people in positions of power.

Chase had a husband and a son both of whom she loved dearly. She'd pushed them away.

Now they were better off without her.

And she'd thrown herself in her work, the only thing she'd done in her life that would qualify as remotely 'good.' She'd stopped a man before he killed Stitts and herself, she'd put a woman behind bars who was responsible for the murders of three women, she'd stopped a man from blowing up a hockey arena filled with twenty thousand people.

And Chase had *finally* saved her sister. After all these years... not in the way that she'd hoped—it lacked a certain Hallmark reunion quality, that was for sure—but Georgina was at last free from the clutches of two men who had brainwashed her.

Somewhere in the back of her mind, Chase detected moisture on her cheeks, but it was an abstract feeling and non-distinct.

Chase couldn't do drugs anymore; the doctor had made it clear that if she did, she would die. She couldn't fuck anymore, because she was bound to contract some sort of venereal disease that couldn't be cured with a good dose of antibiotics.

She was left with one of two choices: live or die.

It was as simple as that. As dichotomous a decision as there was.

And for the first time in a long time, Chase surprised herself by leaning toward the former.

She could work. That was good; that part of her was good. Chase was a good cop and a better FBI agent.

And the desire to stop murderers, rapists, kidnappers still ran strong in her.

"I'm ready, Stitts," she said, or thought she said; at this point, whatever they'd given her was starting to turn her memories into dreams, or vice versa. "I'm finally ready to get well."

Chapter 8

"ANYBODY... ANYBODY SMELL THAT?" Chase asked, looking around the room. All eyes were suddenly on her.

In total, there were five of them at the meeting: Louisa, herself, a woman named Petrova or Petri dish or some other shit, Marissa, and Dr. Matteo.

Somewhere just outside the doors, there were two others, Chase knew: two overweight orderlies with itchy thumbs just waiting to inject anyone who got out of hand with a cocktail of sedatives.

Although the woman named Petri Dish annoyed the hell out of Chase on a regular basis, the fact that she visibly started sniffing made her smirk.

"Yep... yep. I know what it is," Chase continued. "It's bullshit. That's what I smell, bullshit."

Dr. Matteo removed his glasses and rubbed his bald forehead.

"Are you gonna cause trouble again today, Chase? Because if you are, I'm going to send you back to your room with Kyle and Donnie. Is that what you want?"

The smile slid off Chase's face and she slumped back into her chair.

She hated group session. Unlike the private sessions with Dr. Matteo, which made sense to her and seemed to be helping, the group was useless. Sitting here, listening to others talk about their crappy lives and crappier problems? How was that supposed to help? Listening to Louisa made sense because they'd shared so much, but Petri Dish and Marissa? The only thing she had in common with them was tits and a clit, and judging by the thickness of Marissa's mustache, the latter might even be questionable.

"Look, I don't mean to be an asshole, but how does this help, Doc? How does it help to listen to *their* problems? How could that possibly help *me*?"

Even to her own ears, she sounded incredibly selfish and self-centered, but wasn't that why she was here? To heal herself. She fought the urge to defend her comments by saying something like, 'well, to be honest, I just want to do what's best to make sure that when I leave here, I don't kill myself by injecting carfentanyl or by sleeping with a serial killer with AIDS.'

She chewed her lip and said nothing instead.

Dr. Matteo ignored her. When he waved his hand above his head, he even looked a little bored.

Chase sank deeper into her seat.

It was like this day in and day out.

A moment later, Kyle and Donnie were asking her to get to her feet. She'd resisted previously, of course, but that had ended poorly. The two men had been forced to physically remove her from the room. And if she fought them?

Well, itchy trigger thumbs were bound to make an appearance.

"Fuck this," she said out of the corner of her mouth. She rose to her feet and when Donnie reached for her arm, she pulled away from him. "I'm going, just don't touch me."

"Thank you again for your participation, Chase," she heard Dr. Matteo call after her.

"Is sarcasm a crucial part of your treatment strategy, Doc?" she said over her shoulder as she left the room. "Cause if so, you fucking nailed it. Congrats, douchebag."

Chapter 9

"GOD, I WISH I HAD something to drink," Louisa said as she wandered into Chase's room. "I mean, just one drink. A beer, a shot, something. *Anything.*"

Chase watched as the woman made her way to the mirror and looked at herself. She'd lost quite a bit of weight since the incident back at the trap house.

Since Chase had saved her life.

That had been Louisa's rock bottom, but she'd been fortunate enough to have the means to come back to Grassroots Recovery. Chase wasn't sure what her deal with Dr. Matteo was, if it was as militant and strictly enforced as her own—*If you fuck up, do not pass go, do not collect two hundred, go directly to jail*—but whatever it was, she was here, and she was trying to get better.

Chase saw a lot of herself in this woman. Despite their obvious shared experience, they both had a family and struggled with addiction.

But while they'd shared a lot throughout their time together, it was clear by the fact that neither broached the subject that what had happened all those years ago was off limits.

And this was fine by Chase; she could do without reliving the past.

Live in the present.

"I could do a drink," Chase said. "Close the door."

Louisa pulled herself away from the mirror and then did as she was told.

Chase lifted her mattress and then reached inside the cover as far as she could. Her fingers hit something hard, and she pulled her hand out again. In her palm were two miniatures of whiskey. She tossed one to Louisa who was so surprised that she almost dropped it.

"Unfortunately, it's Jameson—Irish whiskey always tastes like piss to me—but it's all I got," Chase said as she unscrewed the cap. She air cheersed and then downed half the bottle. It had been a long while since her last drink, and she felt it; the whiskey burned all the way down. And yet it was a familiar burn. Something she was used to, something she knew well.

It wasn't enough to take the edge off, not nearly enough, but it was... how had Louisa put it? *Something*.

For several moments, during which Chase finished her bottle in silence, Louisa simply stared at her, gobsmacked.

Then the woman shrugged and chugged her bottle in one go. When it was empty, she sighed loudly and looked around for somewhere to put the bottle.

"Hand it to me," Chase said. "I can't get rid of them here, Mussolini searches the trash, you know."

Louisa grinned and handed the bottle over.

"And the faucets, too, or so I hear."

Chase chuckled.

It still amazed her that Louisa and she had been reunited after all these years. It made her sad in a way; she wished that Georgina was here instead of Louisa, sharing a laugh. No, that wasn't right; she wished she were on a tropical beach with her sister and not in a drug and alcohol recovery center.

When she was younger, her late father had taught her about God.

She didn't believe in Him.

Later in life, Stitts taught her about coincidences.

He didn't believe in those.

"You okay?"

Chase blinked and shook her head.

"Yeah, fine."

"You sure?"

Chase frowned. She detested this line of questioning, and Louisa knew that.

"Yes."

"Then why do you insist on being such an asshole during group?"

Chase immediately stopped putting her mattress back in place and turned to Louisa.

She had to make sure that it was actually Louisa that she'd shared a drink with and not some impostor.

"Excuse me?"

"We're friends, right? I mean, after all we've shared… and I did save your life—"

"—twice."

"Yeah, twice. Well, *I* consider us friends now. And friends are candid with each other, right? So… why are you such an asshole in group?"

Chase stared at Louisa for several seconds.

It was a valid question, she supposed. And Louisa was right; she'd earned the right to ask it.

"It's bullshit," she said, at last, looking away. "Hearing about all these people's problems. You know that girl, Petri Dish or whatever? You know what her problem is? She refuses to take any responsibility for what happened to her. Oh, I get it. She had it tough growing up, she didn't have a daddy, blah, blah, blah. But she was the one who got in that car after drinking. Nobody forced her to. She was the one who hit that kid and then fled the scene."

Louisa stared at her the entire time she was speaking, and it made Chase uncomfortable.

What she was saying couldn't be that shocking; after all, it was true.

Thankfully, there was a knock on the door and one of the orderlies peeked in, interrupting the awkward silence.

"Chase, Dr. Matteo has pushed your private session up an hour. He wants to see you as soon as you can."

Chase smiled to Louisa and rose to her feet, smoothing out her mattress one final time.

"All right, I gotta brush my teeth." She leaned in close. "The Gestapo can smell alcohol on your breath a mile away. I'll see you around, Louisa."

Chapter 10

"REALLY? AGAIN, CHASE?"

Chase slumped in the chair across from Dr. Matteo and shrugged.

"I don't even know what I'm doing at the group sessions. I get nothing out of it. *Nothing.*"

Dr. Matteo pushed his tongue into the inside of his cheek and remained silent.

"Ah, don't you start doing that shit, too. Did Stitts come to talk to you beforehand? Did he share with you his ultimate passive aggressive technique?" Chase said, making air quotes with her fingers.

She'd meant this as a joke, but when Dr. Matteo hesitated, Chase thought that perhaps this was the case.

But then he started to speak, and Chase realized that this was never his intention.

"You don't get anything out of it, Chase, because you don't put anything *into* it. It's as simple as that. Group is an important part of the recovery process, and I'm afraid you're missing out on it."

"Oh, gee, the FOMO is killing me," she grumbled, crossing her arms over her chest. She knew she was being petulant, acting like a child having a temper tantrum, but she didn't care. After all, what is it that he called this place? A "safe space?"

Dr. Matteo sighed. She'd pushed him pretty hard before, and once she'd even seen him break, back when she'd confronted the doctor with Stitts at her side, asking for Louisa's address. He'd snapped then, gone off on a tangent, and had dug his claws into her pretty deep.

But now, the more that she thought of it, the more it seemed staged. Dr. Matteo's behavior that day, and, come to think of it, Stitts's as well, was out of character.

Chase made a *hmph* sound and shook her head.

They'd collaborated to get her back here. Sure, they'd likely not envisioned dragging her half-naked body out of a rock quarry and then wait for a couple of months while she was on the brink of death in a hospital beforehand, but nobody was perfect.

"You've made progress, Chase. I won't deny you that. But you've got to—"

"Made progress? Seriously? That's all I get? I mean, I haven't used in over six months. I haven't tried to sleep with you or Ronnie, Donnie, or Lonnie or any of the morbidly obese orderlies you have working here, either. I also haven't solved any cases, because, well, I'm here. Yeah, I remember what you said about my three 'crutches.' I'd say that that counts for more than progress, wouldn't you? I think I'm doing pretty good, Doc. I think I'm doing *damn* good."

Dr. Matteo stared at her for a moment longer before his eyebrows rose up his forehead.

"True, true," he said as if musing to himself. "I'll give you that. But here's the thing, Chase. You ever seen that show the Biggest Loser? It aired a couple years back on ABC or NBC or one of the BCs."

Chase shook her head. She hadn't seen it, but she was familiar with the premise: obese people were sent away to have their lives realigned and their bodies reshaped.

"No, but I know what it's about."

"Well, you wanna know what happens to these people after they lose hundreds of pounds and then go back to the regular life?"

Chase shrugged.

"They put it all back on, just like with every diet?"

"Yeah, they put it all back on. Because the thing is, all the show is doing is removing someone from their life and putting them in a fishbowl; an artificial environment. Devoid of distractions or any of the triggers that they experience in real life, sure, they manage to lose weight. They don't have their families bothering them, they don't have enablers asking them to go out for pizza, and they don't have to work a regular job where they're stressed out and have no time for the gym."

"What's your point?"

"My point is, while you're doing well here, when you get back out there in the real world, how are you going to do then? Are you sure you can avoid all temptations? Out there, there are bad people—"

Chase made a face.

"You don't need to tell me about bad people, Doc."

Dr. Matteo continued unabated.

"Out there, you'll experience the same triggers as before. Are you gonna be able to deal with them this time? Or are you gonna go back to the self-destructive pattern that has plagued you since childhood?"

Chase scowled; she didn't like this line of questioning. It seemed counterproductive.

"How the fuck should I know? I'm just doing what you tell me to do."

"Yeah, well that's not exactly true, is it? You're not doing what I'm telling you. I'm telling you to participate in group because you can learn from these people."

"What in the world can I learn from Petri Dish?"

Again, Dr. Matteo sighed and sank into his chair.

"You know one of the other reasons that those people failed on the Biggest Loser?"

"They just love food?"

"They went back to their same old life," Dr. Matteo said, ignoring her comment. "The biggest chance you have for success in this world coming out of a program like this? Start over. Start a new life. Forget about everyone and everything you used to know. Move away. Get a new job. Make new friends. In essence, become a new person."

This final comment shocked Chase. How could she possibly change who she was? She was who she was because of her experiences. They shaped her, molded her, *made* her. And to deny herself that was... what? Dishonest? Unfair? Fake?

She wanted to come back with a witty retort but had none at the ready. It had been a while since she couldn't think of something snarky to say to Dr. Matteo.

Instead, her mind was preoccupied with a single thought: *Could I really become a new person?*

Chapter 11

"I SWEAR HE DOES this just to piss me off," Chase said.

Louisa looked over at her as they walked down the hallway toward the meeting room.

"It's always about you, huh?" she jested.

"Well, when's the last time we had two group sessions one day? Umm, never? Yeah, so I think it really is just to piss me off."

Louisa said nothing.

Chase also fell silent. In truth, she was feeling quite low. What Dr. Matteo had said had affected her in a profound way she hadn't expected.

Sure, she'd come here—this time, anyway—with the intention of getting better, of actually listening to what the man had to say and to see if he could help her. Shit, after making it to the other side of withdrawal, she was already a better person.

Or so she'd thought.

But now? Now that Dr. Matteo made those comments?

Chase had become a better person, but she was still the same. She hadn't considered the possibility of becoming a *different* person.

Chase entered the room with Louisa at her side, intending on sitting beside her as they always did during group. Only this time, the circle of chairs had name tags on them.

Chase found her own, picked it up and scrunched it into a ball.

"What the fuck is this? We're back in middle school?"

They were the first ones to arrive and Louisa shrugged before taking her seat, which was directly across from Chase.

Chase reluctantly took a seat in the assigned chair, and then immediately started tapping her foot.

Then she glanced around at all the other pieces of paper on the chairs. When she saw that Petra was to her immediate right, her frustration increased. It doubled again when she realized that there was no chair or name tag for Dr. Matteo.

This is a ploy, some sort of game he's playing, Chase thought and was about to tell Louisa as much when the door opened behind them and the two other women entered. They were chatting and giggling, but when they caught Chase's expression their moods immediately darkened.

"This is new," Petra said, taking up residence beside Chase.

Chase grunted something inaudible.

When they were all seated they took turns observing one another like animals from different cages at the zoo who were suddenly put in a single holding cell.

"Anybody see Dr. Matteo?" Marissa asked.

A smattering of nos.

"Well, do you think we should wait for him?"

"Wait for him? Of course, we should wait for him. What the hell else would we do?" Chase shot back. But as soon as the words came out of her mouth, she realized that this was the point.

Dr. Matteo wanted them to be alone so that they could… what?

Chase just shook her head in disgust.

It's bad enough that I have to listen to these people's sob stories, but now I have to do Dr. Matteo's job, too? Lead the discussion like some sort of Girl Guide Unit Leader?

"Why are you always so angry?" Petra asked. Chase glared at the woman. She had wide-set eyes and a round, pale face with bangs cut straight across her forehead.

It was the type of look that bothered Chase. It was the type of look that made you want to punch the person in the face.

She had to actively unclench her fists.

"I'm angry because I have to sit through all of this bullshit," Chase said. She'd promised Dr. Matteo she would try, that she would give group a chance, but all of a sudden, she wasn't in the mood. What she felt like doing now, was going back to her room and sulking. To wallow in her own self-pity.

And then maybe she would become a new person. Someone who loved long walks on the beach and maybe doted on a man who worked in Wall Street. Get a dog maybe… no! Not a dog, a *cat*. A dozen *cats*.

"You're not helping, you know," Petra said. Then she waved her hands over the group. "We're all here because we want to help one another, to get better. Except for you."

Chase nodded.

"Yeah, you're right; I'm not here to help you guys. I'm here because I don't want to end up in prison," she said, rising to her feet. "But lucky me, nothing in my parole conditions say that I have to put up with this crap. I'm going back to my room. If Dr. Matteo ever shows up here, you let him know where he can find me."

With that, Chase turned and started toward the door. She made it halfway before Petra had to get the final word in.

"You're always running away," the woman said under her breath.

Chase spun around and confronted her, storming right up to her face.

"What did you say?"

To her surprise, the diminutive woman, who was only a few inches shorter than Chase herself, didn't back down.

"I said, you're always running away from your problems. You should—"

Without thinking, Chase reached out and grabbed the woman's arm. She opened her mouth to shout something in her face, to tell her off, to say something clichéd like, you know nothing about me, but as soon as her hand made contact with Petra's skin, she was transported somewhere else.

Chapter 12

"*GET ME A DRINK,*" *the woman croaked. "Petra, get me a goddamn drink."*

Petra looked over at her mother and wondered for what felt like the millionth time why the woman hated her so much.

What did I do? What did I do to deserve this? I've always tried my best to help you out, to make things easier — especially after Dad left.

"Take the glass with you," her mother ordered.

Petra pulled herself out of the couch and grabbed the glass from her mother's hand. The entire time, the woman's eyes were locked on the TV. Petra was fairly certain that if she wasn't quick enough, the woman would just let the glass fall out of her hand and to the floor and wouldn't even notice.

With her head bowed, Petra headed to the kitchen.

I have to get out of here, *she thought.* I need to get out of here, get some fresh air.

Petra tossed the ice cubes from the glass into the sink and then grabbed two fresh ones from the freezer. She squeezed them tightly in her hand, before gasping and dropping them in the glass.

How long has it been since I've left the apartment?

Petra inhaled deeply, then grimaced.

Not long enough to get used to the smell.

She desperately had to get out of the apartment but knew that her mother wouldn't let her. She could wait for a couple more hours until her mother passed out, then slip out the door. So long as she was back before her mother woke up…

But that means sitting in this filth and listening to her insults for two hours.

Her eyes drifted to the bottle of Southern Comfort on the counter. She sighed when she realized that there was still a quarter left.

Or three.

There was another way, of course; if her mom ran out of booze, then she would have to let Petra leave.

Petra walked to the counter and picked up the bottle. She debated pouring half of it down the drain, but why waste it?

A quick glance into the family room to confirm that her mother was still mesmerized, she brought the bottle to her lips.

It wasn't the first time she tried alcohol, she was twenty-four years old, after all. It wasn't even the first time she'd snuck some sips of her mother's bottle.

But it had been a while since she had this much.

Petra's cheeks bulged, and she grimaced with the first swallow. The second and third were easier.

With a gasp, she pulled the bottle away from her mouth and stared at it in awe.

There was only an ounce or two left.

Petra quickly filled her mother's glass, then topped it off with some Coke from the fridge.

Putting on her best fake smile, Petra walked back into the family room. Her mother's hand reached out expectantly as soon as she heard Petra approach, but she didn't look over.

The woman's lips searched for the rim of the glass like two desperate worms vying for a single burrow.

For some reason, Petra's stomach revolted, and she brought her fist to her mouth. It was only a burp, and after swallowing hard she leaned over to her mom.

"You're out—I'm going to get a refill," Petra said.

"Make it quick," her mother snapped back. "Tylko dziwka wychodzi w nocy."

Petra started for the door. She grabbed the car keys from the hook then looked back, her mother's words echoing in her head.

Only a whore goes out at night.

Chapter 13

CHASE DOUBLED OVER AND started to gag. She squeezed her eyes closed and tried to regulate her breathing.

Instead of pulling back from her, Petra actually moved closer and wrapped her arm around Chase's waist to make sure she didn't fall. Chase instinctively tried to spin away, to break free, but another bout of nausea struck her.

This time, vomit rose in her throat, and she couldn't choke it back down again. Hot liquid sprayed from between her lips. The other women had gathered around, Louise included, and they jumped back to get out of the way. Their movements were unnecessary; most of her vomit landed on Petra's loafers.

"Somebody call the doctor," Marissa said.

Chase shook her head, and immediately regretted it. More vomit filled her mouth, but she somehow managed to swallow it.

The last thing she wanted was to see another doctor.

"I'm okay," she managed, wiping her lips with the back of her hand.

It had happened again with a living person. As soon as I touched Petra, I saw what she saw.

Most of what Chase had seen could be logically explained; even though Chase paid zero attention to the woman when she spilled her beans during group, she was still *there*. The words were still entering her brain, even if they didn't register.

But some things… like what Petra was thinking when she'd brought the bottle to her lips, the way she felt both dirty and powerful at that moment, that was something new.

Nothing revolutionary, however, but the effect that it had had on Chase was profound.

It's because it didn't feel like this before... before it felt like I was looking through the eyes of the dead. This... this felt like I was her, like there was no separation between us.

Just the thought of the strangeness of the idea brought about another wave of nausea.

Chase whinnied like a horse then straightened, trying her best to keep a straight face. She wanted to say something funny, to make light of the situation but when she saw Petra's face, she changed her mind.

The woman was looking at her in genuine concern. Not in an 'oh, I should ask if you are okay but not listen to a word of the answer because Captain Social Graces says I should.' No, Petra really looked worried about her.

Chase looked over at Marissa, then Louisa. They were looking at her as if she was insane.

What if the person I choose to become is even more fucked up than I am now?

She shook her head and turned to Petra.

"I'm sorry," Chase whispered, then left the room without another word.

Chapter 14

"I HAVE TO... I have to go," Stitts said, glancing down at his watch. "I've got a flight to catch."

Beckett looked over at Dr. Calderon.

"See? You scared him off with all of your hyper-specialized, overcomplicated douchebaggery."

Dr. Calderon scowled.

While it was true that Stitts's head was spinning from all the technical jargon, and the only thing that they'd concluded over the past hour was that the electroshock therapy and Chase's later drug use had caused structural changes to her brain, he really did have to go.

"Yeah, for real."

Whether or not the changes were responsible for Chase's strange visions was something that Stitts would have to ponder later on his own.

"Seriously?" Beckett asked as he poured a tipple of scotch into his coffee. "I think—"

"Yeah, I have to go. Really."

Beckett sipped his drink.

"What about this?" he asked, holding up the folder with Chase's MRI results.

Stitts instinctively reached for it, but Beckett pulled it back.

"I'll take it."

"You want to—?"

"Fuck, I said I'd take it—I'll tell her," Stitts replied. His face was feeling flushed, but he didn't care. He needed to have a smoke and get the fuck out of the hospital. If he missed his flight...

"Fine, shit," Beckett said, handing the folder over. "You got a prom date, or what?"

The man appeared genuinely stung by the comment, which surprised Stitts. Beckett was usually cold as ice. Sure, the man joked constantly, but the laughter almost never reached his eyes.

"Sorry," Stitts grumbled. "I've got to... look, I've got a funeral I need to attend, that's all. I can't do this right now. I'll speak to Chase when I get back to Virginia, and if you guys want to meet up later, I'm more than happy to arrange something. The most important thing is that Chase gets better. That's all I really care about."

Beckett eyed him suspiciously, which quickly made Stitts uncomfortable.

"Sorry," he repeated.

Beckett offered his drink to Stitts without a word, and he took it.

"That's all we want, too," Beckett said when Stitts put the Styrofoam to his lips and took a tremendous gulp.

Chapter 15

CHASE ENTERED DR. MATTEO'S office without knocking. She stormed up to his desk, but he finished reading whatever paper was in front of him before even bothering to look up. If he was surprised by her presence, he didn't show it.

Clearly, Chase had been right about the whole no doctor group session being a set-up. Louisa might contest that everything wasn't about her, but more often than not, it was.

"Live in the moment... you know that hippie bullshit you're always talking about?" she said, jumping right into it.

Dr. Matteo raised an eyebrow and waited for her to continue.

He didn't have to wait long.

"It's not about that, is it? I mean it is, but it isn't."

Her words were even confusing herself, so when Dr. Matteo suggested that she take a seat, Chase didn't hesitate.

"I used to think that was all about the fact that I can't change the past or the future. But... you know when you told me that my life could be distilled down to three things: drugs, sex, and my job?"

This time, her words elicited a reaction from Dr. Matteo. Chase got the impression that the doctor had hoped she'd forgotten all about that.

Well, aren't we stuck in the past, Kimosabe?

"I didn't mean—"

Chase shook her head.

"It's not about the present, not really; it's all about control, isn't it? It's always been about control. You encourage me to live in the moment because that's the only thing I can control. What happened in the past is already done, and the future is unpredictable. But I can control what happens *right now.*"

Chase paused to take a breath. She knew that Dr. Matteo was doing the Stitts thing again, letting her ramble, but she was oddly excited about her revelation and couldn't stop.

"And that's why I use, why I inject heroin. Whenever I'm overwhelmed, whenever there's shit going on in my life that I can't control, I shoot up. Same with having sex with other men. Again, trying to regain control."

Another deep breath.

"And my work? Same thing. I can't control the crime or the actions of the perpetrator, but I can control the end result. And a case will always come to a conclusion. Even with—" *Georgina,* she almost said, but caught herself— "the tough cases, I carry them out to the end."

When she was finally done, she looked across the table at Dr. Matteo expectantly. All of the pieces fit, all of the psychobabble she'd overheard over the past three months finally made sense to her. Truth be told, she hadn't even been listening, but her subconscious…

Ah, except for that.

She had no control over *that*; what happened to her when she'd first touched the corpses in Alaska and had progressed to touching living people, like Petra, and somehow *becoming* them.

Stitts might be convinced that this was just her subconscious acting up, but the more vivid and real these visions, or whatever they were, became, Chase was beginning to have doubts.

"Chase, this whole lack of control issue goes back further than when you took your first hit. It goes all the way back to the day that you were taken, the day…" he smiled and interlaced his fingers. "… well, a long time. But understanding why you do the things you do, why you are so desperate for control, isn't enough."

Chase felt herself becoming frustrated again.

So much for my great revelation. I guess there's going to be no sweet sixteen party for me after all.

"It's not?"

"No," Dr. Matteo continued, "it's not. The thing is, it is inevitable that there will be many facets of your life that are outside of your control. Moreover, there are going to be times when you *shouldn't* have control. You need to allow the ones you trust to take over once in a while. To truly get better, Chase, you need to willingly relinquish control."

Things had taken an unexpected darker turn, once again throwing Chase into discomfort.

"The people I trust? How can I trust anyone, when they always fuck me in the end? Doesn't it just make me an idiot, a lackey, a goddamn Pollyanna, to trust people who have already lied to me?"

Dr. Matteo shook his head.

"No, Chase, that doesn't make you an idiot or any of those things. What it does make you, however, is human. See, the thing is, when you always need to be in control, the consequences of your decisions are severe. If anything happens, it becomes your fault, because you've tricked yourself into believing that you were in control of everything. I won't deny that what happened to you and your family is horrible. But none of it was your fault. You've punished yourself for years for something that you did when you were a child. Think about it… are you really responsible for running away? For being so absolutely terrified that your autonomic nervous system took over, your flight impulse kicked in, and you ran?"

Chase wiped tears from her cheeks and shrugged.

"It is my fault," she whispered.

Dr. Matteo leaned forward even further.

"No, Chase, it's not. You were a kid. It's not your fault, it's not your sister's fault, and it's not your parents' fault. All this time you've been struggling to forgive yourself, but you don't have to; because it's not your fault."

Chase was sobbing again. Only this time, to her surprise, these weren't tears of pain or frustration or guilt. They were something else. Tears of… what, exactly?

Acceptance? Understanding? Joy?

Maybe I have been doing this all wrong, she thought with a deep, shuddering breath. *Maybe I don't have to be the person I was before. Maybe I can start all over again.*

Dr. Matteo suddenly reached out and almost put his hand on top of hers.

Chase instinctively pulled back.

If she were to become someone new, she was going to have to stop having those damn visions, that was for sure.

"Chase, you can start again. I've seen it. I've *done* it."

Chase nodded and leaned back in her chair.

"Maybe… maybe I can. Do you think… do you have some gloves I can borrow?"

Chapter 16

As SOON AS THE officiant said his final words and the casket started to lower into the ground, Stitts turned his back on his mother and lit a cigarette.

He'd been so concerned with Chase that he hadn't paid attention to Mrs. Torts when the kind woman had told him that his mother's condition had deteriorated.

She died two days after the message that Stitts never even bothered replying to.

The people who were there in the end—Belinda, a few friends, a woman that used to do business with the family—told Stitts that it didn't matter, that she was barely lucid.

But they were only being polite. Just like the doctors had lied when they said it was old age, a weak heart, general poor health that led to her demise.

His mom knew that he wasn't there, and she'd died because she had abused opioids for decades.

And he'd enabled her.

With a heavy sigh, Stitts used the butt of one cigarette to light the next. As he did, someone approached from behind.

"Got one for me?"

Stitts turned and was surprised to see that the question had come from his father. The man had barely changed over the years; sure, his hair was a little lighter, the skin on his cheeks a little looser, but not like Mom. He looked ten to fifteen years younger than she had near the end.

Stitts pulled a cigarette out and offered it to his dad. Then he handed over the lighter.

"I love your mother very much," the man said as he lit up.

Stitts nodded and turned his eyes to the sky above.

It was true, he knew; his dad loved his mom. But the things she'd done… she'd stolen his prescription pad so many times and forged his name that it was a surprise the man still had his medical license. Stitts didn't blame him for cutting the ties. He could only lie so many times to protect her before placing them all in jeopardy.

"Hey, Dad?" Stitts asked quietly.

"Yeah?"

"You remember when you were an intern in Tennessee? When those girls went missing?"

The pause that followed extended for so long that Stitts was forced to turn to make sure that his father hadn't walked off.

"Shit, you okay?"

His father was crying. Stitts had never seen his father cry; not *ever*.

The man wiped his face.

"Sorry."

The comment confused Stitts.

What is he sorry for? For crying? For what happened to Mom? For what he did to Chase?

Stitts took another drag. He knew that this was probably the worst possible place and the worst possible time to be asking this question, but he couldn't help it.

He had to know.

"Do you remember?"

Dr. Ben Stitts flicked his barely smoked cigarette to the grass and shook his head.

"No," he said, but Stitts instantly knew that his dad was lying.

And Stitts was surprisingly fine with this. After all, he knew what the truth could do to someone.

It could tear you apart.

He didn't blame his dad for what happened to Chase any more than he blamed the man for what happened to his mom.

A curt nod and his dad started to walk away. But he only made it three or four steps before turning and walking back up to Stitts. The man's face was red, and he was still crying. At first, Stitts wasn't sure what to do. A moment later, his father hugged him.

Who is this man? Stitts wondered. *First the apology, then the tears, now this? What's next? He's gonna tell me he loves me?*

But Dr. Ben Stitts didn't say I love you. Instead, he said something else; something that perhaps carried more weight.

"I should've never let your mother go," he whispered. "I should've been there for her. Jeremy, if you really love somebody, don't ever let them go. Not ever. Protect them, nurture them, help them, but don't let them go."

Chapter 17

"I'M GOING TO BE honest with you, Jeremy, I don't think it's a good idea."

Stitts reached into his pocket and caressed the pack of cigarettes inside.

"Shouldn't we leave it up to her? Of all people, I'd think that she would want to make *that* decision—well, every decision, really. I mean, I'm just saying that she *can* come back to work. Eventually, she'll need to work, right?"

Stitts cringed, hoping that the words didn't sound as desperate and defensive to Dr. Matteo as they did to himself. Not to mention it was a lie; Chase had poker money stashed away, and if that ran out, she'd proven capable of hanging with the best at the poker tables in Vegas.

She didn't *have* to work.

Dr. Matteo caressed his bald forehead. Twice the man looked like he was going to say something but decided against it.

The longer the silence went on for, the more Stitts started to doubt himself.

Was this the right thing? Was he doing what was in Chase's best interest by inviting her back into the FBI, or was this just what he wanted? What he *needed*?

"You think you know Chase. I thought I knew Chase. But I don't even think she knows herself. At least not before she came here this time around. She's changed, and I think she wants to change. I'm not just talking about giving up the drugs, either, though that's part of it. I'm talking about becoming a different, better person. I know you care about her, and I do too, but, as much as it pains me to say, maybe it's best if we just let her go."

The candid reply surprised Stitts. It was no secret, even prior to this recent admission, that Dr. Matteo had a soft spot for Chase. The man was one of the few who knew everything that she'd been through, and while he'd probably heard dozens of similar stories over the years, there was no denying that she was unique.

Chase was unique because of what happened to her at the fair. She was unique because of what happened at the hospital.

The shock therapy. The rewiring of her brain. The guilt. The pleasure. The pain.

"I don't know… I don't know if I can do that," Stitts replied under his breath.

Dr. Matteo leaned forward.

"I can't tell you what to do, and I can't say for certain that getting her job back is a bad thing. I'll leave it up to you, Jeremy. But, whatever you decide, make sure that you're doing it for her."

Stitts nodded and held out his hand.

"Thank you, Dr. Matteo. Thank you for everything you've done for Chase."

They shook hands then, but when Stitts tried to pull away, the doctor held fast.

"If you ever want to talk, Jeremy—not about Chase, but about *you*—please don't hesitate."

Stitts swallowed hard and pulled his hand back.

"Thanks," he said awkwardly then left the man's office.

Me? I don't need therapy. What I need is my partner back, he thought as he started down the hall toward Chase's room.

But his certainty waned when he saw Chase sitting on her cot from across the hall, a book in her lap.

Stitts did a double-take; it was Chase, only she was *different.*

For one, she had a glow to her cheeks that he'd never seen before. Stitts always thought of her as pretty—most everyone did—but now she looked beautiful. Naturally so. She wasn't wearing any makeup, her outfit was a plain gray tracksuit, and her dark hair was pulled up in a messy bun.

And yet her appearance gave him pause.

Dr. Matteo was right, he thought, *she has changed. Maybe it is best if she… if we… all just move on.*

Breathing heavily, Stitts bowed his head and hurried past her room without stopping.

She didn't even notice him.

Stitts ignored the clerk at the front desk and then sprinted to his car.

"Go," he told himself. "Put the fucking key in the ignition and leave. Go back to Director Hampton, tell him that Chase isn't interested in her job back. Tell him that you want a new partner."

As he pulled another cigarette out and pressed the lighter in the dash, his eyes fell on the folder on the passenger seat.

He almost burned it; when the cigarette lighter popped, he almost put it to the folder instead of his cigarette.

Instead, he lit his smoke and then opened the folder.

Inside were all of Chase's MRI exams, past and present.

Stitts knew then that he couldn't do both; he couldn't tell Chase about what Beckett had said *and* ask her back into the Bureau.

I promised never to lie to her again, but last time the truth nearly broke her. What would it do to her this time?

He closed his eyes tightly, letting the tendrils of warm cigarette smoke drift up his nose. To his surprise, an image of his father, teary-eyed as he'd never seen him before, came to mind.

As did the man's words.

If you really love someone, don't ever let them go.

"Fuck it," he said, shoving the folder into the glove box. Before slamming it closed, he grabbed another folder and Chase's badge and gun and pulled them out.

Stitts stepped back into the rain and flicked his spent cigarette butt.

"Fuck it," he said again as he started back toward Grassroots.

Back to his partner.

Chapter 18

CHASE NEVER EVEN HEARD him coming. She was so engrossed in the book, that it wasn't until the figure blocked part of the light from the doorway that she raised her eyes. Her first instinct was that it was Louisa.

But when she saw his perfectly coiffed hair and the boyish grin, she knew better.

"Stitts?" she exclaimed, leaping to her feet. "What the fuck—what the fuck are you doing here?"

She went for a hug, but Stitts's hands were behind his back.

"Nice to see you, too."

Stitts laughed.

"I just came to congratulate you," he said, bringing one hand forward. "You've graduated."

Chase gave him a look and then took the folder from him and opened it. It took her all of three seconds to realize what it was. It was an FBI dossier describing the assassination of a Senator, and it was dated an hour ago.

She looked up.

"What the fuck is this? Stitts?"

Stitts pulled his other hand from behind his back and showed her badge and gun.

"Dr. Matteo gave me a call, told me how well you were doing. I managed to pull some strings—well, it wasn't all me; your rich sugar daddy in Vegas had something to do with it— so I come bearing good news: if you want your job, you've got it. If a cat has nine lives, Chase, you've got a million."

Chase suddenly stopped smiling.

This was… unexpected, to say the least.

She'd turned a corner on her old life. With Dr. Matteo's help, Chase was able to move on and the prospect of starting

over had become a potential reality. This was in part fueled by
the fact that she'd burned so many bridges that going back
was impossible... or so she'd thought.

"Chase? Are you okay? I didn't mean to—"

"They'll really have me back?" she asked.

It seemed unbelievable, even with Stitts and Stu Barnes'
influence. She'd lied, she'd cheated, she'd broken not just FBI
rules but the law—federal and multiple state laws.

"How? Why?"

Stitts shrugged and grinned.

"A million lives, Chase. A million lives."

Chase tapped the badge on her palm and lowered her gaze.

*A million lives but I'm stuck living the same one over and over
again.*

Stitts sighed.

"Chase, I didn't mean to barge in on you like this. If it's too
much, I completely understand. I mean—"

Chase looked up at her partner. His expression was
serious.

*I tried to exercise control by sleeping with men, injecting heroin,
and throwing myself at my job,* she thought, rising to her feet.

"Promise me one thing?" she said.

Stitts nodded.

"Anything."

"If you call me ma'am or try to protect me, even once, I get
to punch you in the dick."

Stitts grinned so widely that his entire face almost split.

"You got it," he chuckled. "So long as you keep on those
gloves. What's with those things, anyway?"

Chase shrugged.

"I'm channeling my inner Madonna and Michael Jackson."

Before he could ask any more questions, she reached out and hugged him tightly.

Stitts hugged her back.

"I missed you," he said in her ear.

Chase pulled away and crinkled her nose.

"I didn't miss your old man cigarette stench."

Stitts laughed again and started out of the room. Chase followed, only to hesitate in the doorway and look back.

I used to have sex with men, inject heroin, throw myself at my job.

With a sigh, she hurried after her partner.

"Two out of three ain't bad, Chase," she said under her breath. "Two out of three ain't bad."

PART II – Assassination

Chapter 19

PRESENT DAY

CHASE FLIPPED THROUGH THE file on her lap as Floyd sped down the streets of Washington, DC.

Senator Tom DeBrusk. Shot twice in the chest, dead before he even slumped to the ground outside a Dunkin' Donuts. In broad daylight no less, with more than two dozen witnesses, none of whom saw anything other than a low flying drone.

"I'm guessing that ATF is already going to be there?" she said, pulling her head out of the file.

Stitts nodded.

"The ATF and the Secret Service," he said glumly. "Plus, Homeland and the DoJ can't be far behind."

Chase nodded, recalling a story her partner had told her about his past difficulties with multi-agency cases.

Something about a bank robber with a bomb wrapped around his neck.

"Great. None of the witnesses know where the shots came from?" she asked.

"Nope. They didn't even hear them, they just saw him slump to the ground. Like it says in the file, there was a drone really close to the scene, but it's unlikely that it was anything more than a toy."

Chase raised an eyebrow.

"Seriously? These drones can fire bullets? I mean, I know the military has them, but ones that people can just buy?"

Stitts shook his head.

"No, but I wouldn't put it past some nutcase to modify one so that it can fire."

"A-a-agent A-a-adams?" Floyd said from the driver's seat.

Chase raised her eyes from the folder and stared at Floyd in the rear-view mirror. Having him around was a breath of fresh air and she was incredibly grateful that the man had responded to Stitts's call.

They'd only spent a couple of days together in Alaska, but that was plenty long enough for her to come to a decision about him: the man was honest, dependable, and a decent human being. All of which seemed in short supply these days.

It was a no-brainer for her to ask the man to come along and lend a hand.

"Yeah? What's up?"

"There's a strict no-fly policy for drones over W-w-w-washington. In fact, most ma-ma-major cities have restrictions."

Chase nodded, noting that Floyd's stutter was almost nonexistent when he spoke about mechanical objects. She'd noticed this in Alaska, too, when he spoke about trains.

She flipped through the folder until she came across a grainy image taken from a local CCTV camera. She turned it around and showed Floyd the drone.

"Even something like this? Looks like a toy."

Floyd looked up.

"Well, it is kind of a t-t-toy, but a real eh-eh-eh-expensive one. That's a top of the l-l-line personal drone. Costs almost two thousand dollars. It can fly up to fifty miles an hour and has a range of more than five miles."

Chase looked over at Stitts, an eyebrow raised.

Stitts shrugged.

She knew that Floyd knew trains, but she hadn't known that he had a wealth of knowledge about drones, too.

Floyd must've picked up on the exchange in the backseat because he suddenly flushed.

"I-I-I l-l-liked trains and hel-hel-helicopters as a b-boy. D-Drones are like the best of b-both worlds."

Chase was about to leave it at that, especially considering that they were approaching a state trooper wearing a yellow vest, when she thought of something.

"Floyd, can you do me a favor? What I know about drones, I can fold into a blade of grass… are these things registered? Like with the FAA or something? Do the owners have meetups, that sort of thing?"

"I d-don't know about registering, but there are a bunch of online clubs and groups."

"Think you can look into that for me? See if there are any local groups around here? I'm sure the ATF is already on it, but just in case."

Floyd's face lit up.

"Yes, of c-c-course, A-a-agent Adams. No p-p-problem."

Stitts offered her a curious expression but didn't say anything. The state trooper knocked on their window, and Stitts rolled it down and flashed his badge.

The trooper nodded and indicated to a parking spot just inside the taped-off area.

"Secret Service and ATF have been waiting for you. They've set up a mobile command center right over there."

Stitts frowned and tapped Floyd on the shoulder.

"You get that?"

"Yep," Floyd said, pulling into the designated spot.

"Alright, here we go," Chase said under her breath as she stepped out of the car and attended her first crime scene in more than six months.

Chapter 20

"YOU REALLY THINK THAT'S a good idea? Getting Floyd involved like that?" Stitts asked as they flashed their badges and walked by the makeshift barricade.

Chase shrugged.

"Why not? It'll give him something to do. Besides, Dr. Matteo said I needed to start asking others for help, letting someone else take control for once."

Stitts rolled his eyes.

"Yeah, I don't think that's what he meant."

"There you go again, Armchair Psychologist, Dr. Jeremy Stitts."

Stitts opened his mouth to say something, but Chase hustled ahead and held out her hand to the first man in a suit that she came across.

"FBI Special Agent Chase Adams and this is my partner Special Agent Jeremy Stitts," she said. The man, a thick fellow with a pink face and broad features, looked at her gloved hand curiously and then glanced over at Stitts. Eventually, he shook Chase's hand.

"Special Officer Tanner Pratt, Secret Service," he introduced himself with a flat voice. The man's hand was so big that it completely swallowed hers. She pulled it free then looked past him.

In the distance, she could see where the senator's vehicle was parked and noted that both the front and rear doors were open. She could also see a trail of loose sheets of paper leading from the car to a slumped form covered in a white blanket up against a Dunkin' Donuts.

"Agents, we're setting up a small mobile command center over here. I can debrief you inside. The press is already all over this."

Chase ignored SO Pratt and started toward the crime scene. The man's large hand shot out, blocking her path.

"The command center is over there," he informed her.

Chase stared at the man's hand until he eventually pulled it back.

"It's best if you just let her go," Stitts said quietly. "Trust me on this one."

SO Pratt raised an eyebrow.

"Yeah," Stitts continued as Chase made her way toward Senator DeBrusk's body, "You're better off just letting her do her own thing."

***

As she moved, Chase's eyes drifted about, taking in the scene, paying particular attention to the sky where the drone had been spotted.

Based on just the limited information that Floyd had shared about drones, she knew that it had a role to play in this. She had no idea *what* role but didn't get bogged down on the details.

Instead, she just let her mind wander, allowed her subconscious to take in the entire scene.

Most of the papers on the sidewalk had a bullet hole in the center, but she didn't bother reading them. Chase had to do a little dance to make sure she didn't step on them as she made her way to the body. There were maybe a half-dozen Crime Scene techs milling about, but they didn't seem to notice her.

She moved so fluidly among them that it was almost like she was part of the scene itself.

There was blood on the sidewalk; two individual splatter patterns that were indicative of blowback. Judging by the size of the spray, Chase ascertained that a high-caliber rifle was probably the murderer's weapon of choice.

She didn't go directly to the covered body. First, she walked up to the glass and observed the interior of the Dunkin' Donuts. It was well lit. There were dozens of half-empty coffee mugs and packs of donuts sitting on tables, and jackets and purses were strung over the backs of chairs, but there was nobody inside.

Secret Service must've taken them out the back door, she thought. A quick glance to her left revealed that Senator DeBrusk had collapsed in front of the door, blocking the exit. It would have taken only seconds before those trapped inside panicked, thinking that a masked gunman was going to descend on them.

They must have exited out the back and once the police arrived, what was left behind became evidence.

She doubted if the Crime Scene Unit would find anything of value inside the store.

Chase looked skyward one more time then sucked in a deep breath. The air was surprisingly clean and crisp, suggesting that the area that the police had cordoned off was substantial. She realized that she could barely hear any cars, let alone smell them.

Having gotten all that she could from the surroundings, Chase finally turned her attention to the sheet covering Tom DeBrusk. She was already wearing gloves, but they wouldn't do in this situation. After peeling off the right one, she took a purple lab glove out of her pocket and gripped it in her hand like a cloth. Then she reached out and pulled the sheet off Senator DeBrusk.

There was no telling how many dead bodies Chase had seen in her time. Two dozen, maybe three. And yet, every time she saw one, she still got a sickly feeling in the pit of her stomach.

Tom DeBrusk was a large man, with receding brown hair and ears that stuck out from his head.

He might have been one of the most powerful men in Washington DC when he was alive, but here, in this pose, with his mouth slack and his chin tucked into the chest, he looked like everybody else. A common folk.

Death, the ultimate equalizer.

Chase teased the white sheet down another foot until she saw the two blooms of blood, one on his suit jacket just below the chest pocket, and one on his dress shirt.

The fingers on the man's right hand were curled as if he'd been holding something at the time of his death, but they were now empty.

She closed her eyes and pictured the images she'd looked at from the local CCTV camera. Sure enough, she recalled that Tom DeBrusk had been holding a folder to his chest when he'd been shot, which would explain the sheets of paper on the ground around her.

Where that folder went, was another question.

Chase took a deep breath and then put the purple lab glove back in her pocket. But instead of replacing the one she'd taken off, she reached for the senator with her bare fingers.

A second before Chase touched his skin and transported herself into Tom DeBrusk's world, a hand came down on her shoulder.

Chase pulled back and looked up at a young man sporting gold-rimmed spectacles and blond hair that was slicked to his scalp.

"Two rounds, probably Lapua Magnum," the man said without even bothering to introduce himself. "If I had to guess the gun? I'd put my money on an M24 Sniper."

Chase nodded and slipped on her glove again.

"FBI Special Agent Chase Adams," she said, extending her hand.

The man nodded.

"Yeah, I know who you are," he said.

Chase tried to read the man's tone but gave up after just a few seconds.

No, you don't, she thought, a grin forming on her lips. *How could you know who I am, when I don't even have a clue anymore?*

"And who the hell are you?"

The response caught the man off-guard and he nervously adjusted his spectacles before shaking her hand.

"Peter Horrowitz, ATF."

Chapter 21

"**ALL RIGHT, PETER HORROWITZ,** ATF, where did the shots come from? Hmm?" Chase asked, looking around dramatically. The street looked like any other American metropolis, complete with shops, high-rises, and office buildings. The only thing substantially different was the White House looming in the distance.

Peter surprised her by not even hesitating before replying.

"Although I need to wait on confirmation of the specific round type, based on what I think they are and what gun I think was used, it's possible that the shots were fired from over a mile away. But, judging by how crowded the street was, and all of the buildings in the area affecting the air currents, I'm thinking that without a spotter, the max distance was about five-hundred meters." Peter glanced around quickly, and then pointed at a trio of identical high-rise buildings, a couple of blocks to the East. "There. I'm betting the shots came from one of those buildings."

Chase's eyes bounced from Peter to the senator, to the high-rises.

"Not enough information to take that bet," she muttered under her breath. When she was playing poker, Chase usually compiled hours of data on the other players before trusting her reads on them.

"I guess. Good thing I don't gamble."

"Tell me something, Peter," Chase continued. "What was he holding? What are all these papers all about?"

Peter adjusted his glasses, then shrugged.

"I dunno. All I know is that outside of the military, the M24 rifle with Lapua Rounds is not easy to acquire. Not impossible, of course, but—"

Stitts and SO Pratt suddenly appeared behind the man. Both dwarfed his small stature.

"That's classified," SO Pratt said.

Chase made a face.

"What? Was it the secret recipe to the president's favorite blueberry pie? Or maybe the nuclear launch codes?"

When not even Stitts smiled at the comment, Chase shook her head.

"Wait. You're serious? We're all on the same side here, fellas."

"Classified," SO Pratt repeated.

Chase glanced to Stitts who looked like he'd either just had an aneurysm or he'd crapped his pants.

Maybe both.

And this is why he hates these interdisciplinary cases, she thought.

"Blueberry pie it is then. Well, I assume that you've taken dozens of pictures of the area and collected all the footage from local establishments. Far be it for me, a wee woman, to release the scene, but I've seen all I need to. You said you have a mobile command center set up? Is it one of those boys only clubs or can I cover my hair and enter? Take a look at the footage?"

SO Pratt's eyes bulged, but he somehow managed to keep a straight face.

Peter Horrowitz, on the other hand, was practically in stitches.

Pratt cleared his throat.

"We set up a temporary trailer, just over there. Should have everything you need."

Chase nodded.

"Gee, thanks. Now, if you need to work out some extra testosterone, why don't you get Captain ATF to jerk you off over there, just out of sight for the cameras. I've got work to do."

This time SO Pratt did a much poorer job of keeping a straight face.

***

"Jesus," Stitts muttered under his breath. Then he offered Pratt and Horrowitz a tired smile. "Don't mind her. It was a long drive."

Before they could reply, he turned and hurried after Chase, who moved through the crowd with ease. She managed to sidestep all the officers, and then pass through a crowd of people holding cell phones, all trying to capture their own morbid souvenir, without being harassed.

Although he rarely agreed with Chase's methods, he could see why she felt the need to act the way she did. No one gave her any respect. Stitts, on the other hand, didn't make it more than ten feet before a state trooper asked for ID. Annoyed, he flashed his badge and continued onward. He was stopped again after just a few steps, and this time, while he was explaining to the rookie cop that he was FBI, Chase's brown head of hair disappeared in the crowd.

"Chase!" he shouted. The officer was still scrutinizing his badge when Stitts wrenched it out of his hands. "Special Agent Jeremy Stitts, FBI."

His frustration had come to a head, and he'd said the words loud enough for onlookers to hear. Almost immediately, he became the focus of their Instagram Stories or Facebook Live videos.

He scowled.

"Thanks a lot," he grumbled, stepping by the officer. He pressed himself onto his toes, trying to spot Chase in the crowd.

It was only then that he realized she'd been heading the opposite direction SO Pratt had said they'd set up the mobile command center.

Chapter 22

SHE WAS JUST THREE blocks away from the crime scene, but it felt as if Chase Adams had traversed the country. Senator Tom DeBrusk had been murdered not a mile away, and yet nobody seemed to care. And it wasn't as if they hadn't heard about it; she had literally passed a half-dozen people who were watching news updates about the crime on their phones.

The ants were so busy bringing sustenance to the Queen that they couldn't even be bothered to take a moment to consider what had happened. A US senator was about to get his caffeine fix when two sniper rounds had ended his life. She wondered if Tom DeBrusk realized that he had been shot, or if he'd just died thinking about his one cream, two sugars.

Chase forced her way through the throngs of people heading to work then took up residence at the edge of the sidewalk in front of the three towers that Peter Horrowitz had indicated.

She searched for obvious signs first—open or broken windows, casings on the ground—but there were none. It was an office building, not a frat house in the heart of New Orleans during Mardi Gras.

Her eyes drifted to the rooftops above, but they were so high up, and the reflection off the glass was so bright, that she had a hard time seeing anything.

She suspected that the shooter might have had the same problem.

Blinking the tears away, she turned her attention to those around her. As before, they seemed oblivious to anything that was going on around them, content in just weaving at the last moment to avoid Chase, who was the only person standing still.

Forget seeing through the eyes of the dead; that *is an advanced subconscious if I've ever seen one.*

There was no indication that anyone had heard anything, but Chase wasn't entirely sure how loud the sniper rifle would be down at street level.

If I were a betting man, I'd say that the likelihood of them hearing anything would be minimal, she thought in Peter Horrowitz's voice.

With a frustrated sigh, Chase walked over to a bench by the side of the road. A man in rags occupied one corner. His chin was tucked into his chest and he was breathing heavily. Clutched between fingers that jutted from holes in a pair of worn gloves was a Dunkin' Donuts coffee cup. *TIPS* was written on the side of it, but the cup was empty.

Either people weren't feeling particularly generous today, or some asshole stole his money.

As Chase pulled off her glove and reached into her pocket for loose change, she was struck by how similar the homeless man looked to the dead senator just a handful of blocks over.

The great equalizer, she thought again. It took her a moment to realize that these words weren't her own.

They were her father's.

"I miss you, Dad," she said suddenly.

It was a colloquial and clichéd thing to say and it wasn't true. If her dad hadn't died, would she be thinking about him? Planning a visit? Calling to see how his day went?

And yet, even though the rational part of her brain registered this fact, it did nothing to take the sting away.

She might not be thinking about him, but there was comfort in the fact that if she had, however unlikely the case, Chase *could* have called him up.

But not anymore.

A shudder coursed through her, and Chase immediately enacted some of the techniques that Dr. Matteo had taught her to deal with her emotions when things were getting out of control.

In the moment; remain in the moment, Chase.

To distract herself, Chase reached out and dropped a few coins in the man's cup. The cup immediately started to lean and, without, thinking she reached for the man's hand in order to right it.

The second her fingers brushed against the man's filthy skin, her vision started to go dark.

Chapter 23

"WE'VE GOT THE BODY going back to CSU and as soon as they release it, ATF will get a chance to take a look. Shouldn't be long before we know for certain what type of rounds were fired," SO Pratt said as he held the door to the mobile command center open.

Stitts nodded and stepped inside. Then he stopped.

"These guys don't fuck around," he said under his breath.

The trailer looked like it was torn from a scene of Minority Report. There were nearly a dozen men inside, most of whom were huddled over some sort of computer or another electronic device. In the center was a small table, which was littered with photographs. The command center had the dimensions of an oversized RV, but Stitts figured that it drained as much power as a small city.

"Everybody," Pratt said in his booming voice. Eyes turned to face them, and headphones were pulled off in a strangely synchronized manner. "This is FBI Agent..."

It took Stitts a moment to realize that the man had forgotten his name and was waiting for him to introduce himself.

"Jeremy Stitts," he said. Everyone in the room nodded but offered nothing in terms of an introduction, which suited Stitts just fine. The less he knew about these people, the less he had to be in conflict with.

"Agent Stitts's partner will also be working closely with us, but she has gone... gone to look for evidence." Pratt turned to Peter next. "And you all know Peter from ATF. He'll let us know as soon as he has any more information about the bullets or gun used in the assassination."

"Yep," Peter said. It took him a moment to realize that Pratt and his colleagues were actually waiting for him to leave. "I'll be in touch," he said, making his way back out onto the street.

When the door shut behind him, Pratt indicated a burly black man with small eyes who sat at the nearest computer terminal.

"This is Agent McKay. He's running the search of the senator's home. He'll also be coordinating the interviews with the family, unless of course…"

"No, that's fine," Stitts said quickly. He hated breaking the bad news to family members. Pratt must have seen this expression before because he quickly chimed in.

"News outlets are already all over this. Haven't even gotten a chance to inform the man's wife, yet."

Stitts's frown deepened.

At least we have that in common, he thought. *A dislike for the press.*

As if to prove his point, Pratt gestured to one of the larger monitors affixed to the wall.

"Turn that up, would you?"

On-screen, was what Stitts would consider that typical talking head: a man with steely eyes and over-tanned skin, his bald head showing nary a reflection from the harsh studio lighting.

"It is with great sadness that we have confirmed that Senator Tom DeBrusk was assassinated this morning," the man said in a flat tone. "The senator was gunned down in broad daylight not far from Capitol Hill. If the name sounds familiar to you, it's because he was the one who was pushing Bill S-89, the controversial bill, which, in layman's terms, basically eliminates the opportunity for businesses to run efficiently. Senator DeBrusk wanted to put tariffs on—"

The man on-screen paused and put a finger to his ear.

"This guy is the worst," Pratt mumbled. "Will Woodley is a parasite."

Stitts was looking over at the SO when the talking head started up again.

"I just received word that the President will be speaking about this terrible incident sometime in the next ten minutes. We will be there, live, as soon as that happens. In the meantime…"

"What?" Stitts asked, eyes going wide. The command center was fully abuzz with activity now, as all of the men were looking at each for information.

"Anybody hear about this?" Pratt barked. "Jesus Christ, who's on comms? Why the hell weren't we informed that the president is about to speak?"

All he got in response were shrugs and open palms.

"Fuck," Pratt grumbled, a hateful glare aimed at the talking head. "How this ass clown gets his information before we do, the goddamn Secret Service is—"

A phone started to ring from somewhere within the command center, and Pratt swept a bunch of computer equipment aside until he found it.

Stitts watched the man say a half-dozen uh-huhs and yes sirs before hanging up the phone.

"That's it; that was the call. We need to mobilize; the president is set to speak within the hour."

Everything was happening so fast that Stitts was having a hard time keeping up.

"You think that's a good idea? According to ATF, the senator was shot from five-hundred meters away or more."

Pratt pressed his lips together.

"Do I think it's a good idea? Hell no. But you try and tell the man what to do." And then, to the group, he said, "Well? What are you guys waiting for? Let's make sure the president doesn't get his ass shot and start a goddamn civil war."

Chapter 24

A BOTTLE. WHEN HER field of vision finally started to clear, that was the first thing that Chase saw. A bottle of bourbon resting on a worn wooden table.

A young hand reached for this bottle and gripped the sides tightly. It was nearly full, and when the hand raised it, she saw a reflection in the glass.

The face that stared back was young, but the dark circles beneath his eyes suggested that already this man had fallen on hard times. There was a slight hesitation and then he brought the bottle to his lips.

When the hand placed the bottle back on the table, a third of the golden liquid was gone.

The hand that reached for the bottle this time was slightly older, slightly more wrinkled. It was still undeniably a young man's hand, but there were noticeable nicotine stains between the first and second fingers this time. As before, he picked up the bottle and held it in front of his face for a moment before drinking.

His hair had started to pull back from a forehead that had deep lines running its width. It was the same blue eyes buried in those dark circles only now they seemed darker, more intractable.

The bottle was only half-full now, and the man was older still. His once flawless skin was covered in pockmarks, most of which were scattered across his nose, which had become bulbous. The hand that gripped the glass trembled slightly, causing the liquid inside to slosh back and forth.

When the bottle was nearly empty, the hand that held it was shaking so violently that it was a wonder it didn't fall to the floor. And then it did fall; it slipped between filthy fingers and crashed to the table.

Only it was no longer a bottle, but a worn Styrofoam cup with the word 'TIPS' written on the side.

***

Chase gasped and pulled her hand away from the man on the bench. She stumbled backward, bumping into a man in a suit who promptly told her to watch where she was going.

She ignored him.

The man on the bench stirred when someone righted his cup and dropped a quarter in it. When someone nearly tripped over his foot, he opened his eyes.

And then, as if drawn by some sort of strange magnetism, the homeless man locked Chase in his gaze.

It was the man whose reflection she'd seen in the bottle, but Chase had known this already.

Not sure what to do next, she gave him a subtle nod and then looked away. The ants continued to march all around her, once again oblivious to anything and everything.

With a simple touch, Chase had felt the man's loss, his remorse, his regret.

But what she hadn't felt was fear.

The man didn't shoot from here, Chase thought with unexpected certainty. *I don't know where the shot came from, but it most definitely did not come from any of these three buildings.*

Fear spread through a crowd more quickly and effectively than any virus or bacteria. Millions of years of evolution had attuned the human subconscious to detect the subtlest signs of danger, the faintest hint of potential injury. The first person in the group might not notice anything more than a strange smell in the air or, perhaps, something in the distance catches their eye. They look for the cause, but more often than not, they can't identify it. With a shrug, they pass it off as nothing. But that slight hesitation caused their gait to falter, for them to slow down just a little. As a result, the next person in the crowd is forced to change their cadence, while the third has to swerve to avoid colliding into the second. Subtle things on their own, but collectively they served a purpose. And by the dozenth person? The crowd is bumping into each other, tempers are rising, and others near the edges disperse to avoid being trampled.

That was fear in a crowd. That was the species' self-preservation mechanism, a herd warning system. And when it was all over? No one even realizes how close the lions in the tall grass had been.

Watching. Waiting. *Hunting.*

But the man on the bench hadn't felt any of this.

There was no fear here, and there was no shooter.

Chapter 25

"YOU COMING WITH, AGENT Stitts?" SO Pratt asked.

Stitts chewed the inside of his lip and looked around. Half of the agents in the command center—no, not half; three quarters or more—had already left, leaving only a few techs and ATF Agent Peter Horrowitz, who had since been given permission to return.

He wasn't really sure how much help he could provide at the president's presser, besides, that clearly fell under the domain of the Secret Service, which SO Pratt seemed to hold some authority over. What he wanted to do was find Chase and ask her what she'd gotten from looking at—*touching, when she touches someone it seems like a memory to her*—Senator DeBrusk. And he would be lying if he didn't just want to make sure that she was okay, that she hadn't regressed. But he also knew that Pratt's request wasn't really a request; it was a test. A test to see if he would fall in line with all the other soldiers, if the FBI was capable of following the Secret Service's lead for once.

Stitts shrugged.

"I'll go," he said. In these situations, Stitts had found it best to take a backseat. There was nothing to be gained by having a pissing contest at this stage of the game.

There would be plenty of time for that later, no doubt.

"Fine, you come with me, then," Pratt said as he stepped out of the trailer. Stitts double-checked that the gun in his holster was loaded. It was a waste of time, of course; his gun was always loaded. But after what had happened with Chase in Alaska, it had become a habit of his.

Outside, he quickly lit a smoke and then made his way over to Floyd, who was standing behind the yellow tape with the other onlookers.

Frowning, Stitts waved at the man, beckoning for him to come over, but an officer immediately blocked his path.

"He's with me," Stitts said between drags. Instead of answering, the officer looked at SO Pratt who, in turn, looked at Stitts.

"Is he in the FBI?"

Stitts shook his head.

"No, but he's our personal driver."

As soon as the words were out of his mouth, Stitts cursed himself.

Why the hell did I say that?

He knew full well what other agencies thought of the FBI. Thanks to TV shows like Criminal Minds, they'd gotten a reputation of being pampered, overpaid, spoiled brats.

In some cases, it wasn't far from the truth, in particular, the latter.

Pratt made a face that said it all: *personal driver? You've got to be kidding me.*

"Sorry, Stitts. Can't do it."

Another test.

The reality was, however, Floyd had no clearance privileges at all. There was no point pushing the envelope on this one; it was a no-win scenario.

"Give me a sec," Stitts said, puffing aggressively on his cigarette as he made his way across to Floyd.

"A-a-agent Stitts," Floyd said as he approached.

"Floyd, think you can do me a favor?"

"Of course."

Floyd looked so young and naive at that moment that Stitts had a hard time believing that he'd gone through puberty, let alone lived into his thirties.

"Chase took off that way and was heading to look at those three towers, I think. Can you go grab her and let her know that we're heading to the president's press conference?"

Floyd's eyes lit up at the mention of the president.

"Y-y-yes, of course. I'll get A-a-agent Adams and let her know right aw-aw-away."

Stitts reached out and clapped the man on the shoulder.

"Thanks, Floyd."

He took another half-dozen furious drags of his smoke then made his way toward SO Pratt's car. Which, he noted with a grin, was a brand-new Mercedes.

Chapter 26

IT WAS IMPOSSIBLE FOR Chase to make her way back to the mobile command center. A procession of a dozen or so black cars, clearly Secret Service, were led by an equal number of police cruisers. She tried to flag one of the cars down, but almost got herself run over for her troubles. Cursing, she waited for the line of cars to pass with all of the other civilians. Just when she thought it was over, another car, this one a dark gray pulled up to the rear.

Chase ran up to it, a scowl on her face. The window was already down, and she was startled by the young face that stared out.

"Agent Adams?" Floyd said, grinning.

Chase had no idea how the man had found her, but just seeing his face made her relax a little. There was just something about Floyd that made her feel at ease, whatever the circumstances.

"Fuck, am I glad to see you," she said. "Where's everyone off to? What's going on?"

"The president is giving a sp-p-p-peech," Floyd replied. He pulled over to the side of the road and started getting out of the car.

"I got it, Floyd," Chase said as she made her way around to the passenger side. "How many times do I have to tell you, I can open my own door."

"Sorry."

"Don't worry about it," she said, sliding into the seat.

"You want me to follow A-a-agent Stitts? You want me to take you to the Wh-wh-wh-white House?"

The Secret Service parade was almost out of sight, and the ants were returning to their business as usual.

It seemed reckless for the president to go anywhere in public just hours after a senator had been sniped only a dozen blocks away from the White House. But he'd done crazier things during his short tenure.

But if a sniper was going to take the POTUS out, then sending another body on the ground wasn't going to help. Even if she were to head over there, by the time she managed to convince everyone that, yes, she was in the FBI, it would probably be too late anyway.

On the other hand, she suspected that the mobile command center would be fairly empty at this time, which would mean peace and quiet. And none of that 'confidential' bullshit, either.

"No, I don't think so," she said, ignoring the disappointment on Floyd's face. Clearly, he'd been excited at the prospect of seeing the president up close and personal. "Let's head back to the command center, instead."

***

"So, there is no re-re-requirement to register your drone," Floyd informed her, drawing Chase out of her head.

"Excuse me?"

"The drones? You asked me if you had to register them."

Chase had completely forgotten about the drone.

"Ah, yes."

"So, like, you can just buy it and fly it. You don't need a license or n-n-nothing. But it's illegal to fly almost anywhere in Washington. There are a c-couple of drone clubs in the area, and they have spe-spe-special permission to fly places, like abandoned ai-ai-airstrips."

Chase took this information in as Floyd slowly made his way back to the mobile command center.

"Good to know," she said absently. "Just pull over here. It'll be easier to walk."

Floyd did as he was asked. Chase started to get out, but Floyd stayed behind the wheel.

"Aren't you coming?"

Floyd crinkled his nose.

"They told me I need spe-spe-special clearance, and I don't got it."

Chase looked around. Security had thinned considerably with everything going on with the president and those who were left looked as green as they came. She spotted a pimply faced state trooper by the south end of the command center wearing a hat that looked like it used to be his older brother's.

"Is that what Stitts said? He couldn't get you in?" she asked with a smirk.

Floyd shook his head.

"No. He tried, but…"

"Well, I'm not Stitts," she said, gesturing to follow him. "And I'll get you through, don't worry about it. After all, you're not just a driver, you're an FBI Special Assistant."

Chapter 27

"I'VE KNOWN PETER HORROWITZ for a while, and he's a good guy, but the ATF in general? The whole department is as leaky as a sieve," SO Pratt said as he moved to the front of the line of agents.

Stitts raised an eyebrow but resisted speaking. After conceding to his authority twice, Pratt clearly considered Stitts trustworthy.

So Stitts did what he always did: he listened.

"That's why I had to tell you back at the scene that the shit that Senator DeBrusk was holding when he was killed was confidential."

Stitts nodded and tried to keep up as they made their way toward the White House on foot.

Pratt clearly expected Stitts to say something, but he didn't take the bait. The problem with prompting someone, he'd come to realize, is that you guided their line of thinking, biased them toward what *you* wanted to know. Let them just ramble on, however, and you had vastly more knowledge at your fingertips: what *they* knew.

"You see, the thing is Senator DeBrusk was on his way to the Senate. They were gonna vote on his baby, Bill S-89. And from what I hear? It was going to pass. After it made it through Congress, it was pretty much a done deal." Pratt paused for a moment, eying Stitts up. "Ah, I forgot, you ain't from around here. Bill S-89 is essentially aimed at stopping lobbyists. All the big companies with vested interests in what the government does have them: energy, pharma, tobacco, the financial sector, you name it. Republicans are up in arms about it, including that douchebag William Woodley who you saw on TV earlier. They think S-89 is just a gateway into the government having more power and sway in the private sector."

Stitts took this all in. He was familiar with how lobbyists worked; the FBI itself wasn't above their influence. Case in point, Chase being rehired after her... issues.

Stu Barnes was, in essence, a lobbyist. For himself, mostly, but also for others, like Chase, for instance.

And that bothered Stitts. Because he knew that lobbyists never did anything for free. Eventually, there'd be a time when he'd call on Chase to repay her debt and there was no telling what that might be.

But, in this case, S-89 wasn't just a bill, but...

"Motive," Stitts said, surprising himself by speaking out loud.

"Yeah," Pratt said calmly as they approached the concrete barricades in front of the White House. "And you know what happens after a bill is passed and before it goes into law? The president has to sign it. Which makes him a target. Now let's go make sure he doesn't get himself shot, shall we?"

Chapter 28

"HE'S WITH ME," CHASE said, flashing the police officer her FBI badge. Before he could reply, she motioned for him to raise the crime scene tape, which he did, and she slid beneath. Floyd quickly followed, and the officer didn't even bat an eye.

When they were out of earshot, she turned to Floyd.

"See? It's that easy," she said with a smirk. "Look the part, FBI Assistant Montgomery, look the part."

"Thanks, A-a-agent Adams," Floyd said, hurrying to keep up with her. "And I'll try."

"Just Chase, please. You're my assistant, not my slave."

Floyd looked confused by this comment but eventually nodded.

"Good. Now let's get some work done before Captain Confidential returns, shall we?"

Chase wasn't surprised to find the mobile command center nearly deserted; she'd expected as much. But she hadn't counted on Peter Horrowitz being there, punching away at a keyboard.

"Where is everybody? Someone giving out free doughnuts?" she asked, announcing her presence. When Peter looked over at her, his face serious, Chase cringed.

Doughnuts... Senator DeBrusk was just murdered outside a Dunkin' Donuts. Classy, Chase, classy.

"The president is going to give a speech... nearly every cop or agent in the city is doing double duty as security."

Chase nodded.

"Yeah, I know, I was just kidding. This here is, ah, FBI Assistant Floyd Montgomery."

To her surprise, Floyd strode forward and nodded.

"Peter," he said curtly. Chase was so taken aback by the sudden change in attitude and demeanor that she balked. When Floyd's eyes met hers, and she saw a glimmer in them, Chase shook her head and regained her composure.

A quick study, she thought. *Who would've thunk it?*

"Any update on the bullets?" Chase asked, moving closer to Peter and his computer.

He pulled out a chair for her, and she took a seat. Chase looked back at Floyd to indicate for him to gather around as well, but he'd already pulled up to an empty terminal and had started typing.

Who the fuck is this guy and what happened to Floyd?

"No, not yet. Body is still with the ME. I don't expect the forensics on the shells to come back for another hour or so. But I do have something for you; take a look at this."

Peter brought up a black-and-white schematic of what looked like a city grid on his computer screen. As he moved the mouse, the image started to render in 3D and Chase realized that she recognized the location in the center as where Tom DeBrusk had been shot: the Dunkin' Donuts. He clicked a few buttons and the image zoomed in on an outline of the senator's body.

"This new software predicts the location where the rounds were fired. All I have to do is input the 3D images of the senator's wounds, and it works backward to determine trajectory and distance, etc. It's kind of like using string or laser lights in closed spaces to find out where the shots came from."

"But what if Senator DeBrusk twisted as he fell? Wouldn't that throw it off?"

Peter grinned.

"Nope. It actually uses all the data we collect from the scene—including the force of the impact and the weight of the victim—to predict his orientation when he was shot. It uses this superimposition in its calculations."

Chase nodded; she was impressed. This was even more advanced than the stuff they'd shown her back in Quantico about a year ago.

"Now, watch this."

Red lines suddenly emerging from Tom DeBrusk's chest. It was like watching bullets fly in reverse and it made her uneasy. The lines continued to extend outward until stopping at a high-rise three blocks away.

Peter clicked another button and the red lines turned into points. Chase had expected two of them to appear, but was surprised when there were more than a half-dozen.

"The software is having a hard time narrowing it down to just one location, probably because the angle of the first bullet before the senator fell, is unclear. Still, I'm pretty sure this high-rise is the location that the shots were fired."

"Is there a way to do a satellite overlay of the image instead of this black-and-white?"

"One step ahead of you," Horrowitz said, clicking another button. The scene on the monitor suddenly became real, transforming into a satellite image of the building.

It was the same one that Chase had run to when Peter had first suggested this as the probable location of the shooter.

The place that she'd touched the homeless man. The place she'd already ruled out.

"How accurate is this sort of thing? Fifty percent? Eighty?"

"Depends—usually around seventy-five or eighty percent accurate. It's only as good as the data you punch in, including shell and rifle type, which I'm still waiting to confirm. But if you look at this here… at where Senator DeBrusk was shot and the angle the bullets came from? This building is the perfect vantage point."

Chase took a deep breath and debated how to proceed.

Peter was the expert and his theory sounded and looked right based on the images on-screen.

Only he wasn't.

"Any security footage from these buildings? The convenience store, here?"

Peter turned to her and smiled. Even though he had a good ten years on Floyd, their boyish mannerisms were very similar.

"I've already got some ATF foot soldiers on their way over. They're going to grab any footage they can and head up to the roof of all three of the high-rises. I mean, I severely doubt that the shooter is still up there, but you never know. They're also going to ask around. If the shots came from here, somebody had to hear or see something."

I beg to differ, Chase thought absently. *A hand on a bottle, a hand on a Styrofoam cup with TIPS written on the side. How close was I to being that man?*

"You have any friendly judges you can reach out to if the building super doesn't want to give out the footage?" Chase asked.

Peter chuckled.

"This is Washington, Agent Adams, and we have a murdered senator on our hands—an act of terror. DoJ and Homeland have pretty much given us carte blanche. Well, technically, they've given the Secret Service free rein, but by extension…"

Chase nodded. That would make things easier… and it would also speed up eliminating the buildings that Peter had just identified as the location that the shots were fired.

"Great. So, why DeBrusk? Why was he targeted?"

"Not a real popular guy around here. Was heading up a bill to restrict lobbyist power. You know, Bill S-89?"

"No… no idea. I've been on, ah, sabbatical for the last little while. Forgot to keep up on my politics."

"What, you don't get William Woodley in… Quantico, or wherever you're from?" As he spoke, Peter raised a finger to the large monitors on the wall. On it, she saw a bald man with a tan, who looked strangely familiar.

"Nope."

But Chase did think she saw something on the way to the command center, a billboard with his face on it and some text about how in debt the government was.

"Well, he's our uber-libertarian, quasi-republican, fully hypocritical talking head."

"I don't know what that means," Chase said with a blink.

"Yeah, neither do I," Peter said. "Anyways, he seems to get his information about an hour before everyone else. Not sure how. But if you're looking for a motive, it's gotta be Bill S-89. I haven't seen this much—"

The talking head suddenly nodded, and the camera zoomed to a podium with the United States seal on it.

"Hey, turn this up? I think the President is about to speak."

Peter grabbed the remote and increased the volume.

"We are still gathering intel about Senator DeBrusk," William Woodley's voice came through the speakers loud and clear. "But at this point, it is not clear if this was an act of terror or just some—we'll discuss that shortly. But right now, the president is about to take to the podium."

Chapter 29

SPECIAL OFFICER PRATT WAS right of course; it was preposterous that the president of the United States of America would be giving a press conference in such close geographical and temporal proximity to an assassinated senator.

Why the man wouldn't do it *inside* the Oval Office, was something of a mind melt for Stitts. Yeah, he understood all that show them who's boss rhetoric, the alpha male mentality of the current regime, the never negotiate with terrorists dogma, but this was just throwing yourself in front of a moving car.

Pratt had taken a position at the president's flank, just out of view of the media, while he had been relegated to crowd control with a much more junior Secret Service agent.

The crowd itself, which consisted of roughly twenty members of the media and twenty random people that Stitts didn't recognize, had been funneled into neat rows, five by eight. Whether or not they'd been vetted before they'd entered, or even searched and patted down, was a mystery.

"This is nuts," Stitts muttered under his breath.

A collective hush fell over the crowd as the president emerged from the White House and made his way toward the podium. His head bowed, he grabbed the sides of the podium and remained in this pose for a good twenty seconds before speaking.

Anything for a photo-op...

"It is with a heavy heart that I stand here before you today and confirm that a member of Congress, a good friend of mine, and an excellent father, was taken from us. Earlier this morning, Senator Tom DeBrusk was assassinated..."

Stitts zoned out the president's words. It was, unfortunately, a speech that he'd heard dozens of times before about victims from all walks of life. It was almost as if the official speechwriter had gotten lazy and had just reused an old speech, simply swapping out the victim's name.

But he wasn't here to pass judgment on the president's speech or even his policies; Stitts was here to make sure that the man didn't get his ass shot. So, instead of paying attention to the president, Stitts surveyed the crowd.

Pratt had made it clear that he thought that the president was a target, which suggested that taking out the senator could have been a ploy just to get the man out into the open.

The president had happily obliged.

If that were the case, it was Stitts's job as the Bureau's premier profiler to identify the shooter.

Pratt had called the shooting an act of terror, and while he wasn't wrong, it didn't fall into the normal Jihadi suicide mission. Jihadis blew up malls filled with innocent people, or the cowards drove minivans through crowded streets. They didn't typically use a sniper to take someone out from a mile away. So, while others might be looking for a middle-eastern male between the ages of twenty and thirty, Stitts was looking for someone different.

He'd already put together a profile in his mind without even thinking about it; the person they were looking for was a young man between the ages of 35 to 45, Caucasian, likely of medium or slight build. He likely had a military background of some sort, which might be evident in what he was wearing or how he was carrying himself.

Stitts scanned the audience for someone who fit this description, his eyes jumping from one cameraman to the next.

"We will not, and have never, negotiated with terrorists. This cowardly act of violence will be met with the just and swift justice. We will..."

A flicker of movement on the stage caught Stitts's attention. It was SO Pratt and the man seemed agitated. Two fingers were pressed against his ear, and he was speaking rapidly.

Stitts cursed himself for not asking for an earpiece from Pratt earlier. He leaned over and gently nudged the junior agent at his right.

"What's going on?" he asked quietly.

The man, clearly trying to listen to whatever message was being shared over the radio, shook his head. Frustrated, Stitts resigned himself to searching the crowd again for any potential threat.

Everything seemed as it was before, which suggested that the threat might be coming from elsewhere. Long range, perhaps, like—

No, he thought suddenly, his eyes fixating on one man in the crowd. *Something has changed.*

One of the cameramen had lowered his camera—a bulky, archaic thing—from his shoulder and was fiddling with it on one knee. A man fixing his camera, trying to ensure he got the best shot, might not have been strange under normal settings, except this man didn't look like he had any idea what he was doing. Cameramen usually knew everything about their cameras, every trick to get another minute of battery power, every setting to get the lighting just right; after all, their jobs depended on it.

To top it off, this man didn't fit the mold of a cameraman: he was young, late teens to early twenties, maybe, and had dark brown skin and a wiry black beard that fell to the hollow of his throat.

The Secret Service agent at his side suddenly leaned over and whispered in his ear.

"Go—we're a go! *Go, go, go!*"

Stitts looked at the man for a moment, his eyes wide. Then he heard the same instruction repeated through the man's earpiece, even though it was more than three feet away.

"Go! Go get him! Take him out!"

And then all hell broke loose.

Chapter 30

"THIS CAN'T BE A GOOD idea," Chase mumbled under her breath, shaking her head. The president was speaking about the recent assassination of Senator Tom DeBrusk to a crowd of maybe forty or fifty people. *Outside*, no less.

"Since when was having good ideas a prerequisite for becoming president?" Peter Horrowitz shot back.

Chase pressed her lips together.

Good point.

With the president's speech going on in the background, Chase returned her attention to the software on Peter's computer.

"What if the shooter was farther away," she asked. "Like, farther than those three buildings?"

Peter zoomed out of the satellite image that his program had constructed.

"It's possible, but not very likely. Once you get outside of about a half-mile, hitting a moving target without a spotter, or maybe even several spotters, becomes very, very difficult. Especially considering the surrounding buildings, cars, people walking, etc. Even the slightest fluctuation in the wind or temperature can cause a bullet to deviate a few millimeters; a few millimeters from the barrel equates to more than a dozen feet at a distance of a mile or more."

Chase raised an eyebrow and inspected Peter.

He started to blush.

"What? In a past life, I wanted to be in the Army. Even went through the sniper course."

Well, aren't you just full of surprises, Chase thought. This reminded her of Floyd, and she glanced up at him. The man was still at a computer, looking more like a Secret Service agent than the few agents she'd already met.

She shook her head and turned her attention back to Peter.

"How old are you? You can't be—"

A commotion on the monitor on the wall caught her attention and she went silent. The president had stopped speaking and was now surrounded by nearly a dozen Secret Service agents. She even saw SO Pratt as part of this group; he was still shouting commands and pointing at something when he led the president back to safety.

"What the hell?"

The camera suddenly turned to the crowd, but before Chase could see what was going on, the feed cut out and William Woodley's hairless face reappeared.

"America: there has been an assassination attempt on the president of the United States," he said in a tone that was brimming with both excitement and terror. "I repeat, there appears to have been an unsuccessful attempt on the president's life."

The man pushed his fingers to his ears as if listening to someone informing him of what to say next.

Chase bolted to her feet. Her hands were shaking so badly that it proved difficult to pull her cell phone out of her pocket. She hadn't gotten through to dialing Stitts's number when it seemed like every light in the command center—of which there were hundreds—suddenly lit up.

"They got the guy!" a tech said excitedly as he hurried toward the door. "We got the guy who shot Senator DeBrusk!"

Chapter 31

IT WAS THE JUNIOR Secret Service agent to Stitts's right who made it into the crowd first. Stitts, not having the luxury of an earpiece, took a moment to collect himself before sprinting after him.

The young agent was all elbows and knees as he thrust his way through the crowd. The man pounced, going airborne to cover the last three feet between himself and the cameraman.

Still fixated on the camera on his knee, the man never saw the tackle coming.

The Secret Service agent's shoulder struck the cameraman in the side and sent them rocketing backward. Stitts watched as the man's neck was whipped backward before the two men skidded across the pavement.

And then everybody descended upon them. Stitts himself got knocked to the ground by another agent, despite the fact that he had his pistol drawn and was shouting that he was FBI since the ordeal had begun.

"Back! Everyone get back!" someone yelled into the crowd. "Get the fuck back!"

Twenty or so Secret Service agents were on top of the cameraman now, who looked dazed even before the first of the blows came. It was a vicious scene, reminiscent of a stray tourist wandering into a camp belonging to a cadre of starving cannibals.

Stitts couldn't believe it.

The man didn't fit his profile at all; he was just a guy trying to fix his camera, to get a decent video of the president.

And it looked as if the Secret Service was going to kill him.

"Stop!" Stitts yelled. Someone grabbed him by the shoulders and yanked him to his feet. He tried to shake free, but the person's grip was too tight. "Get the fuck off me! I'm FBI!"

"Calm down, Stitts," a familiar voice whispered in his ear. The hands let go, and he turned to glare at the man who grabbed him.

SO Pratt stared back, a grin on his pink face.

"We got him," he said with a chuckle. "We got the guy."

Stitts started to shake his head, to tell him that no, they didn't get the guy, that they had it all wrong when Pratt pointed at the camera lying on the ground beside the fallen cameraman.

"A gun," Pratt exclaimed. And then, to Stitts's surprise, he realized that there *was* a gun there; a small, custom pistol that had been tucked into the camera, somehow becoming a part of it.

"What?" he gaped.

It wasn't the first time his profile had proven off base; case in point when he thought that it was a man who was responsible for the Download Murder killings in New York a couple years back, but that was a simple oversight.

This was just plain *wrong*.

Even now, with the evidence before him, Stitts couldn't see it; Senator DeBrusk's murder had been calculated, specific, expertly carried out.

This, on the other hand, was clumsy and inelegant.

"We got the guy," Pratt exclaimed again. He slapped Stitts on the back. "Way to go, Stitts, we got the fucker."

Chapter 32

CHASE FINALLY MANAGED TO dial Stitts's number as she hurried out of the command center. At the last moment, she reached back and grabbed one of the walkie-talkies sitting in a docking bay and attached it to her hip. Then she gestured at Floyd to get the car running.

Peter Horrowitz was at her side and it was a foregone conclusion that he was going to come with her. This was fine by Chase; she actually liked the man quite a bit. He wasn't like the others. And he also had a dearth of knowledge concerning bullets and rifles, and crime scene re-creations that would probably come in handy.

Just as she got into the backseat of Floyd's car, Stitts answered.

"Chase?" her partner asked breathlessly.

Chase got right to the point.

"Stitts? What the fuck is going on? I saw on TV—"

"Some asshole tried to pull a gun out of his camera and shoot the president. Secret Service was all over him; they're taking him to an undisclosed location now to interrogate him. Jesus, Chase, it was an absolute shit show."

Chase reached out and tapped Floyd on the shoulder to get his attention.

"Tell me where you're headed, and I'll meet you there. I'm in the car with Floyd and ATF Horrowitz."

Floyd had already started to drive, but most of the streets were either still blocked off from the senator's shooting or from the assassination attempt on the president. There was no way that they were going to get even close to the White House no matter how many times she flashed her smile and her badge.

But that was alright; Chase doubted that the 'undisclosed location' would be near the White House.

Plausible deniability and all that.

"Yeah, Secret Service's not going to let me tell you over the phone. Did you bring a walkie? I can tell you over the walkie."

Chase lifted it from her belt and turned it on.

"Yeah, got one."

"Go to channel 2."

Chase looked at the device and tried to figure how to change it to channel 2. The car suddenly came to a stop and Chase lifted her eyes to the window.

"Floyd? What's going on?"

"I don't know, A-a-agent Adams. It seems like this r-r-road is blocked too."

Chase wound down the window and leaned out the window.

A state trooper was blocking the intersection with one hand while using his other to wave a convoy of vehicles through.

"What the fuck is this? The Macy's Day Parade?" she grumbled then leaned further out the window. "We need to get through! FBI and ATF!"

She held out her badge, but the man didn't seem to care; he just continued to wave the procession through.

Horrowitz reached over her lap and held his badge out the window.

"ATF! What the fuck is going on here, officer?"

Chase scowled when the man paid attention to Peter.

Figures.

"I've got explicit orders to escort Congressman Vincente to the White House. No one is to come through—"

As the men spoke, Chase heard something strange.

It sounded like a hairdryer running on low. The noise was barely audible above the sound of Floyd's engine, but it was there. Her eyes darted around as she tried to identify the source.

It wasn't an obtrusive sound, and if she had been inside, Chase would have thought it may be a vacuum cleaner or a particularly noisy fridge compressor kicking in. But here, outside in the open air, it seemed out of place.

"You hear that?" she said to no one in particular.

She saw the line of cars in front of her, then looked back the other way. Traffic had piled up behind her and people were starting to gather on the sidewalk.

"Where the fuck is that coming from?"

And then, by sheer chance, Chase looked up.

"Shit! Floyd, get *down!*"

And then, a split second later, she felt it.

Fear. Fear spreading through everyone like a collective nightmare.

Chapter 33

"CHASE? *CHASE?*" STITTS SHOUTED into the phone.

They were in Pratt's car again, and the man was already ripping through the downtown streets, moving farther away from both the White House and Chase. They were tailing another car, which held the suspect from the presser.

"What's wrong?" Pratt asked, the smile that had been etched on his face finally sliding off.

"I... I don't know," he said, before hammering buttons on both the walkie-talkie and the cell phone at the same time. "I was talking to my partner when she shouted for everyone to get down... then I heard glass shattering."

The cell phone had since gone dead, but the walkie-talkie suddenly burst to life. The sound was so loud, that it shocked Stitts, and he dropped it to the floor. When this failed to dampen the sound, he realized that it hadn't been his walkie at all; it had been Pratt's.

"SO Pratt, over."

He was met by a second of static before a frantic voice broke through.

"There's been another shooting!"

Eyes wide, Pratt looked over at Stitts.

"What? Where?"

More static and Pratt yanked the car to the shoulder, narrowly missing the fender of a parked BMW in the process.

"Fucking focus, James. Who's been shot? Where?"

As he waited for a reply, Stitts brought his cell phone to his ear and dialed Chase's number again. There was still no answer.

"Congressman Vincente," James suddenly replied. "Congressman Vincente's been shot!"

Chapter 34

SHE'D SEEN A DRONE; that was what tipped Chase off. It was also what was making the strange whirring noise. A drone, just like the one she'd seen in the photograph and the video taken outside of Dunkin' Donuts seconds before Senator DeBrusk went down.

But the warning had come too late.

She felt the icy grip of fear first, then heard the sound of breaking glass. Without thinking, she shoved Peter out of her lap and then threw the car door open.

In all the confusion, several armed guards actually aimed their guns at her.

"FBI!" she shouted. "FBI!"

They eventually lowered their weapons and then started running around again like ants dropped into a pheromone soup. Everyone was trying to figure out where the shots had come from, but no one seemed to care where they'd ended up.

Chase's eyes were immediately drawn to the second in the line of four cars. She didn't see the glass, but it was the only car from which nobody had, as of yet, exited.

She sprinted toward the black Lincoln, crouching low just in case more shots were fired. When she reached the door, she didn't hesitate in opening it.

Inside the vehicle, she spotted the target: a large man with thick lips was slumped against his seat. Blood was spurting from a bullet hole in his neck and Chase quickly climbed inside to press her hands against the wound. The blood was hot, and it sprayed from between her fingers.

"Help! Medic!" she yelled over her shoulder. But the force with which the blood was coming out of the wound, and the amount that had already soaked her gloves and the seat, made it clear that they would be too late.

Breathing heavily, Chase looked down at a man whom she'd never seen before. His small eyes, buried beneath thick grey eyebrows, stared back.

The man was terrified, and Chase didn't blame him.

"Medic!" she yelled again.

Someone was behind her and Chase slowly took her hands off the man's neck and slid out of the car.

"Fuck!" she screamed. Her gloves were soaked with blood, as were the sleeves and front of her shirt. "*Fuck!*"

Part of her mind registered that Peter Horrowitz was beside her now, asking her something, but she couldn't hear the words.

All she could hear was that goddamn buzzing sound.

Chase ripped her gun from the holster and took aim at the drone that still hovered above them, albeit higher now. She fired off a shot, then a second, but the drone dipped and sped out of sight.

She was about to fire again when Peter gently put his hand on top of hers. Chase cursed and removed her finger from the trigger. She looked around and noted that the Secret Service and police had already made a perimeter around the cars and were actively shoving onlookers back.

I have to get out of here, she thought, looking down at all the blood on her clothes. *The last thing I want is for Director Hampton to turn on the news and see me like this.*

Chase hurried back to the car. When Floyd saw her, his eyes bulged, and he started to get out.

"I'm fine, stay in the car," she instructed.

Floyd took a moment to collect himself, and then handed her a cell phone as she climbed into the backseat.

"It's Stitts, he's been ca-ca-calling you," the man stuttered.

Chase snatched the phone from him and brought it to her ear. Adrenaline still flowed through her veins, and she found it easy to block all sounds except for those coming from the cell phone.

"Stitts? You still there?"

An exasperated Jeremy Stitts replied quickly.

"What the fuck's going on, Chase? There's been another shooting?"

Chase turned back to the vehicle that had been struck. Several people were standing in front of the open door, shaking their heads.

He didn't make it. The poor bastard didn't make it.

"You said you got the guy," Chase snapped. "You didn't get shit. Another person's been shot, Stitts; another person has been killed."

Chapter 35

SO PRATT SLAMMED ON the gas and yanked the wheel to the left. The tires squealed as they started back the way they'd come. Stitts was thrust backward so violently that his phone flew into the backseat.

"Hold onto your fucking hat there, Stitts," Pratt said out of the corner of his mouth.

Stitts struggled to peel himself off the seat and reach into the back. His fingers had just closed around the cell phone when Pratt made another turn and his face bashed against the seat.

"Goddamnit," he swore. Stitts brought the phone to his ear and Pratt yanked the wheel again. This time, he was able to brace himself before his head smashed into the window.

"Chase? We are on our way to you. Just hold tight," he said, glaring at Pratt.

"There was another fucking drone, Stitts. I took a couple of shots at it, but I couldn't hit it."

"Just stay low, Chase. Stay out of the line of fire. We'll be—" he looked up at Pratt.

"—two minutes," the man growled. "We'll be there in two minutes."

Chase said something but there was too much noise for Stitts to make it out. And then the line went dead.

"Shit," he said, sliding the phone into his pocket. Then to Pratt, he added, "Who the fuck is Congressman Vincente?"

Stitts was nervous about distracting the man—he'd narrowly avoided clipping several pedestrians at this point—but couldn't help himself.

"Before it was Bill S-89 and heading to the Senate, it was Bill C-142. Vincente was the one who made sure that it passed in Congress."

The man swerved and Stitts was hammered against the door. Then he slammed on the brakes just inches before T-boning a squad car. Several officers whipped around, guns drawn and aimed at the windshield.

"Secret Service," SO Pratt yelled out the window.

Following his lead, Stitts shouted his own credentials.

Thankfully, one of the men recognized Pratt and told the others to stand down.

"Jimmy, what we got here?" Pratt demanded as he stepped out of the car. Stitts quickly followed.

"Two shots fired from an unknown location. Smashed the window and struck Congressman Vincente once in the neck and once in the side. Ambulance couldn't get here fast enough."

"Shit."

Stitts was following Pratt, but then he noticed Floyd's car and hurried over. The rear door was open, and he leaned inside.

"Chase? You okay? What—oh my God, is that your blood?"

Chase looked down at herself and then shook her head.

"No, the Congressman's. He didn't... he didn't make it, Stitts."

Stitts nodded.

"Yeah, I heard. Floyd, you got something to help clean her up?"

"I've got some whe-whe-wet naps."

"Great, toss 'em back."

Stitts did his best to wipe some of the blood off Chase's clothes, but it was a losing battle.

"I saw the drone in the sky before the shots were fired," Chase said as Stitts continued working on cleaning her up. "In the sky, just above Vincente's car.

"The same one as before?"

"I dunno… I guess," Chase said. "What about your guy? You think the attempt on the president is related?"

Stitts thought about it; the MOs were vastly different, and even the motive was off. Bill 89 had been a Democratic push. As far as he knew, the president was dead set against it.

"I don't know. Maybe, but I doubt it. Young Arab guy… he had a gun, but it doesn't really fit."

Stitts was considering the real possibility that they'd just had two unrelated terrorist attacks in the past two hours.

"It doesn't fit at all."

A man suddenly popped his head into the car from the other side.

"Agent Stitts," Peter Horrowitz said with a polite nod.

Stitts acknowledged him with a nod of his own.

"Look, I'll know better when I get back to my computer, but see those three buildings right there?"

The man pointed at three high-rises made of glass about a block and a half away.

"Yeah? What about them?"

"Those are the same ones that the program singled out as the most probable location where the shots that took out Senator DeBrusk came from. It can't be a coincidence that they are also the highest point around here, as well."

Stitts couldn't help but agree… especially with the last part. Chase, on the other hand, was shaking her head.

"But didn't you scramble ATF agents to that location after the DeBrusk shooting? You're telling me that our shooter took aim while your agents were still in the building?"

Peter Horrowitz's face twisted.

"Maybe they didn't make it inside, maybe they got called back when all that shit went down with the president," he offered.

"Who called them back?" Stitts asked.

Peter shrugged.

"Fuck, I don't know. I'll find out, though."

"No, those aren't the right buildings," Chase said, still shaking her head.

"But the program—"

"The shots didn't come from there," Chase interupted with such authority, that both Stitts and Horrowitz just stared at her for a moment. Horrowitz waited for her to continue, but she abstained from speaking. Instead, she gave Stitts a look.

That look.

And then he knew.

He knew that Chase was convinced that the shots didn't come from there because someone had told her. Or, more accurately, she'd shared someone's memories.

Horrowitz, if for no other reason than to break the awkward silence, simply shrugged.

"Back to the drawing board I guess," he muttered.

The sound of chopping blades drew Stitts's head out of the car. His first thought was that the drone had returned, and he braced himself for more bullets. But it wasn't a drone; it was a military helicopter.

"Air force is scanning rooftops using infrared and heat signatures," SO Pratt said, appearing out of nowhere. "If our shooter is still out there, they'll find him. DoJ and Homeland already have their people on the ground, fanning out from this location and from where DeBrusk was shot."

Stitts looked around, noticing that the street was now teeming with agents from every agency imaginable. While he was grateful for the sheer number of bodies, he cringed at the thought of trying to get anything done with so many different alphas trying to be in charge.

"We'll get him, don't worry," Pratt said. "You wanna stay here on foot and help the search, or head with me to interrogate our would-be assassin?"

It took a moment for Stitts to realize that while he was proposing this as his own plan, someone else must have suggested it. After all, the Secret Service played second fiddle to both DoJ and Homeland—and the FBI for that matter—when it came to the congressman's and the senator's murders.

But an attack on the president, even a foiled one? That was all Secret Service.

Stitts glanced back into the car at Chase, who was still trying to get the blood out of her clothes.

"Yeah, we'll tag along," he said at last. "We won't be much use here on the ground."

Chapter 36

CHASE FINALLY REALIZED WHY Stitts hated working in multidisciplinary teams so much. No sooner had they arrived at what, to her, appeared to be an abandoned warehouse, were they confronted by Homeland Security. SO Pratt immediately started barking that he was in charge, that the Secret Service had apprehended the man, and that it was their jurisdiction. But while Pratt might have been right, Homeland had soldiers, and eventually, they won out.

When it came down to interviewing the man with the gun, however, it was someone else entirely, who never got introduced to Chase or Stitts. To her, he looked like a lawyer, but it wasn't clear who he worked for.

"You guys stay here," Pratt said. "I'll make sure everything is kosher in the interview."

He was just saving face, of course, after his manhood had been damaged. Chase herself wasn't entirely clear about how they all were supposed to work together. So far, she'd seen agents from the ATF, DEA, Secret Service, Homeland, local law, state law, DoJ, and the IRS of all things. Oh, and the FBI, of course. And aside from the latter, and maybe IRS, everyone thought that they were in charge.

Chase wished that there was some sort of ancestry.com for government organizations.

Regardless, as the only woman she'd seen today, not to mention she was only a hair over five feet tall, Chase knew better than to argue with these men.

"Fine," Stitts conceded for the both of them. Pratt nodded and started toward the door to the interview room, only to be stopped by one of the soldiers guarding the door.

"Our man gets a crack at him first, then you can go in."

Pratt growled, eyed the man's machine gun, and eventually backed down, but not before muttering something under his breath.

Chase smirked; she couldn't help herself.

When she looked at Stitts, she saw that he was staring through the one-way glass at the lawyer who was busy preparing documents at the metal table inside.

"It doesn't make sense," Stitts said. "Long-range sniper attacks—accurate, no wasted bullets, no collateral damage. And then we have this clown, who couldn't even get his gun out of the camera. "

"I'm with you on that," Chase said in agreement.

"But it can't be a coincidence."

Chase tilted her head to one side. It certainly seemed like one, either that or a horribly botched plan. She was about to say as much when a door on the other side of the room opened, and a man in chains was led in.

Stitts had referred to him as a young Arab boy, but his face was so bruised and swollen that this was difficult to confirm.

It looked like he'd spent six months in solitary confinement at Gitmo, not fifteen minutes in a warehouse.

"I want a lawyer," the man said, his lower lip, split and bloody, trembling.

"Sit down, Mohammed," the man at the table said.

Mohammed hesitated, but the soldiers who had brought him into the room assisted him rather roughly into the chair.

"I think you know how this goes," Lawyer-man said. "I ask you some questions here, in this room, with people watching from behind the glass. You answer my questions, and then you get processed. If you *don't* answer my questions, we move to another location. A location where nobody is watching."

Mohammed was on the verge of tears now.

"I want a lawyer," he repeated.

The man in the collared shirt sighed and started to absently spread photographs across the table.

"I'm the only lawyer you need, Mohammed. Let's start this off easy: is your name Mohammed Al-Saed?"

When he didn't immediately answer, one of the soldiers gripped his shoulder tightly.

"Yes, that's me; that's my name. Look, there's been a misunderstanding, I've—"

Lawyer-man waved a hand, effectively silencing him.

"And this is your wife? Naour Al-Saed?"

Another nod.

The interrogator moved a photograph of a young girl front and center.

"And this is your daughter? Sefa Al-Saed?"

Mohammed's eyes went wide.

"Yes, that's her. Please, let me explain."

Another hand wave.

"And you live…"

These mundane questions droned on for an infuriatingly long time, and Chase, still covered in Congressman Vincente's blood, struggled to focus.

Dr. Matteo had told her that her life had been boiled down to three components: her drug use, her sexuality, and her work.

After intensive treatment, she had somehow, against all odds, managed to overcome the former two—at least for the foreseeable future.

But the latter…

"I can't just sit here and watch this shit," she grumbled under her breath. She hadn't meant to speak out loud and blushed when both Stitts and Pratt looked over at her.

She wished that she was back with Peter Horrowitz in the command center. At least then she would be doing *something*. At least then, she would have some semblance of control.

And that brought her full-circle.

Dr. Matteo had told her that most of her problems stemmed from a lack of control. She'd never been given the tools to help her deal with her tragedies.

And, as a result, they kept popping up, time and time again.

"Just watch and wait, I've seen this guy work before," Pratt said. "He's a fucking master."

Chase chewed the inside of her lip.

"He may be a master, but I've got certain skills that he doesn't," she said. Chase moved so quickly to the door that even the soldier guarding it, who had been transfixed by the scene on the other side of the glass, failed to react in time.

"Chase," Stitts hollered after her. "Chase!"

But Chase was already in the room with the terrorist by the time any of them mobilized.

Chapter 37

"SHE'S... DIFFERENT," PETER HORROWITZ said as he typed away at his computer.

Floyd pulled his face away from his own monitor.

"E-e-e-excuse me?"

Peter spun in his chair.

"The agent you drive for. Chase. I just said she's different, that's all. Didn't mean to offend."

Floyd thought back to the time when they'd first met, when he'd driven her around Alaska, blabbering about trains. He knew that she was special back then, and nothing she'd done since—*nothing*—had changed his mind about that.

"She is d-d-different," he confirmed with a nod. He was about to turn back to his computer when Peter looked as if he had something more to say. "Wh-wh-wh-what is it?"

"I dunno... I mean, she was just so certain about the gunshots not coming from the building that I pointed out. I mean, so far nobody we've spoken to in the area has heard or seen anything, and my agents pulled back to support the president before Vincente was shot, but still. You should have seen it... she was absolutely certain of that fact. Shit, if I didn't know any better, I'd think that maybe she was somehow involved."

"She isn't," Floyd said quickly. And yet, he remembered the way she'd learned things about the two victims in Alaska, things that no one else—not the local law enforcement, not the coroner's office—picked up on. She *was* different. But she wasn't bad.

She didn't do this.

"Oh, I know. It's just weird. Here, check this out," Peter said, pointing at his computer screen. Floyd wheeled over and stared at a black-and-white image. "This is where the two bodies were shot, and the algorithm predicts that the sniper fired from this building."

Floyd shrugged. He knew next to nothing about bullet trajectories and shootings.

He knew about trains. And he knew a little bit about drones, too. But not bullets.

"Sorry, I don't know how to help you," he said, turning back to his computer.

"Is she single, by the way?"

"Excuse me?"

"Agent Adams. Do you know if she's single?"

Floyd swallowed hard and he glared at Peter.

"I don't know," he said sharply.

"I was just wondering," Peter muttered under his breath.

Brow furrowed, Floyd tried to focus on the task at hand but found it difficult.

Is she single? Why would you ask that? How is that professional?

He thought back to when they'd found her, bloodied, bruised, and half-naked, lying at the bottom of a rock quarry.

A shudder ran through him and he forced himself to devote all his attention to his work.

He'd managed to come up with a short list of drone clubs that operated out of Washington. One in particular, *Fly Right*, appeared to be the largest. An added bonus was that they met at an abandoned airfield not far from the mobile command center.

Floyd clicked the Contact Us link and was immediately redirected to an email form.

He wrote a quick email inquiring about regulations pertaining to drones in the city.

Floyd signed his name at the end and was about to click send when he paused.

And then, with a smile on his face, he added 'FBI assistant' beneath his name.

Floyd debated deleting the words but then thought better of it. Chase had called him that, twice, if he recalled correctly.

Yeah, Agent Adams most definitely is different, he thought with a smile as he clicked the Send button.

Chapter 38

LAWYER-MAN WHIPPED AROUND when Chase entered the room, but before he could get a word out, Chase instructed him to remain quiet.

"You, too, Mo," she said to the man seated across the table. "Just be quiet."

The two guards behind the prisoner looked at her curiously, but she moved with such authority that they didn't immediately attempt to stop her. She knew though that they would eventually, especially because she suspected that Pratt was already entering the room behind her.

But that was okay. She didn't need much time.

"You ever shot of rifle before, Mohammed?" she asked. She stared at the man intently, looking for any sign of deception: hands twitching, pupils dilating, blood flooding into the ears or nose. Anything from her poker days that would indicate a tell.

"No," he said.

Chase believed him.

"Then why the fuck did you have a gun at the president's press conference?"

"You can't be in here," Lawyer-man said. Chase put a hand on his shoulder and squeezed.

"Some guy gave me a camera... he gave me fifty bucks and a camera and told me to record the damn thing. The camera wasn't working so I tried to fix it. Shit, I didn't know there was a gun in there."

Once again, Chase believed him.

"This man who paid you, what did he look like?"

Mohammed shrugged.

"I dunno… a white dude with slicked hair. He looked like a regular guy, not sketchy at all. I was having a smoke and he came up to me. I didn't even —"

"Agent Adams, can I speak to you outside for a moment," she heard Pratt say from behind her. The man started to approach, but Chase moved to the other side of the table, taking off one of her blood-stained gloves as she did.

And then, just as she felt Pratt reach for her, Chase extended her hand and touched Mohammed Al-Saed's fingers before he could pull away.

Chapter 39

"CAN YOU BELIEVE THIS fucking guy?" Peter said, his eyes drifting up to the TV screen.

William Woodley, the talking head, was back, this time rambling on about Congressman Vincente's murder. Only, this didn't last long; it quickly digressed into a one-sided discussion about Bill S-89.

"We don't need Bill S-89. In fact, that's the opposite of what this country needs right now. What we need is tough love. What we need is stagflation. What we need is a market correction in which inflation shoots through the roof, while unemployment continues to rise. It's coming, people, and while it's gonna be hard, we're going to come out on the other side a better nation and people. We'll be more self-sustained than China, more productive than India, and more technologically advanced than South Korea. We don't need more government intervention, we need less. What America needs is *minimal* government intervention. Only under these conditions can business thrive. Businesses make money, businesses drive the economy. The government spends money and restricts the economy. Don't believe me? Then let me ask you this: if the government is so good at running businesses, why have they racked up trillions of dollars worth of debt?"

Floyd was watching the TV now too, and while he didn't really understand everything that the talking head was saying, he was familiar with the rhetoric. It was as unoriginal as the show's format.

"Not two hours after the assassinations, this asshole is trying to spin it for political gain. Oh, sure, William Woodley wants an economic downturn, because his coffers are probably filled to the brim with gold bullion. And when everything goes to shit? He'll buy up all sorts of commercial real estate only to flip it a decade later for ten times the amount he spent. You know, it's kinda like rich people saying that money has no meaning to them, that it's just a *thing*. Well, I'll tell you who it ain't just a *thing* for: the guy on the corner begging for nickels, or the single mother who is cashing in food stamps just to make sure her kids have something to eat," Peter said.

Floyd wasn't sure if the man was talking to him, or himself, but it didn't matter. He really had nothing to add.

"Minimum wage?" William Woodley continued. "All that does is stifle productivity. What's worse, it makes young people unemployable. Think about it: you have somebody with limited skills, straight out of school, and they want to get a job. Because they don't have much experience and they're still learning a craft, their value to a company is limited. Now, if the minimum wage is higher than the value they can provide, no business can hire them. And we've seen what happens in places like Greece when there are simply no jobs for young people. It decimates the workforce, both present, and future."

Floyd was interested in continuing to watch, but an email notification popped up on his screen. When he saw that it was from brian@flyright.com, he opened it immediately.

Floyd,

Thank you so much for reaching out with your questions about drones and regulations. Currently, we are working hard, trying to get the government to approve more safe fly zones in Washington. As it stands, almost all of Washington DC is currently a no-fly zone. We understand the government's concerns but believe that a happy medium between us droners and citizen safety can be reached. If you would like to discuss this further or see how you can get involved, please email me back or better yet, come on out to the airfield and meet up in person.

Thank you again for your interest,

Brian.

Floyd leaned back in his chair, a wide smile on his face.

Then he grabbed his phone and dialed Agent Adam's number.

Chapter 40

"Hey, how'd you like to make fifty bucks?"

At first, Mohammed didn't even realize that the man was speaking to him. It took a tap on his shoulder to get his attention.

"Fifty bucks—all you have to do is videotape the presidential address."

Mohammed squinted at the man. He was maybe in his late thirties or early forties, Caucasian, with hair slicked to his scalp. There was nothing that immediately sounded alarm bells, and yet Mohammed was cautious.

"What? What are you talking about?"

The man pointed at the camera in his hands.

"Look, I got some shit to do, but my boss wants me to videotape the damn thing. I'll give you fifty bucks—all you have to do is stand there and tape it. Ten minutes, maybe less."

Mohammed squinted again, trying to ascertain whether or not this was some sort of ploy, a prank, or a scam. When he saw no endgame in sight, he shrugged.

"Show me the money," he demanded.

The man didn't hesitate. He reached into his pocket and pulled out a fifty-dollar bill. Then he held it out to Mohammed.

But Mohammed didn't take it.

"I'll record it on my cell phone, send you the footage afterwards," he offered, still skeptical. *"Shit, my phone probably takes better video than that old thing."*

The man shook his head.

"Nah, you gotta use this camera. It's got a live feed or some shit. You want it or not? If not, I'll find someone else out here who could use fifty bucks for ten minutes of work."

The thing was, Mohammed was a man who could use fifty bucks.

He chewed the inside of his lip then reached out and snatched the fifty before the man could pull it back.

Then he took the camera.

"Alright, all you gotta do is push this button here, whenever the president starts talking. You shoot some decent footage, and not your foot or some chick's ass, and I'll give you another fifty bucks when it's over."

Another fifty?

Mohammed settled the camera on his shoulder. It was much heavier than he'd expected.

"Alright, meet me back here when it's over," the man said before he drifted away from the crowd.

Chapter 41

A HAND WRAPPED AROUND Chase's waist and pulled her away from Mohammed, breaking their contact.

At first, she thought it was SO Pratt and she started to struggle.

"Calm down, Chase," Stitts whispered in her ear, as together they moved out of the interrogation room.

"He didn't do it," she whispered.

Nobody in the room, the number of whom had ballooned to a dozen or more since she'd left, seemed to hear her.

They were still too busy trying to act like they were the ones in charge to care about anything else.

Pratt came up to her first.

"Agent Adams, you need to get out here," Pratt barked, his face turning a shade of pink. "You sabotaged everything—"

"Take it easy," Stitts cut in. "We're leaving."

He guided his partner toward the exit.

"He didn't do it," Chase said a little louder this time.

"Say one more word, and I'll have you arrested," Pratt proclaimed. As if to back up this claim, several Homeland Security officers stepped forward.

Oh, now you guys can work together, Chase thought.

"Calm down," Stitts pleaded. "Everyone just calm down."

"He didn't even know about the gun," Chase said.

And that was it. Before either of them knew what was happening, the nearest soldier yanked Chase away from Stitts and slapped a set of handcuffs on her.

Chase didn't struggle, but she was going to get her voice heard; she made sure of it.

"He didn't do it! *He didn't even know a gun was in there! Mohammed Al-Saed is not your guy! He's not the shooter!*"

PART III – Drone

Chapter 42

"**WHAT THE FUCK WERE** you thinking, Chase?" Stitts demanded.

Chase waited for the officer to unlock her cuffs before answering. Then she rubbed her wrists and immediately slid her gloves back on. Stitts had, thankfully, rinsed them out, and while they weren't completely clean, they weren't soaked in blood anymore.

"It's a waste of time in there; Mohammed didn't know shit about the shooting or the gun. I have no idea who gave him the camera, but that's the guy we should be looking for."

Stitts just stared blankly at her for a moment before replying.

"Yeah, I told you, I feel the same way. But you can't just barge in there and start mouthing off. There are rules and regulations."

Chase rolled her eyes and moved toward the door.

"It worked, didn't it?"

Stitts gawked.

"Chase, if it wasn't for the fact that Lawyer-man somehow knew the man who represented Drake, and Screech called to vouch for you, you'd be in prison right now. Fuck, that prick Pratt might have even labeled you a terrorist."

"The lawyer who represented Drake? What are you talking about?"

Stitts sighed and shook his head.

"You're missing the point. You can't do that. Not here."

Chase hated being lectured by anyone, but it was somehow worse coming from Stitts.

"I'll behave, Daddy. Promise."

Fuck, I did it again.

"Sorry," she grumbled and Stitts's expression softened.

"Don't apologize to me... you have to apologize to Pratt. Seriously."

"You got to be kidding me," she said, cringing at the very idea. It was all part of this fucking machismo bullshit.

God, I wish I had a dick and didn't have to deal with this shit.

"No, I'm not kidding. You have to apologize to the man. I mean it, Chase."

You need to relinquish control, Chase, Dr. Matteo's words echoed in her mind.

"Fine," she said under her breath. "Where's the asshole, anyway?"

"He's watching the botched interrogation from the other side of the glass. Sometimes, Chase... there's someone out there, sniping Congressmen and Senators, and we have to waste time doing this shit. Sometimes, Chase. Sometimes..."

The comment seemed out of character for Stitts, but Chase chalked it up to him needing a cigarette.

"Fine, I said, fine. I'll just—"

The phone in her pocket buzzed and she immediately answered it. It was Floyd.

"Yeah?"

"Agent A-a-a-adams? It's Floyd."

"Yeah, I know, your name shows up on my phone when you call. What is it?"

"I looked into the drone stuff that you asked for. I found out that there is a club that operates not too far from here. The man in charge, Brian Doucette, said he'd be happy to discuss rules and regulations. We can go meet him now if you want. I can pick you up."

Chase had forgotten all about the drone that she'd fired two shots at. It was one of the few avenues that they hadn't explored yet. And it also gave her an out.

"Come pick me up. I'm at—" she looked at Stitts who started to shake his head. "On second thoughts, I don't know where I am. I'll grab a cab and meet you back at the command center. Then we can head out to the club."

Before Floyd could answer, Chase hung up the phone and started down the hallway. A few seconds passed before Stitts hollered after her.

"Chase? *Chase?*"

Chase turned and held her hands out to her sides in an apologetic gesture.

"I'm sorry, I gotta run. You go ahead and do the apology for me and we'll meet up later. Truly, Stitts, I'm grateful."

Chapter 43

As STITTS WATCHED CHASE go, he couldn't help but think that despite Dr. Matteo's claim that she'd changed, it was still the same old Chase. He was grateful that she seemed to have lost the urge to use, and so far as he knew, she hadn't fucked any of the Secret Service, but as soon as they'd arrived in Washington, she'd gone back to her old ways. Now that they were on the hunt for a killer, nothing else seemed to matter to her. She would insult and hurt anyone who came in her path and break any and all rules that she had to in order to find whoever was responsible.

"Where's she going?" a gruff voice demanded.

Stitts whirled around and faced Pratt, his face now a perpetual scowl.

"She had to... she had to go. Look, I'm sorry about what happened in there. Sometimes—well, Agent Adams has her own way of doing things and sometimes it can lead to... fuck. Sorry about that, Pratt."

Stitts hated the fact that he was apologizing for Chase. She was constantly admonishing him for looking out for her, but she had no problem letting him get her out of trouble.

If there wasn't a maniac still out there somewhere, I wouldn't be covering for you, Chase.

But that was a lie. He owed her.

Pratt made a noise that was halfway between a grunt and a sigh.

"You guys still working on Mohammed in there?"

"No; either he's the world's best liar, or he really was just a scapegoat. We're going to take him somewhere to sweat a little more, but I doubt anything of value is going to come out of it."

Stitts nodded.

"Doesn't fit the profile."

Pratt's scowl deepened even more. Stitts knew what the other departments thought about profiling. All you had to do was bring it up, and invariably the conversation would degenerate to some famous cases where the profiler was way off base.

It didn't matter how many you got right, of course; one bad apple spoiled the whole bunch.

They stood in the hallway long after Chase had left, not saying anything. For the first time in a long time, Stitts wasn't sure what to do next. He could hurry after Chase, but that would not go over well with respect to interagency relations. He'd already proven himself a loyal soldier in the eyes of Pratt and his men. Going after Chase would ruin that. But to stay in role, he also couldn't go ahead and start telling Pratt and others what to do next.

Thankfully, a Secret Service agent appeared behind them and broke the impasse.

"SO Pratt? We've got men stationed outside the homes of most of the senators and congressmen who were in favor of Bill S-89."

It was the junior agent that Stitts had been standing beside during the presidential address, and he nodded at the man.

The agent didn't nod back.

"Good. Tell them not to leave their homes, to stay away from windows. You know the drill. I want to amp up security around the White House, as well," Pratt said. The young Secret Service agent nodded, but when he didn't immediately leave, Pratt added, "Anything else?"

The agent started toe digging.

"What?" Pratt barked. "What is it?"

The man took out his phone and held it out for both of them to see.

"There this video I think you should see. The bald dude was showing it on his talk show, or whatever."

One glimpse of the bald man's face, and Stitts knew exactly who the man was talking about.

"William Woodley."

"What kind of video?" Pratt snapped.

"From the drone."

"*What?*" Stitts nearly gasped.

Clearly, Pratt wasn't catching.

"The drone? What drone?"

"The one that was seen when Senator DeBrusk was murdered," the young agent clarified.

"You've got to be kidding," Pratt said, grabbing the phone from the man's hand.

"I wish I was."

Pratt pressed play and they all watched the video, their mouths going slack with every horrifying second that passed.

They saw DeBrusk exit the car and make his way to the door. He was smiling, and he waited patiently for the sidewalk to clear before crossing it. Just as he grabbed the door, he turned back and looked up.

For a brief second, the camera locked onto Senator DeBrusk's face. At first, he looked confused. But when his body was thrust backward, a bullet hole directly in the center of the binder he was holding, his expression changed.

The man looked terrified.

Chapter 44

FLOYD WAS WAITING BY his car when Chase hopped out of the cab. She waved at him and he waved back enthusiastically.

"Are you ready to go?" he asked.

Chase nodded. She wanted to go, all right. She wanted to get as far away from SO Pratt and his goons before they decided to lock her up again.

"Yeah, let's get going."

Floyd reached for the rear door, but she shook her head.

"No, I'll get in the front."

But to her surprise, the back door opened from the inside.

"Peter said that he wanted to come along. I hope that's all right," Floyd said.

Chase lowered her head to look at Peter Horrowitz in the backseat.

She nodded.

"Fine by me," she said as she slid in beside Peter.

As Floyd drove out to the abandoned airfield, he updated her on some of the details about the drone club.

"The drones are expensive and while I couldn't get exact numbers on how many are in Washington, the best estimate I could get put the number around a hundred and fifty," he said. "The good news is, *Fly Right* has at least a hundred members."

Chase listened closely. Like when Floyd spoke about trains, his stutter was almost nonexistent.

"The most common drones in this price range have a maximum range of about five miles. But that's without interference or anything like that. In practical settings, like in the city, you're looking at more like three and a half miles, tops."

Chase thought about this for a moment, trying to figure out how the drone was related to the shooter. She turned to Peter Horrowitz, who had his laptop out and open on his lap.

"Can you use your computer program to figure out where the drone might've come from? Can you triangulate its location based on the maximum distance these things can travel?"

Peter shrugged.

"I can get a maximum distance it could have come from. Not sure if I can get anything more specific than that."

Chase waited for the man to type in the information, and then the screen transformed into the black-and-white image again. This time, however, there were two large circles overlaying the image.

"If we assume that the operator didn't move between the shootings—meaning, the drone took off from the same location both times, we're looking at this area here—a strip of about a mile long and nearly that wide."

Chase stared at the image. It was still a large area, and they'd made many assumptions along the way, but it was a start. She also noted that the three buildings that she'd visited were within the highlighted area.

"What the fuck does this drone have to do with the shooting, anyway?" she grumbled.

Peter shrugged.

"I can tell you with a hundred percent certainty that the bullets didn't come from the drone. There is just no way that an object with such little mass would be able to propel a Lapua Magnum round. But other than that…"

"We're here," Floyd said as he stopped the car. Chase turned her gaze out the window and saw that they'd arrived at something that looked like an airplane hangar... from three or four decades ago. It was a semi-circle made of corrugated aluminum, and it appeared as if it had seen better days.

Chase instinctively looked up and saw several low flying drones buzzing about on the opposite side of the hangar.

Yep, we've come to the right spot, that's for sure.

Chase stepped out of the car, as did Peter. But when the driver's door remained closed, she turned back and beckoned to Floyd.

"Hey, FBI Assistant, you coming, or what?"

A smile broke out on the man's young face.

"Yes, of course," he said, jumping from the vehicle so quickly that the door almost smacked into Chase's hip.

"All right, let's see if one of these nerds can help us out, figure out where the damn drone came from and what role it has to play in all of this."

Chapter 45

"JESUS," SO PRATT SAID when the video finally ended. Stitts turned to the junior agent.

"And this asshole aired the video on live TV?"

The man nodded.

"He's been playing it on loop for the last fifteen minutes or so. It's going to be another half hour before all the networks are showing it... for a price, of course. So far as I can tell, he's the first to get the footage."

"Unbelievable," Stitts muttered. He couldn't help but think of Senator DeBrusk's family; his wife, his kids.

Fuck, nothing is sacred anymore... not even murder.

"We have to go talk to this guy," Pratt stated. Then he looked up and repeated the statement more aggressively. "He's the biggest opponent of the Bill S-89. He's got motive."

Stitts pressed play and watched the video a second time. It wasn't any less horrifying. Then he thought about the profile, about how Peter Horrowitz had marveled at the accuracy of the shots.

"Does William Woodley have a military background?" he asked.

Pratt shrugged, but the junior agent confirmed that this was the case.

"Ex-Marine; honorable discharge when he tore his ACL. He talks about it on the show all the time. And I mean, *all the time.*"

Was it possible that this man, this public figure, was dumb enough to murder a congressman and senator then air the evidence on his very own show?

Stitts didn't know William Woodley from Adam, but he didn't think so. It took a certain personality type to make it to the point where you could afford massive billboards in the middle of the city, and while there was no guarantee that he was a rocket scientist, there was only a slim chance that William Woodley was an absolute moron.

"I don't know what this means," Stitts admitted. "But I'm thinking that we should have a little chat with our talking head."

Pratt looked at Stitts and then snapped his fingers.

Moments later, a handful of Secret Service agents appeared in the hallway behind the junior agent.

"Damn right we are."

Chapter 46

CHASE LED THE WAY, while Peter and Floyd picked up the rear. They nearly made it to the door before it opened and a man with curly brown hair and light-colored eyes stepped out. He had a huge smile on his face.

"Welcome, welcome," he said cheerily. He gestured for them to enter.

"FBI Special Agent Adams," Chase said, shaking the man's outstretched hand. When he saw her stern face, his smile faltered, but only for an instant.

The man looked exactly the way Chase expected somebody who was head of a drone flying club to look: slightly overweight, a little bit awkward, and a whole lot of geek.

"Brian Doucette. It's a pleasure to meet you."

Chase hooked a thumb over her shoulder.

"This is my assistant, Floyd, and ATF Agent Horrowitz. I think Floyd spoke to you about drones via email?"

Brian nodded and held the door open for them. Chase stepped inside and was immediately surprised. From the outside, the hangar had appeared to be a complete semicircle. Only it wasn't; the back half was cut off and opened to a large field.

"Yes, he said he was interested in more information about regulations?"

Instead of answering right away, Chase continued to walk into the makeshift hangar, her eyes drifting left and right. In front of her, stood three men with remote controls, while there were two others on her left, talking on cell phones, and a third on a laptop. To her right was a man hunched over a workbench performing what looked to her like drone surgery.

"Something like that."

"Well, anything I can do to help. But I gotta be honest, your guys' rules about where we can fly these things? I mean it's so—"

"Those aren't our rules," Chase said, interrupting the man. "That's the FAA and the local government. FBI has nothing to do with that."

Brian stared at her blankly for a moment and then nodded.

"Oh, okay, sure. What is it you want to know?"

Chase strode forward, and all three men followed her towards the open field.

"Do you need to register your drone with any official agency?"

"No, you don't have to register it, although every operator is supposed to put their name, address and phone number on the bottom of the drone."

Chase frowned.

"What about you guys? Do you have to sign up or show ID to use this field? To fly here legally?"

Her presence was starting to draw the attention of the three men flying their drones. They looked at her curiously, trying to get a read, clearly worried that their precious airfield was about to get shut down.

"Yeah; to fly here, you need to join the club, which means you need to provide ID. We also ask for a very small registration fee to use the place. The guy who owns it is a droner himself, but we all pitch in to keep the lights on."

"I'm going to need to see that list," Chase said the words with such authority that Brian didn't even hesitate, even though he was about to break nearly a dozen privacy laws.

"Sure, no problem. I'll go—"

One of the men had started to pack his drone up in a big black briefcase when Chase spotted something within that caught her eye; some sort of goggles. Without thinking, she walked over to him and stopped him just before he closed the case.

"What are those things? The newest Oakley's?"

The man, who wore thick glasses and had a hairline that started by his temples, looked at her for a moment before grinning a gap-toothed smile.

"These? These are my racing goggles."

Without her even having to ask, the man opened the case and took them out. They were huge, and they reminded Chase of some VR goggles she'd seen advertised during one of the online poker tournaments she'd played a while back.

The droner held the goggles out to her, and she noticed that inside the hood were two video displays; one for each eye.

"Put them on, try them. Trust me, it's the closest thing you can get to flying, without an airplane," the man insisted.

Chase politely declined the offer.

"I think I'll pass. Listen, do you—"

She stopped. Something that Peter had said a while ago occurred to her.

"Wait—with these goggles, do you see what the drone is seeing?"

The man nodded.

"Yeah, FPV—uhh, first-person view. It's amazing; it's like you're inside the drone. Like you're—"

"You know what? I think I will give them a try, if you don't mind of course," Chase said with a sheepish grin.

She didn't have to ask twice; the geek was probably overjoyed that a woman was finally taking an interest in his hobby.

"Sure, let me help you out."

After casting a glance over her shoulder at Peter and Floyd, who both looked incredibly confused, she allowed the man to put the goggles on her face. For all their size, they were actually lighter than they looked and relatively comfortable.

As for the field of view, however, all she saw was black.

"Hold on, I'll power them up," the guy said. Chase felt his hand touch the side of her head. Suddenly, her entire field of view exploded into colors and some sort of logo.

Chase gasped. The immersiveness of the experience of just seeing the logo was mind-blowing. Sure, she'd spent the last six months in a rehab facility, where the most exciting thing was Taco Tuesday, but still.

"Amazing," she muttered.

"Oh, you think that's amazing? Just wait until you see this."

Chase heard and felt air on her face and then the screen changed, and she stumbled backwards.

Chapter 47

SO PRATT DROVE LIKE a maniac. Stitts had thought that this was only the case when someone was in danger, but that proved untrue. He drove like a madman at all times, it seemed. Thankfully, William Woodley's studio wasn't far.

His *shared* studio, that is.

The junior agent in the back seat, who had since introduced himself as Darren Trotter, had informed them both that most of these guys shared a studio.

This surprised Stitts.

"He's got a big ass billboard on Massachusetts Avenue; you're telling me he can't afford his own studio?"

Darren shrugged.

"The production company probably fronted the money for that."

Pratt leaned out the window and started reading off civic addresses.

"One-two-four, this is it?" he asked.

Stitts shared the man's skepticism. One-two-four Avon Road was a plain, six-story apartment building. It was hard to believe that there was a state-of-the-art studio inside.

"Yeah, this is it," Darren confirmed.

They hopped out of the car, with SO Pratt leading the way up the front steps, his hand firmly on his gun that was still in its holster, Stitts noted.

He was amped up, eager for action. Clearly, the scene back at the warehouse hadn't lived up to his expectations.

Stitts stepped in front of Pratt, and while the man made a face, he didn't protest. Pratt might be able to push it, say that this had to do with the attempt on the president's life, and therefore, Secret Service jurisdiction, but it was just easier to let the FBI take the lead.

For now, Stitts knew that at the first chance, Pratt would reclaim his throne as the alpha dog.

Stitts knocked three times on the door, holding his FBI badge in plain view of the peephole.

After about thirty seconds, he heard the door unlock from the inside.

"FBI, I'm—"

But Stitts didn't even finish his sentence before Pratt rushed in front again, nearly knocking him back down the steps in the process.

"Get down! Get down on the ground!" Pratt shouted.

The door swung open and a thin man with dark hair was tackled to the ground.

Several other Secret Service agents came out of nowhere and stormed the building.

"For fuck's sake," Stitts grumbled as he regained his balance. "Pratt!"

The man was in a blind rage and didn't hear him.

Stitts hurried inside and grabbed Pratt by the collar and yanked. The man got to his feet and glared at him. For a split second, Stitts thought that Pratt was going to crack his skull open right there.

But Darren stepped between them.

"Pratt, the FBI should take this one. It's their jurisdiction," he said, clearly trying to diffuse the situation.

Pratt looked at Darren, then back to Stitts. Eventually, his eyes fell on the man on the floor, who was being 'helped' to his feet by agents Stitts didn't recognize.

Jesus, Stitts thought as he stared at the big man with the heaving chest. *Pratt flew off the handle at the drop of a hat.*

Eventually, he backed down and Stitts approached the man who'd been knocked down.

"I'm sorry about that, things have just been a little amped up after what happened this morning." The man brushed his hair back with both hands and nodded. "My name's Jeremy Stitts, and I'm with the FBI."

He flashed his badge, but the man didn't even look at it.

"I'm guessing you here to see Will?" the man asked in a soft voice.

"Yeah, we need to have a chat with him," Pratt growled from behind them.

"He's in his dressing room, follow me," the man said.

With that, he spun on his heels and started down a narrow hallway, none the worse for wear after being tackled. Off to the left, they passed an open area, and Stitts glanced inside. There was a semicircular desk made from some sort of imitation marble in the center and behind that a large green screen. There were several cameras aimed at the desk, which was empty.

"In here," the handler said, indicating a door with the name 'Woodley' scrawled on a chalkboard.

The man knocked once and then opened the door.

"Will? There are some FBI agents here to see you."

The lights were so harsh inside the dressing room that Stitts had to cover his forehead with the blade of his hand and wait for a moment for his eyes to adjust. Even then, he didn't immediately see anyone inside. Eventually, he saw the outline of a man in front of a mirror lined with light bulbs. The man turned. He was bald, deeply tanned, and had napkins spread out from the collar of his shirt.

And he didn't look happy to see them.

"Gentlemen, what can I do for you?" he asked. It was clear by the way he inhaled deeply before speaking that this was his commanding voice, his television voice.

Stitts flashed his badge and stepped deeper into the dressing room.

"FBI Special Agent Jeremy Stitts. I want to—"

"Well, you can't have it," William said quickly.

"Excuse me?"

William waved a hand at the man who had led them to the room, and said, "You can go now, Fred. And make sure the set is ready for my next show in fifteen minutes. I'll be going live again."

The handler nodded and left them alone in the room. Pratt stared him down as he passed, but Fred wanted nothing to do with him.

"You can't have it. You can't have the tape, and you can't have my source," William reiterated.

They hadn't even asked any questions, and already the man was coming up with answers.

Shit, Stitts realized suddenly. *He knew we were coming. And he* wanted *us to come.*

After all, what would look better to an audience of Republicans than the government storming a private studio, strong-arming poor little William Woodley into hand over privileged information?

They would eat that shit up.

Which is probably why the man aired the tape in the first place, Stitts concluded.

"Where'd you get the tape, Woodley?" Pratt demanded.

Stitts saw the faintest hint of a smile form on William Woodley's lips, and he wished that Pratt would just stay out of it; he was sprinting headlong into the man's trap.

"A senator and a congressman were shot dead this morning. While you might not agree with the bill that they were pushing, you must respect their right to free speech. After all, I'm guessing that you support the first amendment as much as the second, am I right?"

William stopped smiling, but then he shook his head and the grin returned.

"Nice try. You almost had me there for a second. I'm shocked and saddened by the death of two Americans, but I simply can't give up the tape or my source. I took an oath as a journalist and my sources trust me. I won't break either. What do I know, anyway? I just report the news, read a teleprompter filled words that people smarter than I put together to form coherent sentences."

"Journalist," Pratt mocked.

Once again, Stitts ignored him. Chase may be unpredictable, and he rarely agreed with her methods, but at least she had a purpose, a goal. Shit, an idea even.

Pratt had no clue. He was just seeing red.

"This guy's not done yet, William. Tomorrow it could be another senator or congressman who's targeted. Pratt, how many senators were expected to vote in favor of S-89?"

Pratt didn't answer; he didn't even acknowledge the question.

Stitts turned to Darren, who was standing in the doorway.

"Darren?"

"Fifty-one."

Stitts nodded. Fifty-one meant that the bill was going to pass.

"So, there are fifty more potential targets, William. And however many congressmen voted to—"

"More than two-hundred," Darren said.

Shit, that's a lot of people who need protection, Stitts thought.

"Just give up your source, help us out here."

William shook his head.

"Can't do it. You're going to need to get a search warrant and good luck with that."

Now Stitts was starting to get frustrated. The man didn't give a shit about dead Americans.

All he cared about was ratings; ratings and whatever game he was playing.

"We don't need a subpoena you smug bastard," Pratt said with a laugh. "These shootings were acts of terror."

The big man was right, Stitts realized. The normal rules that governed their actions didn't apply; they were blurry, at best.

And yet, William Woodley must've known this, being the patriot that he was. But he didn't seem at all worried.

Something smelled fishy, and Stitts paused to look around. On the makeup table were tubes of creams and lotions, a bottle of beer, and a set of keys.

And then he spotted it; there, not a foot from William's elbow, tucked behind a bottle of hairspray was a small red light from the camera that was recording them.

"Yeah, you heard me. We're gonna shut you down, Woodley. Shut you down and tear this place apart. You're going to—"

Stitts whipped around and put a finger to his lips. Pratt made a face.

"What? What are you—"

Stitts hushed him again and then tried to get him to vacate the dressing room. The man didn't budge.

Stitts cursed under his breath and then pointed at the red light behind the hairspray bottle.

"He's recording us. Don't you get it? This is what he wants," Stitts said low enough that he hoped the microphone didn't pick it up.

William chuckled and crossed his arms over his chest.

The prick was enjoying this.

As soon as Pratt picked up on the gesture, the veins in his forehead started to bulge. He opened his mouth to say something, but Stitts quickly intervened.

"We'll come back," Stitts said. "It's too bad that you couldn't cooperate with the government. It's too bad that if anyone else dies, it's gonna be on your conscience, William."

This rattled the man, and he sat bolt upright in his chair.

"It's my right to keep my sources private. I made an oath!"

Stitts practically had to shove Pratt through the door.

"We'll be back," Pratt repeated over his shoulder. "We're gonna fucking come back, Woodley! Mark my words!"

As they made their way toward the front doors, Stitts cast a glance into the studio and saw that the handler was now cleaning the desk.

The bastard's going to go live in ten minutes, and guess who's going to star in the feature story?

"Yeah, and I'll be waiting!" William Woodley predictably shouted back.

Chapter 48

CHASE FELT AS IF she were flying. At first, while she was still getting used to just how immersive the experience was, she'd only seen grass. But even that was so vivid, so real, that she had to stop herself from reaching out and trying to touch it. And then she was airborne, staring down at the earth as she hovered.

"You can move your head around," the man controlling the drone said. "I've set it up so the camera will mimic your head movements."

Chase hesitated. She was worried about getting nauseous, as she did at the end of all her visions, even though this wasn't one of them. Eventually, curiosity took over, and she turned her head to the right.

Her entire world shifted. But it wasn't jittery or choppy, it was smooth, even, *real*.

"Wow," she whispered, staring at a forest in the distance. Just when her eyes started to focus on the individual trees, the drone took off, zipping through the air at breakneck speeds.

Chase found herself in the clouds next, living in them, breathing them in.

All of a sudden, the drone did a three-sixty and started rushing back toward the hangar.

As it neared, Chase saw herself, standing with her knees slightly bent, one hand at her side, the other outstretched just a little.

"Too much," she gagged, pulling off the goggles. "It was too much—I saw myself."

The geek landed the drone and then looked at her.

"Sorry about that. Sometimes I get carried away. But it was pretty amazing, wasn't it?"

Chase nodded. It *was* amazing; she couldn't deny that. The only strange part, the only nauseating part, was when she'd seen herself live.

But this wasn't a social outing.

She turned around to look at Floyd and Peter who were staring back, slack-jawed.

"I know why the drone was there," she almost whispered. "I know—"

Brian Doucette suddenly returned with a sheet of paper in his hand.

"These are the names of all our members," he said. "I'm sure—"

Chase reached out and grabbed the paper.

"Thank you, Brian," she said. And then she thanked the man who'd let her try the drone goggles. She gave a smile, too, and thought that she detected a slight bulge in the front of his slacks, right between the two front pleats.

"What did—" Peter began, but Chase shook her head.

"Let's go," she said, hurrying toward the door. "I know exactly what the drone was there for."

Chapter 49

"THAT FUCKING PRICK WAS recording us? *Us?* Does he not know—"

"Who cares?" Stitts shot back.

"Who cares? *Who cares?* I fucking care, that's who. You can't just—"

"This is what he wants, Pratt. He wants you to get pissed off and say or do something stupid. You wanna throw him in jail? His ratings will go through the roof—then he'll sue, claim that his first amendment rights were violated. And he won't give a shit that you ruined the studio. You want to know why?"

Pratt swerved, sending Stitts and the two other Secret Service agents in the back seat rocketing toward the window.

"Well, for one, it's not his studio but more importantly, the tape isn't there. Nor was there any video or evidence of whoever gave him the damn thing. *If* they even brought it personally, which I highly doubt. I wouldn't be surprised if someone didn't just email it to him." This last part gave Stitts pause. If it was an email transfer, then a file that big was probably stored in the cloud somewhere. And if that were the case, they might be able to trace it. "Maybe we could track it down."

"Track it down? What do you mean?" Pratt asked, finally calming down.

"If it was sent digitally, maybe we can trace who sent it."

As Stitts was thinking this over, his phone started to buzz, and he took it out of his pocket. It was Chase.

"Chase? Everything all right?"

As was her style, his partner got right into it.

"I know why the drone was there," Chase said.

"You saw the video, too?"

Another short pause.

"Video? What video?"

"You know that asshole William Woodley, the one we saw on the TV back at the command center? Well, he somehow came across footage shot from the drone. He aired the entire assassination of Senator Tom DeBrusk live on his news channel."

"You have to be kidding me."

"I shit you not. Me and Pratt went to go talk to him, but he's not going to give up the source, no way in hell. This is his ticket to becoming Rush Limbaugh's heir, and he knows it. Where are you?"

"I'm on my way back to the command center. I'll be there in five."

Stitts looked over at Pratt and covered the mouthpiece with his hand.

"How long until we get back to the command center? My partner will be there in five."

The mention of Chase made the man scowl, but he answered anyway.

"Ten," he said, swerving, and picking up speed. "Maybe eight."

"I'll meet you there in ten," Stitts said to Chase before hanging up.

If the psychopath behind the wheel doesn't kill us first.

Chapter 50

FOR THE SECOND TIME that day, Chase could barely believe her eyes. And both times had to do with drones, albeit under dramatically different settings.

She was watching the video that William Woodley had shown on his TV program, the one that revealed Senator Thomas DeBrusk's last moments on this earth.

It was sickening.

But she had a job to do, a murderer to catch before he struck again. Woodley would get what was coming to him, she was sure of it.

Something at the beginning of the video caught her eyes. Right before focusing on DeBrusk, there were a whole bunch of indicators on the screen. She'd identified the GPS signal, as well as the current height of the drone, but didn't understand any of the rest.

"What's all that crap at the beginning on the screen?"

"That's flight information for the pilot," Floyd answered. "Didn't you see it when you put on the goggles?"

Chase shook her head.

"No, none of that crap was there."

"The operator must've set it on full s-s-s-screen mode. This is what you normally see when you're flying it with the con-con-controller."

Chase got Peter to rewind the tape and then squinted at the numbers, trying to figure out what they all meant.

"What's—"

The door to the mobile command center suddenly burst open and Pratt barged in.

When he saw Chase, he actually growled.

Stitts followed the much bigger man and somehow managed to weasel his way by him.

"You see the video now?" he asked. He'd brought the foul stench of cigarette smoke in with him, and Chase crinkled her nose.

"Yeah, I saw it; it's on screen now."

Stitts shook his head in disgust.

"The drone was there to videotape it all," he said.

Chase gave him a look.

"Yeah, maybe. But I've got another idea, too."

"What's that?"

She hadn't told Peter or Floyd her theory yet and everyone turned to look at her. For a moment, she was transported back to group therapy, when she was supposed to open up and share her feelings.

Chase forced the sensation away.

"It was something that Peter said… he said that the shooter was most likely holed up in one of these high-rises based on the range of the gun and rounds."

"Which were confirmed to be from an M24 Sniper with Lapua Magnum rounds, by the way. And my men searched those buildings and have found nothing. Nothing on CCTV footage, either."

Chase nodded, this was news to her, but she'd expected as much.

"Yeah, but the program you used spat out those coordinates because you didn't think the rifle could fire any farther, right?"

"The M24 has a range of nearly eighteen-hundred meters; what I said was that without a spotter and on a busy street corner, I wouldn't expect this kind of accuracy outside of half a mile. In fact, even with a spotter—"

"Exactly," Chase interrupted. "But that's with a human spotter. I'm talking about a mechanical one."

Peter and Floyd looked confused, Pratt looked angry, but Stitts started to smile.

"The drone. The drone is the spotter," he said.

Peter suddenly jumped to his feet and approached the paused video on-screen.

"You know what, I think you're right. Look at this: this is the wind speed at the drone and this is the temperature. And with a camera this good? You could literally use it as a second scope, extend your shot by another half-mile or more."

Chase closed her eyes and envisioned how it had felt wearing the goggles, how immersive, how *real*.

"Exactly."

"So, we find the drone and we find the shooter, is that what you're saying?" Pratt piped up.

It was Stitts who answered.

"We find out who owns the drone, and I'm pretty sure they'll lead us right to the shooter."

SO Pratt slapped his big palms together, causing Chase to jump.

"So, what the hell are we waiting for?"

"It's not that easy," Chase said. "You're not required to register a drone, and they can be purchased from dozens of retailers, including online. There's no way of knowing who this particular drone belongs to."

"We've got this," Floyd interjected, holding up the sheet of paper that Brian Doucette had given them back at the hangar.

Stitts raised an eyebrow.

"It's a list of names of people who signed up as a member at the *Fly Right* club," Chase informed the group. "It's by no means inclusive."

"Yeah, but to use the drone as you described it, you would need to be pretty skilled, I would think," Peter said. "And given that you can't practice anywhere in Washington, I think there's a good chance that our shooter's name is on that list."

Pratt strode forward and reached for the paper in Floyd's hand. But Chase was faster and grabbed it first.

"Peter, can you cross-reference this list with anybody who would have access to a sniper rifle? Ex-military, that sort of thing?"

Peter nodded.

"Stitts, you think we might be able to trace where the video came from?"

"Maybe, if you know someone with a particular set of skills."

"I might know a guy," Chase replied.

"Yeah, and I have my men looking for a connection between William Woodley and Mohammed Al-Saed," Pratt added.

Chase had forgotten all about Mohammed and the outburst. She still didn't know how he fit into the whole picture, but it was just too much of a coincidence to overlook.

You're starting to sound like Stitts, she scolded herself.

Still, Chase felt a little giddy. Finally, they seemed to be getting somewhere. All it took was a little good old-fashioned—

There was a knock at the command center door and a Secret Service agent poked his head in.

"You guys seeing this?" he asked, eyes wide.

"No, what?"

"Somebody put this clown William Woodley up on the big screen," the agent said, and all the giddiness that Chase felt was suddenly gone.

Chapter 51

THEY ALL STARED AS the horrible last few moments of Congressman Vincente's life played out on live TV.

"Holy shit," Peter whispered when it was all over.

They all felt the same way about what they'd just seen: disgusted.

And when William Woodley's matte, tanned face returned to the screen, Chase wanted to claw the despicable creature's eyes out.

"We gotta find the person taking these videos," Stitts said in a voice suggesting that he was speaking to himself.

"I feel horrible showing you guys these images, but I believe it's in the best interest of our country to see them," William Woodley said in a flat voice. "Only by seeing the depraved atrocities committed by terrorists on our soil will we know the true extent of their evil."

"Yeah, right, I bet you feel horrible," Pratt said. "I told you we should have fucking brought that guy in."

Chase looked to Stitts for an explanation, but her partner shook his head.

"We don't even know if he's involved," Stitts reminded them. "Anybody could have sent him that video."

But the man's tone betrayed him; Chase could tell that he wished he'd hogtied that prick, Woodley.

"Let me talk to him," Chase said softly.

Pratt glared at her.

"No. I don't think that's a good idea."

Chase ignored him. She'd dealt with egos twice the size of Pratt's in her time.

And she knew that ignoring them was worse than fighting back.

"Stitts, let me talk to him. I know the type; you do, too. He won't talk to you guys, but he'll talk to me."

As she spoke, Chase held up a hand and mimed removing one of her gloves, hoping that Stitts would catch the hidden meaning in her words.

Eventually, he must have caught on, because he slowly nodded.

"Yeah, it's worth a shot," he said.

"I don't think this is a good idea," Pratt repeated.

Stitts suddenly spun around.

"No one fucking asked you; your job is to protect the president. We have over a hundred potential targets out there… why don't you try and protect them, as well? We'll figure out who's taking the goddamn videos."

SO Pratt was so surprised by Stitts's outburst that he physically recoiled.

Rather than allow the man time to recover from the assault, Stitts quickly turned back to Peter.

"So, there's no way of figuring out who owns this drone?"

Peter shook his head, but then stopped. He brought up the footage of the drone taken from the Dunkin' Donuts CCTV.

"Wait a second. Brian at the hangar said that you were required to write your name on the bottom of your drone. I wonder if there's any way to get an image of the underside."

"You really think that someone who's using a drone as a spotter to kill a senator and congressman is going to write their name on the bottom of it?" Pratt asked, his face now turning the same color as an eggplant.

"Well, you seem to think that William Woodley is dumb enough to air footage of his own kills, don't you?"

"William Woodley is pond scum," Pratt shot back. "A fucking virus."

What the hell has gotten into Stitts, Chase wondered. She decided to intervene quickly before it came to blows.

"Fellas, let's just take it down a notch. Who knows, maybe we'll get lucky."

Peter, also sensing the need to diffuse the situation, said, "I'll mess around with the image, see if I can get a good shot of the bottom."

"Well, if you see a name, compare it to the list of members from *Fly Right*. As for tracing where the video might have been sent from," Chase said, turning her gaze to Floyd. "Give my friend Screech in New York a call. I think you've met before?"

Floyd immediately fell into character.

"Of course, Agent Adams."

"Good."

Chase rose to her feet and indicated for Stitts to lead the way toward the door. She could feel Pratt's eyes on her the entire time. It took all her willpower not to say something snarky.

"Well," Pratt asked when they were almost out the door. "What the hell are we supposed to do?"

Stitts turned.

"How about your job? How about you keep the rest of the congressmen and senators safe? How about that?"

Chase was glad that she was out of the command center before the smirk crossed her lips.

Chapter 52

"**WHAT THE HELL WAS** that all about?" Chase asked when she and Stitts were inside Floyd's car.

"Nothing," Stitts said. "Pratt just lost his cool with Woodley. Kind of like what happened with you and Mohammed Al-Saed."

Chase cringed.

"I guess I deserved that. I'm sorry; I'll apologize to the Secret Service later, send them a fucking postcard. But right now? Right now, we have to make sure that nobody else who supports that Bill gets capped."

Stitts didn't reply and for the next several minutes, the only words spoken were intermittent directions from her partner.

Out of the corner of her eye, she saw Stitts fidgeting with a package of cigarettes, but he refrained from lighting one up.

"I don't know if I ever thanked you," Chase said, surprised by how easily the words came.

"What?"

"I don't know if I thanked you. If you didn't come that day and drag me out of the quarry, I'd be squirrel meat by now."

Stitts, who had clearly been deep in thought, chewed the inside of his lip before speaking.

"You saved my life, too," he said, deflecting.

"You also rescued me from that sick bastard Brian Jalston. Every time I try to crawl out of a hole, you're there with a hand reaching down to grab me. Thank you, Stitts. I mean it."

Stitts had become so uncomfortable that he brought a cigarette to his lips, pulled it out, then jammed it back in.

It was clear that both of them were still tiptoeing around the final elephant in the car.

She'd thanked him, and Stitts deserved it for all he'd done for her over the past few years. But that didn't change the fact that their entire relationship had started with a lie and she wasn't about to continue that trend.

Chase hadn't said I forgive you, because she wasn't sure she had.

"I hope you aren't thinking about lighting that thing in here," she said, trying to lift the mood. Stitts took the cigarette out of his mouth and started to roll it between his thumb and forefinger.

"No need, we're here."

Chase pulled the car over and glanced at the plain apartment building to their left.

"This? This is that asshole's studio?"

Stitts stepped out of the car and immediately lit his smoke.

"That's exactly what I said—one more thing: when Pratt and I came before he was recording us. I wouldn't be surprised if he tapes us, as well."

"I'll be on my best behavior," Chase said with a chuckle. "Promise."

***

Stitts knocked on the door and waited patiently for close to a minute. Like before, the man with dark hair opened it.

Fred… Fred the Handler, he thought. *No, Fred the Fluffer; that sounds better.*

He flashed his badge, as did Chase, but the man barely glanced at them.

"We need to talk to William again," Stitts informed him. "We didn't bring the juice monkey with us this time; it's just me and my partner, and all we want to do is chat. That's it."

The man stared at Stitts's open palms and then nodded. He stepped to one side and held the door open for them to enter.

Stitts didn't wait for an escort; he hurried down the hallway toward Woodley's dressing room. He was nearly there before he realized that Chase wasn't by his side.

"Chase?"

He found her staring into the 'studio', observing the faux-marble desk and the green screen.

"This is it?" she grumbled.

On TV, William Woodley looked like a superstar, the Dan Rather of right-wing news. The reality was much more underwhelming.

"That's it. Come on, Chase."

When they got to the door with Woodley's name still scrawled across the chalkboard, Stitts knocked once, then opened it.

The scene was strangely familiar. As before, Woodley was seated at the makeup chair, staring at himself in the mirror. Thankfully, however, the bulbs on the frame were off this time, and he didn't have napkins rimming his neck.

Woodley startled when they burst through the door and pulled his cell phone away from his ear.

"You guys are back already? And I see you've brought a friend? Lemme guess, First Amendment Lawyer Lady? No, no; Seventh District Supreme Court Judge?"

The man was putting on a show, trying to act tough, but Stitts noticed that he was looking past them to see if they'd brought Pratt along.

"We just want to talk," Stitts said, trying to calm the man's nerves. "This is my partner, FBI Special Agent Adams."

"Well, sorry to say, Special Lady, but you've wasted your time. I'm just gonna repeat what I said before: I won't give up my source or the tapes."

Stitts frowned and looked over at Chase; it was her idea to come here, to speak to this ass-clown. He hoped she had some sort of plan.

He did a double-take; Chase was smiling, and it was… unnerving. Stitts couldn't remember the last time he'd seen his partner smile. If he didn't know any better, he would have thought that she was fanboying.

As Chase slowly walked over to the makeup table, she started to remove one of her gloves.

"This your hand cream? I get the worst cracked hands," she asked pointing at an innocuous bottle of cream on the makeup counter.

"Yeah," Woodley replied hesitantly. Clearly, he was as mesmerized—or confused—as Stitts was.

"Mind if I borrow some?"

"Okay… sure."

He reached for the bottle, as did Chase.

"Sorry," she said with a giggle, pulling her hand back. Only she wasn't quite fast enough, and her fingers brushed against William Woodley's forearm.

And then, Stitts saw Chase's eyelids flutter.

Chapter 53

"I'LL BE DAMNED," **ATF** Agent Peter Horrowitz said, looking closely at the computer screen. Floyd leaned over. "What does that look like to you?"

Floyd squinted and tilted his head to one side.

"R, K, space, Y, A," he said.

"That's what I see, too. I think our lady friend might be right; I think the idiot who videotaped the shooting put his name on the bottom of the drone."

Pater grabbed the sheet of paper that Brian at *Fly Right* had given them and started to search the list. He used his finger to zip along, but he moved so quickly that Floyd couldn't keep up.

"Look here," Peter said, tapping the sheet of paper. "Mark Yablonski—R, K, space, Y, A."

Floyd had to look to the image and then back at the list twice to see what Peter was indicating.

Excited now, Peter turned to his computer and loaded up a program that to Floyd looked something like the phone book they used to have in Alaska up until a few years ago. He punched in Mark Yablonski and Washington, DC. Three addresses popped up. Next, he dragged these addresses directly onto the program that he had been using to map out where the shots had come from.

Then he leaned back in his chair.

"I'll be damned," he whispered.

"What? What is it?"

"I think we… shit, I think we found the guy!" Peter shouted as he scrambled for his cell phone.

Chapter 54

CHASE PULLED HER HAND away and then took a step backward. Out of the corner of her eye, she saw Stitts staring at her, a strange expression on his face.

"Don't you want the cream?" Woodley asked.

Chase shook her head and turned to Stitts.

"Let's go."

Stitts continued to stare for a moment longer before nodding.

"What? That's it? You're not gonna beat me up? You're not even going to threaten me?" Woodley said as they started toward the door.

Chase knew that the man was recording them—she'd seen the red light on the makeup tray. She also knew that saying anything else would likely come back to bite her in the ass.

But Chase could only give up so much of her old self in such a short period of time. She turned and glared at the despicable creature who made money by posting videos of people being murdered for everyone to see. Including the victims' families, and their loved ones.

Back in Seattle before she'd gone undercover, they used to have a name for money that was begotten by ill means, be it drug money, money from prostitution, robbery, or murder.

Dirty Money, they'd called it. Now, looking at William Woodley's smooth face, his smirk, his slightly raised eyebrows, she realized that there was something worse than Dirty Money.

Then there was what this piece of shit did. There was Dirty Money and there was *Filthy Money.* And every cent that this man made by exploiting the deaths of others was *Filthy Money.*

"No, I don't want your hand cream," she said with a sneer. "Wouldn't want to deny you the pleasure of beating off to your own reflection. Because there's no— "

Stitts grabbed her by the arm and pulled her out of the room. He didn't let go until they were outside.

"Smooth, Chase," Stitts said, shaking his head. "He was recording in there, you know."

"Yeah, I know. So, what? Now he has something else to beat off to, the conceited prick. Wait—did you say *smooth*? Was that a hand cream joke?"

Stitts sighed and lit a cigarette.

"It's not him, is it?" he asked between puffs.

Chase turned back to the apartment building as she opened the door to Floyd's ride.

"No; he may be showing the videos on his stupid fucking show, but he didn't take them. And the only thing he's shot recently is his load into a napkin. "

She slid behind the wheel and Stitts flicked his butt away before getting into the car.

"You sure?" he asked.

Chase was about to confirm but hesitated.

Am *I sure*?

The honest answer was no. If she bought Stitts's idea that the visions were a construction of her subconscious, she had no idea how reliable they were. They were also subject to interpretation or, in the case of when she'd touched Louisa, *mis*interpretation.

"No, not sure. Pretty sure, but not a hundred percent."

With that, she started the car and put it into drive.

"What's it like, anyway?" Stitts asked as they made their way back to the mobile command center. "When you do your voodoo thing?"

The question caught her off guard and she was forced to think about it for a moment before answering. The truth was, despite how visceral and important these visions were, she hadn't put too much thought into what they felt like. Stitts was the only other person who knew about them, and this was the first time he'd asked.

"It's like… it's kind of being like an actor in a movie, a CAM movie… Blair Witch style, you know?"

Stitts nodded encouragingly.

"Only I feel sick afterwards. It's… it's not pleasant. Like I'm intruding on someone or something?"

Again, Stitts nodded.

"You know, come to think of it, it was not so unlike the drone I got to fly earlier in the day. With the goggles on."

Now, her partner gave her a look.

"You flew a drone?"

"Not exactly. I 'experienced' it, I guess. Didn't steer or anything like that."

"Huh," Stitts said, slumping into his seat. They drove in silence for a few more minutes, and Chase hoped that the man would let it go.

Just talking about it brought about an uncomfortable feeling in the pit of her stomach.

But apparently, Stitts wasn't quite done yet.

"And you have no idea what things you picked up on in there before you touched Woodley? You don't know what the clues were that led to your vision?"

"No. I just—"

Chase paused again. She hadn't really done any sort of retrospective analysis of the scene after one of the damn visions. Sure, the theories that came out of them were often proven correct later on, usually by a third party, but the sickness she felt immediately following one of them always ensured that she got the hell out of there.

"It was the way he was sitting, I think," Chase started slowly. "That, and his facial expressions. He knew why we were there but didn't seem the least bit worried about it. Even a cocky bastard like him would have shown a trace of fear. I mean, there's no way that he kept any information about his source at the studio, but still. I would've seen *something* if he was responsible. Pupil dilation, maybe, a twitch of his fingers."

As Chase let her words sink in, she realized that she was describing everything as a vision, but that wasn't what it felt like at all. To her, it felt oddly like a memory; *her* memory.

She shook her head.

"That's what I think, anyways. But I'm no doctor."

Before Stitts could ask anything else, her cell phone rang.

"Adams."

"W-w-w-we f-found the g-g-guy. Y-y-you have to come with u-u-u-us—*fuck*—us. Pratt wa-wa-wa-wants you to lead the ch-ch-ch-ch—the raid."

"Floyd, slow down. Take a breath," Chase instructed; she had a hard time understanding what the hell he was saying.

"We f-f-f-found the g-g-g-guy with the dr-dr-dr-drone."

"Deep breath, Floyd."

She heard the man take not one deep breath, but three.

When Floyd spoke again, she finally understood what he was trying to say.

"We found the m-m-man who owns the drone and we're h-heading there now. Sp-sp-special Officer Pratt says you have to be there."

Sweat suddenly broke out on Chase's forehead.

"Give me the address, Floyd. We'll meet you there."

Chapter 55

"MARK YABLONSKI, FORTY-TWO YEARS old, did two tours in Iraq," Stitts said, relaying the information to Chase. "Peter says that they got lucky, got a partial name on the underside of the drone that matches one of the members of the drone club. He also says that the man lives in range of where both the congressman and senator were shot."

Chase tried to focus on the road while taking in what Stitts what saying.

She couldn't imagine that this Mark character would be so stupid as to put his name on the drone that was used as a spotter during the assassinations.

But apparently, he had.

"I guess that's why they're criminals," she muttered under her breath.

"What's that?" Stitts asked.

"Nothing."

"Caucasian, ex-military, early forties. Fits the profile," Stitts confirmed as Chase pulled up to a barricade. She flashed her badge and he let her through.

She pulled up behind a black Secret Service vehicle a half a block down and then got out of the car.

After a good stretch, she took her time looking around. The street that Mark Yablonski lived on was the type where every second house had bars over their windows and the residences that had front lawns were overgrown with weeds. It amazed her that such a place existed not twenty blocks from the White House.

Chase quickly spotted SO Pratt and a handful of other men huddled over the hood of a car tucked into an alley and out of sight.

"There," Stitts said, pointing at the men with his cigarette. "They're over there."

"Yeah, I know," Chase replied, starting in their direction. "Just taking in the sights, is all."

As she neared, Chase saw that Pratt was pointing enthusiastically at a large piece of paper that was covered with red markings. Everyone was paying so much attention, that they didn't notice her approach. Chase didn't mind; it was better than having to bash heads with these Neanderthals.

All the men were in plainclothes, and some of them sported shirts or light jackets with the DoJ or Homeland Security emblems on them. Several police officers were hanging out by the mouth of the alley, but they seemed disinterested at best.

Chase recalled Floyd's words on the phone.

SO Pratt wants you to lead the ch-ch-ch—raid.

She glanced over at Stitts, but he was too lost in thought, and in sucking every last nugget of nicotine from his cigarette, to notice her.

Pratt wants me and Stitts to lead the raid because the Secret Service has no authority to be doing house calls, she realized.

Back at the warehouse, where the interrogation of Mohammed Al-Saed was supposed to take place, Homeland and the DoJ had put Pratt in his place. He needed somebody with jurisdiction to serve the warrant on Mark Yablonski. Somebody who he thought he could control, push around.

Fat chance of that happening.

"Hey boys," Chase said at last, announcing her presence. Pratt looked up and then turned to his team.

"This is FBI Special Agent Adams and her partner Agent Stitts," he said as ways of an introduction.

Oh, he remembers my name… that's good. By the end of all of this, I'm going to make sure he never forgets it.

Clearly picking up on something in her face, Stitts stepped forward and took the reins.

"Which house are we hitting?" Stitts asked, lifting his chin to the map on the hood of the car.

Chase scowled and was about to elbow her way forward when she remembered her lessons from Dr. Matteo.

Sometimes it's in your benefit to allow someone else to take control.

And this, she surmised, was one of those times. Taking charge now would only make Pratt look bad in front of his men. While Chase would've liked nothing more, pissing the man off minutes before a raid wasn't ideal. Something like that had the potential to explode, to lead to a friendly fire incident inside confined spaces.

She'd seen it before and judging by the way that Pratt had a propensity to blow his top, she wouldn't put it past the man.

There would be a time to deal with Pratt, but that time wasn't now.

"Bungalow, three down from our present location," Pratt said, indicating a spot on the map marked with a big red X. "Local law enforcement has the street cordoned off—no one in or out. I've got a sniper stationed on the roof over there, and they've reported that there are two bogies inside. Both are on the main floor."

"And you've procured the warrant?" Stitts asked.

Pratt grinned and handed over a sheet of paper. Stitts took a cursory glance at it and then nodded.

"So, what's the play here?"

"FBI leads the way, serves the warrant," Pratt offered.

"FBI serves the warrant," Stitts agreed, glancing around. He pointed at a battering ram leaning up against the wall. "Local law enforcement does the breach, then FBI goes in first. Secret Service comes next."

The vein on Pratt's forehead bulged, but he surprised Chase by not only not complaining, but by agreeing.

"Sounds good," Pratt said. "FBI serves, local breaches, FBI enters."

Something isn't right here, Chase thought. She'd seen Pratt exchange a look with his men before agreeing to Stitts's plan. But before she could get a grasp of what this meant, Stitts turned to her.

"You ready, Chase?"

Chase withdrew her pistol from her holster.

"Ready as I'll ever be," she said as she made the first move toward the end of the alley. "Ready as I'll fucking ever be."

Chapter 56

"IT'S UNLOCKED," STITTS SAID, pulling his hand back. The officer on the stoop with him nodded and put the battering ram down. Then he moved back behind the line of Secret Service officers. "One knock, then I'll enter. Chase you follow, then the Secret Service. Got it?"

Chase nodded, as did Pratt who was crouched behind her. In total, there were seven of them on the stoop and roughly the same number up against the side of the house.

"One knock," Stitts repeated under his breath.

He looked back one final time at Chase. She seemed to be keeping it together, which was a good thing; he needed her. Chase wasn't the best shot, but he could count on her to watch his back. Pratt, on the other hand, was unpredictable.

Stitts stood up straight.

"FBI! Search warrant!" he shouted at the same time that he knocked. He didn't wait for a response, he just grabbed the door handle and then shoved. "FBI! On the ground!"

Stitts burst into the house, leading with his gun. A woman screamed, and he whipped his head in the direction of the sound.

A woman with a mess of frizzy gray hair took one glance at the gun and dropped to her stomach.

"FBI! Stay on the ground! *Stay down!*"

Chase was behind him now, shouting.

In the kitchen, Stitts spotted a man sitting at the table, partially blocked by the wall.

"Get down!"

Now it wasn't just he and Chase shouting, but a dozen people or more.

"Get on the—"

The man at the table's hand shot into the air, and for the split second, Stitts thought he had a gun in his hand.

But it was only a fork, and it clanged loudly as it crashed to the floor beside the whimpering woman.

Knowing that trigger-happy Pratt was right behind him, he shouted for the man to get on the ground again, all the while running toward him.

"I can't! *I can't!*"

Stitts grabbed the man by the collar and tried to wrench him off the chair. But the man appeared to be stuck, and it toppled with him.

"Get—"

Stitts looked down at the man and realized in horror why he hadn't obeyed when they'd burst through the doors, why he hadn't dropped to the floor.

PART IV – Green Screen

Chapter 57

WHEN HIS PHONE RANG, Floyd's first thought was that it was Chase, and his heart started to pound in his chest. But, when he looked down at the screen, he saw the number was unlisted.

His second thought was that something horrible had happened to her, that it had all gone wrong, and this was someone calling to break the bad news to him.

With a trembling finger, he answered the phone.

"H-h-h-hello?"

"Floyd, my man. How are ya?"

Confused, Floyd couldn't even manage a single syllable.

"Floyd?"

He cleared his throat.

"F-f-f-fine. Is sh-sh-she okay?"

"What? Floyd, it's Screech. What are you talking about? Is everything alright in the nation's capital?"

Floyd exhaled loudly, and he closed his eyes, trying to calm his heart.

It's Screech. It's not the DoJ or Homeland or the Secret Service.

"F-f-fine. I'm f-fine. Everything's f-fine."

"Okaaay… well, I got your message, but I'm not really sure what you want me to do. You want me to trace some sort of digital file?"

"Yeah, s-something like that. We're trying to tr-tr-track down the source of a f-f-file, where it came f-f-from."

Floyd looked at Peter to make sure that he was relaying the information correctly. Peter indicated for him to put the call on speakerphone, and Floyd graciously obliged.

"Screech, this is Peter Horrowitz from the ATF."

There was an awkward pause, before Screech said, "Uh, okaaaay. Hi. Floyd? You have a warrant for all the shit, right?"

Floyd again looked at Peter, who leaned in close to the cell phone.

"This has to do with an Act of Terror; we've got carte blanche from the FBI and ATF to use any means necessary to track down where that file came from."

Another pause, shorter this time.

"Alrighty then. Where is the file hosted? Facebook? YouTube? Twitter? It'll be next to impossible to break into any of those powerhouses."

"No, it was played on a local TV station, then looped on YouTube. But we just want to know where the file came from, not gain access to it. I can give you the IP address of a series of computers in the studio here in Washington that I'm assuming it was uploaded from."

"How long is the video? The resolution?"

"About three minutes and 4K."

"Uncompressed, that's gonna be a decent size file. I'm guessing it was dropped into the cloud then grabbed from there. Send me those IP addresses and I might be able to backtrack to the source. If there's any sort of dummy servers in Asia somewhere, it's gonna take some time. A *lot* of time."

"Anything you can do will be helpful," Peter replied.

"And this is… uh, everything is above board here, right? I mean, we got some problems here with the local yokels… wouldn't want to add to our situation."

"Definitely."

"All right, I'll see what I can do. Put Floyd back on the line."

Floyd picked up the phone and took it off speakerphone. Then he turned his back to Peter, who went back to his computer, presumably to prepare the IP addresses from the studio.

"Y-yes?"

"How's she doing, Floyd?"

At first, Floyd wasn't sure what the man was talking about. Then he remembered how he'd felt when the phone had first rung, when he'd been convinced it was Chase.

"B-better. F-f-fine, really. She's working hard."

"Wait, she's *with* you? Let me talk to her."

"No, sh-she's not with me. I mean, sh-she's here, but at a crime scene. Wor-working—

"Fucking hell. Is that a good idea? I mean, I thought she was gonna take a break from all this stuff."

"Sh-she w-w-was. But Sti-Sti-Stitts got her out, got her j-j-job b-back."

Screech sighed.

"These fucking cops and their jobs," he muttered. "Would it hurt them to take some time off? Pick up a hobby, maybe? Underwater basket weaving?"

"Underw-w-water what?"

"Never mind. You look out for her, Floyd."

"Sti-Sti-Stitts—"

"Never mind about Stitts. Keep an eye on her. Chase might look fine on the outside, but nobody goes through everything she's been through and comes out the other side with butt cheeks that squeak when you walk, if you know what I mean."

"Wh-wh-wh-what?"

"Never mind. Just look out for her, is all."

"I w-will."

"Oh, one more thing, Floyd. You sure that this is all kosher? The last thing I need right now is some douchebag from Cyber Crimes who moonlights as a Geek Squad tech tearing down my door, *capiche*?"

"Uh, yeah. C-c-capiche."

The phone went silent for a moment, leaving Floyd to wonder if he had answered correctly. The truth was, he'd only understood about a quarter of what the man had said.

"Talk soon then. *Peace.*"

The phone went dead, and Floyd turned to Peter, eyebrows raised.

"D-d-d-do we have clearance?"

Peter shrugged and centered his chair in front of his computer.

"Yeah," he said hesitantly. "Sure. I mean, I think so."

Chapter 58

"WHAT'S GOING ON?" CHASE demanded as she burst into the kitchen. Stitts had dragged their suspect to the floor, but now, inexplicably, he was helping him back up again.

And he was being oddly... *polite* about it.

"Stitts, what the fuck?"

After righting the man in his seat, her partner looked over at him, a deep frown on his face.

"What? Tell me what's—" For the first time since entering the kitchen, Chase looked down. "Shit."

Others were trying to get into the kitchen now—mostly Secret Service, but some of the local PD—and when their eyes fell on Mark Yablonski, they stopped.

"What the hell is this all about?" Mark demanded, his face beet red. "What the—"

SO Pratt suddenly barged into the scene, oblivious to pretty much everything.

"This him? Hey, asshole, you Mark Yablonski?" he shouted.

"Yeah, I'm him. What the fuck is this about? You barge into—"

"Oh, ho, ho, ho," Pratt mock laughed. "You're in real—"

Chase stepped in front of the big man.

"What the fuck's wrong with you?"

A confused expression crossed over Pratt's face.

"What? This asshole just killed—"

Chase grabbed his arm and yanked him hard into the other room. Pratt was so surprised that he actually went with her.

"He didn't do the shootings, you idiot."

Pratt's eyes narrowed.

"Oh, yeah? This one of your fucking tricks, again? Like with Mohammed Al-Saed?"

"No, not a trick, you tool. I know he didn't do the shooting because he's in a wheelchair. You ever seen a man with his legs amputated above the knee crawl onto a roof? 'Cuz if you have, I'd love for you to share the video."

"Wh-what?"

Chase couldn't deal with the man's sheer incompetence any longer. She slipped her pistol into the holster and pushed her way through the crowd of agents and back outside.

Stitts hurried after her, immediately lighting up.

"You know, he could still be involved, Chase," he offered between drags. "The whole drone thing... it can't be a coincidence."

Chase took a deep breath and turned her gaze to the sky above. It was a completely cloudless day, and she found herself wondering what it would be like to be up there—with the goggles, of course. What it would be like to be essentially hovering, weightless, free, absolutely—

"Chase?"

"Yeah, you might be right," she said suddenly. Then she started back toward the door.

"Chase? Where are you going? Don't do anything—"

—*stupid.*

Chase didn't hear the final word—there was too much chatter among the Secret Service agents—but she didn't need to.

She knew what was coming.

Since when I have done anything stupid? She thought with a grin. *When have you known me to do* anything *stupid, Stitts?*

When she made her way to the kitchen, she saw a police officer trying to cuff Mark Yablonski to his own wheelchair.

Since when have I done anything this *stupid?*

"Don't be an idiot," she said, sounding almost bored. "Take the handcuffs off him."

The officer looked at her, then his eyes darted over to SO Pratt, clearly seeking approval.

"I said, take the fucking cuffs off him," she repeated.

The man did as he was asked. He didn't look pleased being spoken to this way, but Chase didn't give a shit.

Her attention was focused on the man in the wheelchair, and when she addressed him, the rest of the room went quiet. Even the woman who'd dropped to the floor, presumably the man's wife, who was being led to another room stopped her jibber-jabbering.

"I just have a couple questions for you, Mr. Yablonski."

"Oh, yeah?" he shot back. When he spoke, the left side of his face wasn't quite synchronized with the right.

Fucking hell, how did we miss this?

"Well, I have a couple of questions for you, too. Like, for starters, what in the fuck you are doing in my house?"

"We have a warrant," she said, holding her hand out behind her and snapping her fingers. A second later, someone jammed a sheet of paper into her palm and she put it on the table in front of Mark. The man barely looked at it.

"A warrant for what?"

"Look, I just have a few questions for you."

Mark glanced around nervously. He was pissed, sure, but he was also scared.

Chase didn't blame the man; they'd probably triggered his PTSD by barging into his home like this.

"Like what?"

"A drone," Chase said simply. "Do you have a drone?"

The man looked confused but eventually nodded.

"Yeah, I have one, so what? I fly it every morning at around six a.m." He pursed his lips and gestured to his wheelchair. "Not like I can get out much."

"What about today? Were you flying it this morning?"

Mark's eyes narrowed.

"Yeah, but…" he let his sentence trail off.

"But what?"

Everyone in the room was staring at her now, desperate for an explanation. But she didn't have the time nor the desire to spell things out for them.

"But it wasn't working too good. Lost sight of it a couple times and couldn't get it to return to home. Eventually, it came back online, so I brought it back in and charged the battery. About an hour later, I took it out again, but the same shit happened. Might have to take it to the repair guy at *Fly Right*, see if he can tell me what's wrong with the damn thing."

Chase grabbed her forehead with one hand and squeezed.

They were right about the drone, she realized. *But they were wrong about who was flying it.*

Chapter 59

"**How the fuck were** we supposed to know?" Pratt demanded as he exited the house in a huff.

Chase looked the man up and down, but instead of answering, she just shut her eyes.

"Hello? Hey, I'm talking to you!"

Chase held out her hand.

"Just let me fucking think, all right? Give me a goddamn second here."

She didn't need to touch Mark Yablonski to know that he was telling the truth. She'd seen it in his face.

The man had no idea why they'd raided his house and thrown him to the ground.

But the drone… we are right about the drone.

"Doesn't make sense…" she muttered.

"Fuck this," Pratt snapped. "I'm gonna arrest this guy. See what he knows."

Chase opened her eyes.

"Oh, that's a fucking great idea. Is that how you do things around here? Just toss innocent people behind bars, see what happens? Rough 'em up a little? How did that work out with Mohammed Al-Saed, huh?"

Pratt's eyes became narrow slits and his face started to turn the same shade of pink she'd seen before.

"Fuck this. I don't have to listen to this shit," he said, turning back to the house.

"No, you don't. You can fucking go home. Put your feet up. After all, you have no jurisdiction here at all."

Pratt whipped around and pointed a finger at her chest.

"You're here because I'm letting you stay here. You ever wonder why the DoJ and Homeland have stayed out of the picture? Why you've had such freedom to do whatever the hell you wanted?"

"The DoJ can suck my dick," Chase spat back. "And if you keep pointing that stumpy finger at me, I'm going to bite it off. On second thought, you'd probably like that, wouldn't you?"

Pratt laughed.

"Oh, this is just fucking great. You know what? If it weren't for us bringing in Al-Saed, DoJ and Homeland would be in charge. And if you think I'm an asshole, those guys—"

"You are an asshole. A 'roided up juice—"

"Would you fucking stop arguing!" Stitts suddenly shouted. All eyes were on him now. "We're on the same fucking team here! Pratt, you're right about one thing, the FBI is in charge here and it doesn't matter why that is. We're in charge. And Chase, it was good intel, and Mark fit the profile. It's not our—"

"Fit the profile?" Chase chuckled. "Caucasian, ex-military, early forties," she said in her best impression of Stitts's voice. "What about cripple, huh? Double amputee? Does *that* fit the profile?"

Stitts's face softened, and Chase knew that she'd taken it too far. Even Pratt seemed taken aback by her words and tone, and he didn't strike her as someone who shocked easily.

They fell silent for a moment and Chase fought the urge to fill the void with an apology.

The truth was, they'd fucked up—they all had. All they needed was for William Woodley to get a hold of what happened here, and she wouldn't be surprised if DoJ or Homeland *did* step in. She couldn't fathom a bigger asshole than Pratt, but too many cooks always spoiled the stew.

Instead, she took the time to think. Then, without saying anything to the men who were staring at her, she pulled her cell phone out of her pocket and dialed Floyd's number.

"Thank g-g-god you're ok-k-kay, Chase. I was—"

"Floyd, I need you to put me in touch with Brian Doucette from *Fly Right*. Think you can do that for me?"

"Yes, of course. I'll send you his contact information."

"Anything new on tracing the file? From Screech?"

"No, not yet."

"All right, thanks. I'll see you soon."

After hanging up, she turned to Stitts and Pratt who were still staring at her.

"Go get the drone from Mark, inside," she said. "I've got an idea."

Chapter 60

"**I'M DOING THE BEST** I can here, Chase. I don't have your superpowers, I can only work with what I've got."

They'd been silent the entire drive to the hangar. Now, as Chase pulled Floyd's car onto the grass parking lot, he decided to speak up. She wondered if this was a deliberate strategy so that they couldn't get into a deep discussion.

Fine by me, she thought. The truth was, she was sick of talking. All she'd done for the past six months or so was talk. Talk about her problems, about her addiction, about her goddamn menstrual cycle.

I don't want to talk anymore. I just want to catch this asshole before he strikes again.

And there was no doubt in her mind that he would strike again. She didn't need her 'superpowers' to deduce this. Someone had it out for those who supported Bill S-89, and it was only a matter of time before another senator was targeted.

"Just stressed," she said, stepping out of the car. Stitts tucked Mark Yablonski's drone under his arm, then lit a smoke. "You've got your fix, but I've had all of mine taken away from me."

Except for one.

Predictably, Stitts remained silent.

She strode toward the door with purpose, but when she reached it, she paused.

The man who had taken out Senator DeBrusk and Congressman Vincente had some military training, of that there was no doubt.

But what if he has ordnance training as well? Why take out those who supported the bill one by one when you can take them all out in a single swoop?

"Shit… they were supposed to vote on Bill S-89 in the Senate today, weren't they?"

"Yeah. Senator DeBrusk was on the way there when he was shot," Stitts replied.

"And did they announce when they'd moved the vote to?"

"Tomorrow."

Chase gawked.

"*Tomorrow?* You can't be serious."

Stitts nodded and flicked his spent cigarette butt.

"Serious. Pratt says that—"

"—he's gonna increase security," Chase finished for her partner. "A lot of good that's going to do when a sniper is picking people off from a mile away. This is so ridiculous."

Stitts opened his mouth to reply, but Chase pulled the door open and stepped into the hangar before he could spout the virtues of SO Ronnie Coleman.

"Brian?" She called. "Brian, you still around here?"

There were four or five new droners by the open end, but she went directly for the man who had lent her the goggles earlier.

"Have you seen Brian?" she asked.

The grinning man pointed at someone who was hunched over a drone, his back to them.

"You want to try the goggles again?" he asked.

Chase looked over at Stitts, who offered her a curious expression.

"Maybe later," she said, hurrying over to Brian. "Brian?"

The man in the striped T-shirt turned and looked up at her.

"Agent Adams, it's a pleasure to have you back. What can I do for you?"

Chase nudged Stitts and he held the drone out to the man. It wasn't much bigger than a VHS tape, folded up the way it was.

"I've got a question about this drone," she said.

Brian's face grew serious as he turned the drone over in his hand.

"A fine piece of machinery. Top of the line consumer drone. And it's been modded, too."

"Yeah, great. Listen, I have a couple of questions about this particular drone that I hope you can help me with."

Brian raised an eyebrow.

"Sure... whose is this, anyway? Is it yours? Are you getting into the game, Agent Adams?"

Chase shook her head.

"No—it's a friend's. When I had the goggles on earlier, the guy was controlling it with the cell phone connected to the remote. Is there any other way to control these things? Like two remotes per drone?"

"No, each drone is individually coded; one remote per drone. Otherwise, in places like this, the signals would get crossed and you'd have some pretty expensive accidents. Sometimes, there's a little interference, but—"

"Can you hack it?" Chase interrupted. "Is it possible to change these codes so that it can be controlled from another remote?"

Again, it looked as if Brian was going to snap answer no, but then he hesitated. He turned the drone over in his hand and pulled back a plastic tab to reveal a port.

"To be honest, I'm not sure. I guess if you could somehow get the individual code from it, it might be possible. I mean... hold on. I'm not the best person to ask about this. Tim is our main repair guy, and he knows everything about them. If you can hack it, like you said, he would know how."

Brian raised his free hand and pointed across the hangar.

The man whom Chase had seen earlier in the day hunched over the drone worktable, looked up.

"Tim, you got a sec? Agent Adams here has a couple of questions for you."

Tim nodded and slowly put the drone that he was working on down on the table.

"Sure," he said.

But instead of coming toward them, he spun and started to run.

Chapter 61

FLOYD WATCHED PETER HORROWITZ type at his computer. His fingers moved so quickly that they were a blur.

He'd overheard the man tell Chase that he'd been in the military, but Floyd was beginning to think that he'd also been some sort of data entry specialist.

"So, if we take Chase's theory that the drone was used as a spotter and extend the M24 Sniper System range all the way to 1,500 meters…"

Something on the TV on the wall caught Floyd's attention, and he looked up from Peter's computer.

William Woodley's fake n' baked face filled the screen, and he appeared particularly irate.

"Then, if we take into consideration that the drone took off from Mark Yablonski's porch… *Bingo*."

Floyd's eyes drifted back to the computer screen.

It was the black and white schematic this time, only there was a cluster of red dots near the center.

"Anything look familiar to you?" Peter asked.

Floyd shrugged. To him, they looked like chickenpox.

The TV flickered, and he looked up again.

Woodley was still front and center, but there was an image in the upper left-hand corner now that nearly took his breath away.

"Agent Adams," he whispered.

Peter made a face.

"What?"

"Look," Floyd almost shouted, pointing at the TV. "Turn it up! It's Agent Adams!"

Peter scrambled to find the remote and turn the volume up.

"I'm not usually at a loss for words, but I'm having a difficult time expressing exactly how it feels to have my dignity taken from me. Earlier today, I had two FBI agents barge into my dressing room while I was preparing for this segment. The woman you see here made several disparaging comments about me and my sexuality. I was appalled that an FBI agent would behave this way. So much so, that I had to do a little digging to make sure that her badge wasn't an excellent reproduction. And you're not going to believe what I found out about FBI Special Agent Chase Adams. Here, take a look."

The grainy image of Chase faded, only to be replaced by a video.

"No," Floyd moaned.

"Watch."

The video started to roll, and both Floyd and Peter stared in horror. Chase looked terrible, with dark circles under her eyes and her skin was waxy and thin. Her shoulder length dark brown hair was wet with sweat.

Floyd wasn't sure when the video had been taken, but Chase looked a lot like she had the day they'd dragged her out of the abandoned rock quarry.

"Yeah, this is her. My sources tell me that Agent Adams spent six months in an addiction recovery center just prior to coming to Washington DC. *This* is the person that the FBI sends when Washington is on high alert for more terrorist attacks? She comes to my studio with no warrant, and demands my sources?"

Woodley paused for effect and Floyd could have sworn he saw the man smirk.

"No, he can't—he can't d-d-do this."

"This is only the tip of the iceberg, people. Apparently, Agent Adams's problems run even deeper than this. And you guys know me, I'm all about transparency. So, here's what I'm going to do: because Agent Adams violated my civil liberties, I will be airing a new video of her every day this week, until she comes and apologizes to me in person. So, Agent Adams, if you're out there and watching this—and, let's be honest, who isn't—come on back and pay me a visit. I know you know the address."

Floyd couldn't take it anymore. He started toward the door, only to stop when he realized that Chase had taken his car.

"Floyd? Where are you going?"

He spotted a set of keys on the table and scooped them up, not caring who they belonged to.

And then he was on the move.

"Floyd? *Floyd?*"

Chapter 62

STITTS KNEW THE MAN was going to bolt the second he looked up from the drone.

"Shit!"

Pulling his gun from the holster while starting to run was no easy task, but he managed. Still, Chase caught him after just a couple dozen strides and then passed him.

"Stop!" he shouted between breaths. "FBI! *Stop!*"

But it was clear that this man, drone repairman Tim, had no intention of stopping.

"Fuck," Stitts muttered under his breath. He considered just letting Chase take him down—he appeared, after all, to be in his mid-fifties or early sixties—but his partner had a propensity to fire her weapon at the wrong time.

Stitts bore down, fighting the burning in his legs and limbs, and quickly overtook his partner.

Tim veered left, heading not for the door, but for the open part of the hangar.

Stitts had no idea where he intended to go; it was just a wide-open field beyond the hangar. But he didn't much care, either.

He wanted to tackle the man, but he was starting to feel light-headed and the best he could do was shoot a leg out. Stitts's toe just clipped the back of Tim's left heel and the man's legs pretzeled.

He flew, face-first onto the grass, even skidding a few feet before coming to a stop. Stitts, on the other hand, fell backward on his ass, where he remained.

There wasn't enough strength or oxygen left in his body to subdue the man.

But before Tim could scramble to all fours, Chase was on his back, wrenching the man's wrist behind him and pressing them up to his shoulder blades.

"Calm down!" she shouted. It took three or four such shouts before the man started to relax.

"Okay, okay! *Okay!*"

Stitts was overcome with a hacking fit, coughing so badly that spit flew from between his lips. He leaned onto one side and then gagged. By the time he managed to get enough oxygen in his blood, he saw that Tim was already seated in front of him, his hands cuffed behind his back.

Chase was glaring down at him with a stare so patronizing that had he been able to draw a full breath, he just might have told her off.

"You okay?" she asked but didn't wait for an answer before turning to Tim. "How about you? Just trying to get your ten thousand steps in, or what?"

***

"You're telling me that you have no clue why this strange man wanted you to hack the drone, is that it? Oh, and you didn't see the news... at all? About the shootings? How's your math, Tim? Can you fuckin' put two and two together for me?"

Tim looked at his toes.

"I didn't know that any of this was related to the murders," he said quietly.

Chase grabbed him roughly by the chin and raised his face.

"What's that? You want to confess?"

Tim shook his head and pulled away from her hand.

"The guy just said he'd give me fifty bucks—fifty bucks to install some software he provided into a drone—so long as it was a good one with a long range, he didn't even care which one. I didn't know what it was all about. I think he said something about a research project or something. I had no idea this was all related... man, I liked Congressman Vincente."

Chase glanced over at Stitts. She didn't know if it was Dr. Matteo's influence, or her sudden joie de vivre; but she thought she believed this guy, too. She believed Mohammed Al-Saed, she believed William Woodley, and she believed Mark Yablonski.

And now she believed Tim the drone repairman.

For fuck's sake, I went from being Eeyore to a Pollyanna in six months. What's wrong with me?

"What's the guy's name? What did he look like then? Whose drone did you install the hack into?" Stitts asked, finally rising to his feet.

Tim shook his head.

"He never gave a name and the light in the hangar messes with my eyes, man. He was a regular dude. White, kind of thin. Black hair. As for the drone, it was the guy's in the wheelchair. Mark something."

Chase chewed the inside of her lip. She believed the man, but there was believing and then there was *believing.*

She stepped forward, teasing off one of her gloves at the same time.

The last thing she wanted to do was touch this guy; she was starting to feel like Woody Allen at an orphanage.

But it just wasn't adding up. Just like Mark Yablonski putting his name on the bottom of a drone that was used during an assassination didn't make sense.

"He called it 'research'? That's what he said? You really didn't know that he was installing a secondary control?"

Tim's eyes went wide.

"A secondary control? No, I had no idea."

"But it is possible, right?"

"Yeah, I guess so. But I didn't know that's what the software was all about. He just needed a drone."

Stitts coughed again and then spat onto the grass.

"I don't think you understand how serious this is," he said. "This isn't just some invasion of privacy bullshit. The entire city is on lockdown, on high alert. You aided and abetted a terrorist, Tim. Whether you intended to or not."

Chase watched as Stitts inhaled three times. He looked terrible, psychotic, even.

"You're a terrorist."

Tim shook his head back and forth.

"No! *No!* I'm a patriot… I didn't… man, I liked Vincente. I didn't want any of this to happen."

Chase, fully convinced now, put her glove back on. Then she racked her brain for what to do next. If they called Pratt and let him know what had happened, he'd come roaring out here and throw Tim in jail with the others—maybe send them to Gitmo. But none of the men knew anything of value.

They needed a subtler approach. Something clandestine.

"Tim," Chase said. "You said that this guy gave you the program to install in the drone."

"Yeah, he did. He just gave me—"

"Do you think you can get the program off the drone and make some modifications?"

Tim made a face.

"I'm not… I'm not sure. Maybe."

"You helped a terrorist murder two people, Tim," Stitts reminded him. "You say you're a patriot? Then prove it."

Tim swallowed hard.

"I think I can. What changes do you want me to make?"

Chase hesitated.

"I want you to add a third controller. I want you to keep the ones already in place but add a third. You think you can do that?"

"Yeah. Yeah, I can do it. Just let me up, and I'll do it."

Chapter 63

FLOYD WAS FURIOUS. HE couldn't believe that William Woodley would exploit Agent Adams's life like that.

She didn't deserve it.

Agent Adams might have her problems, but she was a good person. He'd seen her solve crimes that no one else could, which saved lives.

And she'd been kind to him, as well.

William Woodley was a bully, plain and simple. And growing up in rural Alaska with a terrible stutter, Floyd had had his share of run-ins with bullies. After a while, it was just easier for him to keep his mouth shut, rather than try to stutter his way out of a confrontation. But the time to keep quiet was over. If anyone needed to shut up, it was William Woodley.

Floyd pulled up to the address for the studio and then did a double-take. It was a plain apartment building, which was not what he'd expected. But after making sure that this was the correct address, he got out of the car, and hurried to the door.

"William W-w-w-oodley!" he yelled at the windows as he knocked. "G-get down here!"

Predictably, there was no answer. Sometimes all you had to do was push back and a bully would leave you alone.

But that wasn't good enough here. Floyd couldn't let this coward air more videos of Chase on his stupid TV show.

He knocked again, but when there was no reply, he tried the door. It was unlocked, and Floyd peeked inside.

The interior was dark and when he shouted, his voice echoed back at him.

He knew that he shouldn't enter, that he had no authority to enter, but he saw Chase's face in the darkness. Not the way it was now, but the way it had been.

Defeated. Bruised. Broken.

What William Woodley had shown was terrible, but the rest was even worse.

I can go inside, Floyd thought, *trying to rationalize his actions. I can go inside… I'm just a man looking to rent some studio space.*

He cleared his throat and shouted once more.

"William Woodley! Wh-wh-where are you?"

I'm also an FBI assistant… and Agent Adams is my boss.

With another deep breath, Floyd built up as much courage as he could muster and finally entered the building.

It was nearly pitch-black inside, and he was grateful for the light that spilled in from the door behind him. He had no idea where he was going, but the flow of the place led him to the right, down a narrow hallway. He continued to announce his presence as he went, making sure that if Woodley was actually here, that he'd know he was coming.

Eventually, Floyd came to an opening on his left that led to a desk that he recognized.

It was the desk behind which the bully had sat when he played the video of Chase.

Seeing that desk with the green screen behind it enraged him further.

"W-w-w-william W-w-w-woodley! G-g-get your—"

Something struck him in the back of the head and even before Floyd could finish his sentence, the floor rushed up to meet him.

Chapter 64

"THAT'S IT? YOU'RE DONE?"

Tim the drone repairman nodded and handed Chase her cell phone.

"The app's right there, on your home screen. If the drone becomes active, you'll get a notification. Load up the app and you can take control. I've made you the master, while the other two are slaves."

Chase took her cell phone and opened the app. Although the video feed was dark—the drone wasn't on—she recognized all of the meters and numbers from the video she'd seen on Woodley's show.

She knew that in order to actually fly the damn thing that she should practice, but the sun was already starting to set, and time was of the essence.

The Senate was planning on meeting tomorrow and if someone really wanted to put a stop to the Bill, they'd strike again in the morning.

And if Mark Yablonski flies it every morning, that's when the shooter will take control of it.

Still nervous at the prospect of flying the damn thing, she looked around. Eventually, her eyes fell on a man crouching over a large black case.

A thought occurred to her then.

"Hold on a sec," she said to Tim, Stitts, and Brian. "Wait here."

Chase hurried over to the man and put on her best fake smile.

"Hi," she said softly.

The man nearly fell over.

"I'm sorry, I didn't mean to scare you."

When he saw who it was, the man's face broke out into a smile.

"Oh, no, problem. I was just packing up. I can… I can take it out again if you want…"

"Well, actually, I was hoping you could do me a favor."

The man's smile never faltered, and Chase knew at that moment, that she could ask for his firstborn child and the man would've handed it over, no questions asked.

"Your goggles. I was wondering if I could borrow them for a day or two."

The man's eyes darted down to the case.

"You want to… borrow them?"

Chase nodded then hooked a thumb over her shoulder at Brian who was standing about fifteen feet away.

"Yeah, I'm thinking of joining the club, but I need to give this a try first. I've already got a drone, but I love the goggles. I'll tell you what, let me borrow them for a day or two and then we can meet up and talk about it over drinks, maybe?"

The man surprised her by hesitating.

He'd give up his firstborn, but not his precious goggles.

"I can give you some cash? As a retainer?" Chase added.

The man shook his head and grabbed the goggles.

"Nah, no need for that. We're a growing community and I'd love to get someone else involved. Here, take 'em. I'll be here tomorrow if you're done with them then."

Chase nodded then handed the man her business card.

"Call me if you need them back sooner."

When she turned back to Brian, Tim, and Stitts, the smile slid off her face and she looked skyward.

"Tim, you think you can set it up so I can control the drone with these goggles?"

"Sure, it'll only take a minute."

Chapter 65

PETER TRIED TO RUN after Floyd, but the gangly bastard was quick and elusive. Peter, on the other hand, had spent way too many hours behind the computer becoming skinny-fat.

He liked Floyd, he liked Floyd a lot. The man was good on the computer, and he seemed to have a knack for absorbing knowledge about mechanical things, like drones and trains.

Peter got the impression that Floyd was often considered dumb or slow because of his stutter, but that clearly wasn't the case.

It was also apparent that the man had a thing for Chase—or Agent Adams as he insisted on calling her—which had become obvious the second that Peter had inquired about whether she was single.

"Floyd?" Peter called out when he lost sight of him. There were no longer any amateur vloggers around trying to catch a glimpse of the scene—Senator DeBrusk's shooting had happened almost twelve hours ago and was old news already—but enough people were walking by that when they turned to look at him, he blushed.

Eventually, Peter just gave up and made his way back to the mobile command center. Now that it was completely abandoned and silent, he thought he could get some real work done.

Right before William Woodley had played the video of Chase, which was clearly a fake as was all the bullshit out of his mouth, he'd gotten a hit on the predictive software.

Peter brought up the black-and-white background image again and then zoomed in on the smattering of red dots. There were four of them that fit all of the criteria: within the M24

Sniper's range, within range of both assassinations, and within range of Mark Yablonski's drone.

One of them was the tri-towers that he'd pointed out several times but had led to nowhere.

Is it possible that someone was shooting from the rooftop when ATF was inside the building? Peter thought, recalling what Chase had said.

The answer was yes, of course—it *was* possible—but Chase had been adamant—

"What the hell?" Peter whispered as he looked at each of the dots more closely.

He quickly pulled up a list of addresses and confirmed the listing. Then he went back and double-checked the variables he'd inputted.

Everything was as it should be.

Peter swallowed hard and hovered his cursor over the red dot in question. A pop-up indicated that the program considered this location as the likely one with a confidence of eighty-eight percent.

"Oh, shit," Peter shouted as he scrambled for his phone.

Chapter 66

"**LET ME GET THIS** straight," Pratt said, crossing his arms over his chest. "Not only do you want me to let this guy go, but you want me to give him back evidence from the assassinations *and* you want me to tell him to go about his business? To fly the drone again tomorrow morning, even?"

Chase nodded.

"Not only that, but I want you to tell Senator Torey McBain, the next biggest pusher of Bill S-89 aside from DeBrusk, to head up to Capitol Hill tomorrow around six. Tell him to go ahead with the vote."

SO Pratt laughed. And this wasn't a chuckle, either; it was nearly a gut-buster. When Chase didn't join him, he looked to Stitts.

"I know your partner has problems, but she's all out of whack here. There's no way—"

"What? I have problems? What the hell are you talking about?"

Pratt smirked.

"You haven't seen the latest video from our pal Woodley, have you?"

"What video? What are you talking about?"

"Looks like you made a friend in Woodley. He's been airing your dirty laundry all afternoon."

It took a moment for Chase to figure out what the man was talking about.

Of course, she thought glumly. Woodley was pissed that they hadn't given him what he wanted. Mainly, some sort of abuse caught on camera.

Instead, he'd just gone and done his research on her, which was arguably worse.

Chase was furious, and her first instinct was to find Woodley and wring his neck.

She took a deep breath and thought of Dr. Matteo's teachings.

There are things that are outside of your control, Chase. Trying to control them is a waste of energy. Just let them happen.

Grinding her teeth, she struggled with this advice.

If I don't at least make an effort to control things, what's stopping others from just walking all over me?

For the first time in a long time, Chase felt the familiar tingle in her fingertips. The urge to use wasn't nearly as strong as the other times, but it was still there.

And, Chase thought miserably, *it's probably something I'm going to have to deal with for the rest of my life.*

She shook her head.

"This isn't about me. It's about catching this bastard. As Stitts pointed out before, the FBI is in charge. So, why don't you just go ahead, and do as I ask."

Pratt looked around for support, eventually finding it in a middle-aged police officer.

"I mean, we can fine him for flying his drone, maybe even take it away. But that's about it."

Pratt scowled.

"If anything happens, it's on you," he spat, reaching for the drone and snatching it from her hands.

Chase knew that she should let this go, that she'd already won, but, like with William Woodley, she couldn't help herself.

"No, it's not; it's on *you*. The Secret Service is supposed to be protecting these people, not the FBI. Let us knock down doors, you just keep these people safe."

Pratt was walking away now, but she willed him to turn around.

Come on, turn around. C'mon.

Pratt just kept on walking. When he was out of earshot, Stitts pulled out a cigarette and lit up.

"You're on fire today, you know that?"

"Blazing."

"What you want to do now? When will you get some rest?" Stitts asked between drags. "Mark won't be flying the drone again until the crack of dawn, and until Screech gets back to us about the file, I'm not sure what else we can do."

Chase thought about this for a moment. It made sense. Getting sleep now meant being clearheaded in the morning when Mark took his drone out again.

But she didn't feel like sleeping. What she felt like, was a drink.

"What about grabbing something to eat... and something to drink, first?"

"You sure?"

Chase rolled her eyes.

"Let's grab Floyd along the way. I'm thinking he might need a drink, too."

If there was anyone truly out of their element here, it was her new 'Assistant'.

"I could have do a cold one or two," Stitts admitted with a shrug.

"Let's go then before Pratt changes his mind."

Chapter 67

"*I DON'T BLAME YOU, Chase. You were only a kid. So was I.*"

Chase stared blankly at her sister's face.

"*You* do *remember me,*" *Chase barely whispered. "I knew it... I knew it.*"

Georgina scrunched her nose. She looked so much like she did that day when she'd gone missing thirty years older, that it was uncanny.

And it broke Chase's heart.

She couldn't imagine what it must've been like for her sister to be abducted, to be brainwashed, to be renamed, and to have God only knows what else happened to her in that house.

"*I missed you,*" *Georgina said, reaching for Chase. Before they could wrap their arms around each other, someone came between.*

Someone also named Georgina.

Chase smiled and tousled the girl's hair. It wasn't as orange as her sister's used to be, but it had a hint of strawberry mixed in with the blond.

"*You're always getting into trouble, aren't you, little one?*" *Chase said. She bent down and gave the girl a wet kiss on her cheek. Georgina wiped it off with the palm of her hand and made a face.*

"*Gross,*" *she whined.*

Chase laughed.

Then the little girl looked up at her mother and said, "Riley, who is this woman?"

Chase felt her entire body start to tremble.

She tried to ignore the use of her sister's adopted name, Riley, and the fact that Georgina didn't even know who she was.

It's okay, she's still getting used to it. This isn't her fault — none of this is her fault.

"*I'm your auntie,*" *Chase said, trying to keep her tone even.*

Georgina backed up and huddled against her mother's legs.

"No, you're not."

Chase offered a wan smile.

"Your mother and I are sisters, sweetie. I know —"

The little girl shook her head violently.

"You're not my mommy's sister. Those are my mommy's sisters," she said, pointing off to her left.

Chase swallowed hard and followed the girl's pudgy finger.

And then her heart skipped a beat.

There, standing by the edge of the woods, were three women.

Three women wearing long, flowing white dresses.

Sue-Ellen, Portia, and Melissa.

Fighting back tears, Chase turned toward her niece only to find that she wasn't there anymore. In her place was a man with a salt and pepper beard and nicotine-stained teeth.

"I knew you'd come back," the man said in a southern drawl.

Chase tried to reach out and shove the man but couldn't even move her arms.

Panic-stricken now, she looked down and saw that her arms were wrapped tightly against her chest in a white coat.

A coat with buckles across the front.

"No!"

This time, when Chase raised her gaze, it wasn't Brian Jalston, but Jeremy Stitts.

He was leaning into her, trying to shove something big and black into her mouth.

And he too was smiling.

"Here, Chase, put this in your mouth. Put this in your mouth so you don't bite your tongue off."

Chase whipped her head to the side, but Stitts grabbed her chin and forced the mouthpiece between her pursed lips.

It tasted horrible, like melted plastic.

Then Stitts, his smile impossibly wide, leaned forward again. This time, he put an electrode to each of her temples.

Chase heard a fizzle in the air and then it felt like every hair on her body was standing on end.

A second later, she started seeing triple.

Chapter 68

"CHASE, WAKE UP. WAKE up!"

Chase's eyes snapped open and she sat bolt upright.

She had no idea where she was. In fact, she didn't even know if she was still dreaming. Somewhere above her was a persistent pinging sound, and there was a harsh light aimed directly into her eyes.

"Chase! Chase!"

A hand came down on her shoulder and Stitts's familiar face came into view. He was also holding something out to her, and she immediately moved her head to one side, thinking that it was that damn rubber mouthpiece.

But it was only a cell phone.

Her cell phone.

The harsh light, she realized, was the dome light and the pinging was the door open indicator.

"You okay?"

Chase, still not fully recovered, said, "Must've fallen asleep."

"You passed right out the second we got into the car. I tried waking you a few times, but you were having none of it… but then you started shaking…"

Chase cast a glance out the window and realized that it was pitch-black out.

"Jesus, what time is it? How long was I out for?"

"It's almost two," Stitts said guiltily.

"Two? Fuck off. No way it's two o'clock."

The clock embedded in the dash confirmed what Stitts had said.

"What the hell… how is that possible?"

Chase shook her head and then winced. Something in her neck was pinched, and she started to massage it.

"What the hell were you doing this whole time?" she grumbled.

Stitts indicated toward his open window. Outside on the asphalt were more than a dozen cigarette butts.

"Gross."

Stitts just shrugged.

"Can we go somewhere so I can get some real sleep?" she asked. "Are the cutbacks so bad that the Bureau makes their agents sleep in the car now?"

"Already got us a room," he said, starting the car.

Chase's brow suddenly pinched.

"What about Floyd? Weren't you going to pick him up? And why did you give me my phone?"

"It was ringing… didn't want to answer it for you. As for Floyd, I couldn't find him. Went back to the command center and it was deserted."

For some reason, Chase got the sneaking suspicion that the sleep she'd gotten was all there was to be had this night.

"Couldn't find him? What about Peter?"

Chase's phone buzzed in her hand and she answered instantly.

"Floyd? Where are you?"

"Sorry, babe, but this ain't Floyd."

"Screech?"

"Guilty as charged. But speaking of your man Floyd, I was trying to get a hold of him, but no luck. Given all the traction the shootings in Washington are getting on the news now, I thought I'd give you a call."

Chase rubbed her stiff neck again.

"What the hell are you doing up? At this hour?"

"Yeah, I don't really sleep that much anymore. Not since…
well, anyway, I have an update on that file trace that you
asked for."

"And?"

Chase nodded at Stitts and then pulled the phone away
from her ear and turned on speakerphone.

"Well, not sure this is the news you wanted, but I couldn't
find a file of that size arriving at the IP address Peter sent me."

Chase grimaced. She knew it was a long shot, but she also
knew that if anyone could find out where the file had come
from, it'd be Screech.

"Couldn't find it, huh. Well, thanks—"

"No, you don't get it. There were no files of that size
downloaded by any of the IP addresses Peter gave me."

"What do you mean?"

"I mean, nobody downloaded it at the studio. Nobody
downloaded anything that large today."

The pain in her neck had spread to between her temples
now.

It wasn't downloaded? But she'd seen it played on
Woodley's TV show. Or had she imagined that, too?

"Shit," Stitts said, putting the car into drive.

"What? *What?*"

"It wasn't downloaded, because someone either personally
brought the video in or—"

"—or it was William Woodley's video all along," Chase
finished for her partner.

Chapter 69

"DOOR'S OPEN," CHASE SAID, pointing toward the studio.

Stitts nodded and they both pulled out their guns.

She still couldn't believe that it was William Woodley. She'd touched him, she'd stared into the man's face.

They hurried across the street and Stitts indicated the door and then pointed to his left. Chase nodded and then he aimed a finger at her before pointing to the right.

Evidently satisfied that she understood his silent commades, Stitts crept forward and then stepped into the studio.

Chase followed.

It was darker than she'd expected inside, and for the first few seconds, she was just blindly fanning her gun across the expanse.

Slowly, her eyes started to adjust, and she crept down the hallway with more confidence. Stitts made it back to her side just as she arrived at the mouth of the studio.

"I'll go tight, you go wide," he whispered in her ear. "On three."

With his free hand, Stitts held up one finger, a second, and then a third. He pushed himself away from the wall and then entered the studio. Chase took a deep breath and followed, keeping to the right.

It was empty. The dim LEDs that had been left on as part of a budget security system reflected off the semi-circular desk, but there was no one there.

She turned her head back to look at Stitts and nodded. Stitts returned the gesture, then pointed down the hall toward Woodley's dressing room.

Chase acknowledged this and stepped in that direction. She'd taken a half-dozen steps before she heard a low-frequency hum.

A bright light suddenly filled the studio, completely blinding her.

"Get down!" Stitts shouted. "Chase, get down!"

Chase could hear her partner's voice, but the damn electrical buzz was so loud in her ears that she had no idea where it was coming from.

"Fuck!" she shouted, squeezing her eyes closed and pressing her palms against her ears.

Only the buzzing continued to get louder and louder.

And then she tasted melted plastic in her mouth and bit down on the mouthpiece.

Chapter 70

"GET AWAY FROM ME!" Chase tried to shout, but all she managed was to slobber all over the mouthpiece. It tasted horrible on her tongue, and she tried to spit it out, but it was too big to dislodge.

Stitts was smiling like a crazy person. His tongue, which was impossibly long slipped from between his lips and he licked both electrodes at the same time. They sizzled, and a small tuft of smoke drifted up from his mouth.

He inhaled it with his nostrils.

"No, no, no, no!" Chase mumbled again, whipping her head side-to-side.

But there was no escaping this. This was her penance, her punishment for abandoning her own sister in the clutches of a madman.

Stitts put the electrodes to her head and every muscle in her entire body contracted at the same time.

Chapter 71

"**Stop shooting! For fuck's** sake, stop shooting at me!"

Chase blinked several times, trying to force her mind back into the present.

"Chase!"

Her head was aching, and she heard a strange clicking sound undercutting the buzz.

I'm back, she realized. *I'm back in the studio.*

Another couple slow blinks and she found herself staring at the green screen above the desk. Squinting, she realized that there were six holes in the screen.

What the hell?

It took her another moment to put it all together. She pulled her finger off the trigger and lowered it.

"Stitts?" she said, a tremor in her voice. Her only saving grace was that she'd already heard him speak.

"Chase, I'm coming out! Don't shoot!" Stitts called.

She spotted him pressed against the wall, his own gun at his hip. He was frowning and shaking his head.

"Is she done shooting?"

Chase immediately dropped to a knee and spun toward the green screen again.

"Fuck! Don't shoot!"

Chase squinted.

"Peter?"

She saw the man's hands first then his head as he rose from behind the desk.

"What the hell?"

"Don't shoot!"

Chase slipped her gun back into her holster and Peter stepped away from the desk. His eyes were bulging out of his head.

"Jesus, you almost killed me!"

Chase swallowed and stared at the bullet holes on the green screen.

What the hell happened? I don't remember firing a single shot, let alone emptying my magazine.

Stitts put a hand on her shoulder.

"It's okay, Chase," he said quietly enough so that Peter couldn't hear.

"What are you doing here?" Chase demanded.

"Me? *Me?*" Peter shot back. "What the hell are you doing shooting at me?"

Chas grimaced.

The buzz was still in her ears and she had a wicked headache now.

"I'm sorry," she said, forcing the air out of her lungs in an audible *whoosh.*

"It's okay," Stitts repeated.

But it wasn't okay, not really. She'd nearly killed an ATF agent, and she couldn't even remember pulling the trigger.

"I'm sorry," she said again.

Peter made his way over to her.

"Shit, it's fine. Close, but I'm fine."

"What are you doing here, Peter?" Stitts asked.

For a moment, Peter seemed confused, as if he'd forgotten.

"I came here looking for Floyd. He ran off when he saw you on the news. I tried calling him, and I tried calling you, but you FBI guys don't seem to ever answer your phones."

"Floyd came here? You sure?" Chase asked.

"Pretty sure. I just got here and was turning on the lights when you tried to shoot me in the face."

"You came here at two in the morning?" Stitts asked.

Peter shrugged.

"Couldn't sleep."

Chase would've thought this strange under normal circumstances, but Stitts and Screech had essentially said the same thing.

"All right, let's clear this place then get some sleep," Stitts said.

Chase took a step backward and then her heel skidded across something wet. She looked down, then immediately leaped to one side.

"Shit!"

She'd stepped in a puddle of blood. Stitts must have seen it too because he broke off into a sprint toward the dressing room. Chase and Peter followed closely behind, but by the time they got there, Stitts was already coming back out again.

"It's empty," he said, shaking his head. Then he pulled his cell phone out of his pocket and started to dial.

"Who are you calling?" Chase asked.

"Pratt. We need everyone we can get to search for William Woodley. Now reload your gun and let's get ready to move."

Chapter 72

THE SUN HAD JUST started to rise over Washington when the tactical force was finally assembled at the end of Bank Street.

It had taken some convincing to get SO Pratt to round up the troops, which Chase had found surprising, given how much the man despised Woodley.

I guess he hates me more.

But the evidence was compelling: Woodley had aired the videos on his show, the studio was one of the locations that Peter's software had identified, and the video file had been brought there on USB.

After Pratt had agreed to organize the raid, he'd gone full bore. Twice, Stitts had to remind the man that they couldn't just fill Woodley full of lead, much as they all wanted to.

Chase couldn't help but think that part of that message was for her, too.

This time, Stitts conceded the plan to Pratt. Chase wasn't sure if this was him extending an olive branch, or if he was just too damned tired to care. Either way, when Pratt was done, Stitts came up to her privately.

"You gonna be okay going in?"

Normally, this sort of question would piss her off, but the truth was, she was still shaken up about what had happened back at the studio.

"I'll hang back, pull up the rear."

Stitts nodded and helped her adjust the heavy ballistic vest that was strapped to her chest.

"What happened back there?" he asked before quickly shaking his head. "Never mind."

Chase reached out and grabbed his arm. Stitts stopped, while the others, Pratt included, continued toward William Woodley's home.

"I had some sort of flashback. A dream or memory or something," she admitted. Normally, Chase would keep something like this to herself, but she figured she owed him an explanation. Peter too, maybe. "It was the lights or the buzz or something. It was like I was being shocked."

She left out the part about Stitts's long tongue and how he'd licked electrodes before pressing them to her temples.

Because, well, that was insane.

Something crossed over Stitts's face then, but it vanished a second later.

"You think that he's in there? Floyd, I mean?" she asked. She had a bad feeling about that, too.

"I don't know. I have no clue."

Chase moved her hand to her hip as they hurried to catch up to the others. But instead of pulling out her gun, she grabbed her cell phone instead. She switched it to video mode and started to record just as one of Pratt's men smashed the door off the frame with a battering ram.

"FBI!" Stitts shouted. "FBI!"

Chapter 73

THEY FOUND WILLIAM WOODLEY in the shower.

It was Stitts who yanked back the curtain revealing the man in all his spray tan glory.

Woodley was so startled to see them that he slipped, sending a spray of bubbles all over Stitts and the Secret Service. Pratt grabbed the man by the arms and dragged him out of the tub like a slippery salmon. He was confused, he was scared, and he was naked.

Not a good combination to be caught on film.

"What? What?" Woodley's prattle went on for nearly thirty seconds before he was cuffed and hoisted onto the toilet seat.

Pratt threw a towel over his crotch.

Slowly, Woodley started to regain his senses.

"What the hell are you doing here? This is harassment! I'm going to—"

Pratt dropped to his haunches and got within inches of the other man's face.

Woodley's fear returned in spades.

"You shot the senator and congressman, you coward. Used a drone to do it, too. For all your big talk on that show of yours, you didn't even have the balls to face your victims before you killed them. You are a disgrace to Marines everywhere."

Woodley's face went through a series of convoluted changes, as he tried to settle on a particular expression.

Chase watched through her camera lens, trying to feel him out again. She wanted to take her glove off and touch the man, but given the circumstances, she decided that that wouldn't go over well. She didn't know what that would prove, either, given that she'd already touched Woodley and confirmed that he wasn't involved.

Or so she'd thought.

"I didn't do anything!" Woodley finally said, settling on a pout. "I didn't kill those people! I just reported them! That's not a crime. That's not a crime!"

"You sure did. You shot them both."

"What? I didn't—fuck, this is crazy!"

He was close to tears now, and Chase made sure to get a close-up.

"And you paid Mohammed Al-Saed to videotape the president's speech, didn't you? With all your connections, you probably knew that the president was going to speak, and you set up Mohammed as a decoy to take out Vincente."

Woodley just blubbered incoherently.

"Get him up," Pratt ordered. Two Secret Service agents hoisted the man to his feet and the towel covering him slipped to the floor. Eventually, someone helped him into a pair of sweatpants and a shirtless Woodley was led from the bathroom.

It was a pathetic sight, fitting of a pathetic man.

Chase filmed it all.

"We're going to take him to the warehouse, have the lawyer speak to him," Pratt informed both her and Stitts. This time, there was no invitation to join them. That was fine by Chase.

In fact, everything had come together nicely, except for one thing.

"Where's Floyd?" she demanded as Woodley was paraded by.

At first, when he looked at Chase, the man didn't seem to recognize her. But then his eyes slowly widened.

"You! You're behind this," he accused.

Chase ignored the comment.

"Where's Floyd?" she asked again. Chase stopped recording and slipped the phone in her pocket. Then she started to remove one of her gloves. "Tell me where Floyd is."

"I got no fucking clue what you're talking about, lady. I think you're off your fucking meds."

Chase growled and lunged at the man, leading with her bare hand. But before she could grab him, a thick body came between them.

"You've done enough here," Pratt said.

"Get out of my way," Chase shot back. She tried to get around the man, but there was no chance that she was moving his bulk.

Stitts hooked an arm around her waist and gently pulled her back. The whole while, Pratt was smirking at her.

"Thanks for your help," he said sarcastically.

Chase tried to lunge again, but Stitts held her tight.

"Have a nice trip back to Quantico," Pratt hollered after her as Stitts practically dragged her toward the door.

Now that they'd gotten Woodley, Pratt wasn't holding back. He didn't need the FBI anymore.

"Stitts, let me go. We have to find Floyd. We have—"

But Stitts wasn't going to let go and Chase had no choice but to once again relinquish control.

Chapter 74

"**He doesn't give a** shit about finding Floyd," Chase spat. "All he cares about is getting his face on the news."

"Calm down, Chase."

"We do all the leg work, find all the evidence, and he gets to drag Woodley in."

"Take it easy, Chase."

"I bet their government-affiliated torturer doesn't even ask about Floyd."

"Take it easy."

"Would you stop saying that? It's annoying as hell. I am taking it easy, for Christ's sake!"

"You getting all wound up about it isn't going to help, Chase," Stitts shot back at her. "You think running back there and assaulting Pratt is going to get you anywhere other than in prison? We play this game every time. You get pissed off at some officer who you think isn't doing a good job, and you go after them, leaving me to clean up the mess. *I* have to make sure that you don't get your ass thrown in jail."

Chase visibly recoiled.

"What? What are you talking about? Don't you think that —"

"I get that you're hurting, Chase. I do. But other people are hurting, too. You're not the only one out there with pain."

Chase stared at her partner, who suddenly seemed on the verge of tears.

Where is all this coming from?

"Are you... are you okay?"

Stitts pulled out a cigarette.

"I'm hurting too, Chase. I was a kid back then, and I was traumatized, too. I had to live with it because unlike you, I remembered."

Chase chewed the inside of her lip.

"Shit, I'm sorry, Stitts." Chase reached for her partner then, and the man surprised her by embracing her tightly.

He was falling apart.

"My mom," Stitts said. "She died—I didn't mean to take it out on you."

And then it hit her.

Part of her unyielding desire for control meant that she couldn't listen to other people's problems. How could she possibly help with their issues if she couldn't even come close to dealing with her own? Not to mention that her own problems were so large that she didn't have room for others'.

It had happened with her husband, and he'd left her. And now it was happening with Stitts.

"I'm sorry, Stitts. I didn't know."

She regretted saying that last part. She didn't know, because she didn't ask.

Stitts took a step back and wiped his nose and cheeks.

"Come on, let's get out here," Stitts said. He hooked a chin at Floyd's car and Chase started in that direction.

"Where are we going?"

"We're going to find Floyd. We're going to find him before something bad happens to him."

Chapter 75

"YOU DIDN'T, BY CHANCE, put a tracker in Floyd's phone like you did mine, did you?" Chase asked, trying to lighten the mood.

Stitts was having none of it.

"No," he said flatly. They'd already visited an apartment that Woodley owned but rented out. There was no sign of Floyd. If it was any consolation, the man's current tenants were a bunch of hoarders.

"Peter couldn't come up with anything else? A summer home that Woodley owns where he might be keeping Floyd?"

Stitts shook his head.

"No. He says that the man is struggling to just make ends meet; no summer home for him."

This was another nugget that didn't seem to fit. Woodley was staunchly opposed to a bill that would heavily tax the top one percent and affect the way they ran their businesses. You didn't have to be rich to support lower taxes, of course, but usually, those who were so vocal about it had the most to lose.

"But Peter did manage to get the CCTV footage that you asked," Stitts continued.

Chase took Stitts's cell phone and looked at the photo. It was grainy, but she could clearly make out Mohammed Al-Saed with his hand outstretched, reaching for the video camera. She squinted, trying to focus on the man holding the camera. The picture quality was too poor to make out much detail, but if it was William Woodley then he was wearing a wig; the man in the photo had a head of thick black hair.

"Not much help," she said, stating the obvious.

With a heavy sigh, Chase handed the cell phone back to Stitts. Then she picked up her own phone and tapped it in her palm.

"Where the fuck are you, Floyd?" she said under her breath. It was then, that she realized that, like Stitts, she knew very little about Floyd.

She knew that he was from Anchorage, that he liked trains, and that he had a horrible stutter that seemed to go away when he was talking about anything technical.

"Is there a train museum or something around here?" Chase suddenly asked, grasping at straws. "Because Floyd—"

Her phone buzzed in her hand and she looked down at it. She hoped it was Floyd checking in, but it wasn't even a phone call. There was a gray bar across the top of the screen that she'd never seen before. In white text, the words 'ONLINE' flashed continuously.

"What the hell is this?" she mumbled, turning to face Stitts who was concentrating on driving to nowhere. "Someone hacked my phone?"

"What?" Stitts said, not even bothering to look at her.

Ignoring him, Chase pressed the gray bar. An app popped open and the screen was filled with what looked like blades of grass.

"What the fuck is this?"

All of a sudden, the camera pulled back.

"Shit!" she exclaimed, reaching out and grabbing Stitts's arm.

"What is it?"

For a second, all Chase could do was point at her phone.

"Chase, what—"

"It's the drone, Stitts. The goddamn drone is taking off again!"

PART V – Dirty Money

Chapter 76

"**PULL OVER!**" **CHASE SHOUTED.** "Pull the hell over!"

Stitts still looked confused, and Chase felt the need to explain further.

"It's the drone; Mark Yablonski must be flying it again," Chase said excitedly. Although Stitts finally adhered to her request to pull over, he didn't seem as interested in these facts as she was.

"They've already got Woodley in custody," Stitts remarked. "Mark is just taking the thing out for a joyride like you told him to."

There was still this nagging feeling that Woodley wasn't their guy, gnawing at the lining of her stomach.

"We'll see about that," she said, hopping out of the car, and heading to the trunk.

Inside, her eyes fell on the VR goggles that she'd borrowed from the man at the hangar. She felt silly pulling them out here, at the side of the road, but they really had nowhere else to go. If nothing else, the drone would give her a bird's eye view of the city and if she got lucky—*really* lucky—it might help her locate Floyd.

Chase slid the goggles over her head and switched them on. Again, she was met with a bright light, followed by the animated logo. After the stream connected, Chase was back in first person view.

Careful not to take control just yet, Chase watched as the drone rose up, the camera aimed downward at the operator—Mark Yablonski—and his wheelchair. She promised herself that she would only watch for a few minutes—five, tops—and if all Mark was doing was peeping in his neighbor's windows or snapping pics of the White House, she'd shut it down and get back in the car.

Then she would pull all the strings she had at her disposal, including reaching out to Stu Barnes if she had to, in order to find Floyd.

The experience of being the drone was so immersive that she didn't hear Stitts get out of the car, let alone approach.

"Don't you think we should be out there looking for Floyd?" Stitts said from her left. Chase turned in his direction, only to feel disoriented when her field of view did not change.

"Give me a minute," she said out of the corner of her mouth. And then she focused on the live video before her eyes. The drone continued to ascend, the camera shifting from Mark in his wheelchair to a view of early morning Washington. It paused for a moment as if allowing Chase an opportunity to take it all in, even though the man couldn't possibly know that she was watching.

The drone suddenly took off, zipping above first the squat bungalows in Mark's neighborhood, then rising higher still to avoid several high-rises. The drone blasted through chimney smoke, the camera moving to focus on a man encouraging his dog to do its business, to people in housecoats collecting the morning paper.

Normal shit. Boring shit.

"Anything?"

Chase shook her head, but then regretted it.

Don't move with this goddamn thing on, she thought. *Don't move until you take control. If… if you take control.*

"Nothing," she said. Closing in on five minutes now, Chase reached up with the intention of taking the goggles off. Just as she did, however, her cell phone in her hand pinged and the drone suddenly veered hard to the right. It started to pick up speed, blasting through the calm morning. The steering was not as fluid and Chase got a sinking feeling that Mark was no longer in control.

"Hey," she said, still focusing on the images before her eyes. "Did Homeland lift the terrorist high alert after Pratt took Woodley into custody?"

"Not sure."

Knowing Pratt, Chase wouldn't have been surprised if the man had told anyone and everyone who would listen that they had their guy, that the threat was over.

"What about Senator McBain?"

"What about him? You told Pratt to make sure that he headed up to the Capitol to vote on Bill S-89 today."

Chase frowned.

Maybe that wasn't the best idea, she thought suddenly, second-guessing her plan.

If Woodley was innocent, and this was the shooter controlling the drone, then she was putting a lot of faith in two people to ensure that Senator McBain, or any of the supporters of S-89, remained safe.

It dawned on her that she didn't know either of them well.

Chase's anxiety kicked up a notch when the drone's actions changed from a meandering morning flight to something with more purpose.

"Stitts…"

"Yeah?"

The houses suddenly went from dilapidated, to upscale. Then from upscale to gaudy.

"What is it?"

Chase even thought that the drone passed over the studio where Woodley filmed his show but couldn't be sure.

"I think… I think we might have a problem here," she said hesitantly.

"What do you see? Do you see Floyd?"

Chase didn't answer right away; she was distracted by the fact that the drone had started to hover over a particular house. A house that had three familiar black cars parked out front.

The Secret Service.

"Shit," she whispered.

"Chase? You gonna let me in on this? What do you see?"

The drone did something strange; it rotated on a single axis and then started to descend in a straight line.

It's creating a perfect line of sight, Chase realized in horror.

"I think… I think—" and then the door to the mansion opened and a large man in a blue suit stepped out. He was laughing about something and he slapped the Secret Service agent that was standing beside him on the back as he made his way down the steps.

Chase didn't *think* anymore. She *knew*.

She knew that whoever this man was, that he supported Bill S-89 and that he was going to be the next victim.

"Stitts… Stitts, we have to do something. We have to do something, now!"

Chapter 77

CHASE DESCRIBED WHAT SHE was seeing, how the drone seemed to be focusing in on a congressman or senator— someone important—as he was leaving his house. What made things worse was that this man was carrying a navy-blue binder under one arm, a binder that looked like a carbon copy of the one that Senator DeBrusk had been holding when he'd been shot.

"Where is he? Where's this guy?" Stitts asked.

Chase shrugged.

"I don't know… I don't fucking know. Close, not too far from here."

She heard Stitts pull his cell phone out of his pocket and dial a number. A few rings later, a robotic answering machine came on.

"C'mon, Pratt, pick up your damn phone," Stitts said as he dialed the man's number again.

Something was happening with the drone. It was moving up and down now in a slow, controlled manner like it was sublty correcting for wind and temperature.

As if it were trying to relay the perfect shot.

"Try Peter—call Peter and see if he knows what's going on," Chase said. "This might be Senator McBain. See if he has an address on the man."

Once again, Chase heard him dialing on his phone.

"You better hurry, Stitts. I have a feeling that whoever's doing this is trying to line up the perfect shot.

"Shit—can't you do something?"

"Do what? I can't—"

And then Chase froze.

She *could* do something. She'd completely forgotten that Tim, the drone repairman, had installed a backdoor control for her.

All you have to do is take control; you'll be the master, while the other two will be slaves.

Chase debated doing just that; taking control. She'd fly the goddamn thing over the Atlantic, thus depriving the murdered of his shot.

But that would also mean that she would never get him, either. Whoever it was would know that she was onto him and change up their MO.

Chase cursed under her breath.

"Peter, I think there's going to be another shooting," Stitts said.

"What? Who?" a sleepy-sounding Peter replied quickly.

"A man, in his mid-fifties, thinning hair," Chase said, rattling off information as she observed.

"Well, that pretty much describes every politician in Washington. Gimme something else."

Chase squinted.

"I don't… wait, I see something. I see a tricycle on the lawn. A girl's tricycle. Also, he's coming out of a big house with columns out front. Does this sound like Senator McBain to you?"

"Hold on a second," she heard Peter say over the speakerphone.

"Hurry up, I don't know how much time we have."

Peter returned after a moment.

"Yeah, that's him. It's gotta be him."

Chase ground her teeth in frustration. She'd told Pratt that if anything else happened to someone involved with S-89 it was on him, but that didn't change the fact that this was her plan.

"You gotta get someone out there… get Pratt on the line and tell him to tell his men to take McBain back inside."

"I'll try," Peter said, then the line went dead.

"Can you take control? Mess with his line of sight?"

Chase nodded, and she moved her fingers up to the temple of the goggles, as the man in the hangar had shown her. She was about to take the reins then crash the goddamn thing when a thought occurred to her.

Maybe… maybe I can take control and *find out who's responsible for these murders,* she thought.

"Peter said that if this drone was used as a spotter, it would have to be pretty much in a direct line between the shooter and the victim, right?"

"Yeah, I think so."

"Then I have an idea," Chase said. "Call me with your phone and switch mine to speaker. Then get in your car. I'm going to direct you back to the shooter."

Chapter 78

"CAN YOU STILL HEAR me, Stitts?" Chase asked for what felt like the thousandth time.

"Yeah, I got you loud and clear. You gonna tell me where I'm going because I can only go round and round this neighborhood so many times before someone starts to take notice."

"Give me a second," she said. Senator McBain had already gone toward his house twice—once to kiss his wife who looked so young that Chase considered that the tricycle might be hers—and a second time to exchange words with a member of the Secret Service team. She had to be careful not to take over too soon, and she had to trust herself that she could fly the damn thing using only her head. A week ago, she'd known nothing about drones. Now, someone's life depended on her being able to fly one.

In her mind, she went over the instructions that Tim had given her back at the hangar. She could control the camera with her head, which could also turn the drone, but to move forward she had to use a touchpad on the side of the goggles.

It wasn't going to be easy, but all she had to do was turn one-hundred and eighty degrees and then fly in a straight line. There would be no obstacles to avoid, she knew.

But that would only work once the drone settled into the shooter's line of sight. Which meant that Senator McBain had to stop dicking around and start moving toward his car.

Just then, McBain kissed his wife a second time, waved, then started toward a black car, the rear door of which a Secret Service agent was holding open for him.

"Here goes nothing," she whispered as the done started to settle again. "You ready for this, Stitts? Can you see the drone?"

"Yeah, I see it. Can't get any closer though. You're going to have to tell me where to go."

Chase took a deep breath and raised her fingers to the touchpad on the temple of the goggles.

"All right, here goes nothing."

And then she did it. She double tapped the side of the goggles just as Tim had shown her.

At first, the drone didn't do anything. And Chase tapped again.

"C'mon, c'mon…"

"What's going on over there, Chase?"

Chase ignored him and tried to figure out what was wrong. *Was Tim in on this? Did you just scam me? Why the hell isn't the drone doing anything!*

And then it dawned on her that the drone wasn't doing anything because she had to *make* it do something.

Chase turned her head all the way to the right, and the drone's camera went with her. Then she started to move in a small circle until the drone was facing completely backward.

"Okay, Stitts, here we go. *Here we go!*"

Chase slid her fingers across the touchpad and the drone shot forward at breakneck speed. Her phone buzzed in her hand—presumably, their shooter trying, and failing, to regain control—but she ignored this.

It took all her focus to make sure that the drone was flying in a straight line back to the source.

"Okay, we're headed three streets west of Senator McBain's residence," she said loudly. Her heart was thumping away in her chest now. They had to be quick; once the shooter found out that he wasn't in control anymore, he was apt to bail.

"Alright, heading that way now," Stitts replied.

The drone was flying so fast that it was difficult to focus on anything in particular. Chase found herself doing some mental math, trying to crunch the numbers—the distance, the range, the speed—to guess where the drone was headed, where the shooter was located.

"Where to now, Chase? Anything you recognize? Any turns?"

"No, just keep going... keep going straight. It's—" Chase froze.

"Chase? What's happening? Goddamn it, tell me what's going on?"

It was something that Stitts had said—*Anything you recognize*—that stuck with her. She *did* recognize this area, she realized.

Not only that, but she was there just yesterday.

"Stitts... Stitts! The drone is heading back to the studio— the shooter's at the studio!"

Chapter 79

"**WHAT? ARE YOU SURE?**" Stitts shouted.

"Yeah, hurry! Hurry!" Chase yelled back.

Stitts hammered on the gas and then made a hard right. It wasn't until halfway down the street that he realized he'd gone the wrong way. It was proving exceedingly difficult to follow directions provided by somebody controlling a drone.

Chase wasn't bound by the rules of the road, which, in this case, was mainly gravity.

How can the shooter be back at the studio? And where the fuck is Floyd?

Part of him hoped that this was all a misunderstanding, that Woodley really was their guy.

But Chase was rarely wrong when it came to these things. She had her problems, that was undeniable. But when it came to her 'skills?' They rarely let them down.

You should tell her… tell her about everything you know. Tell her about the electroshock therapy, about Beckett's insights into your brain.

The problem was, Stitts didn't know if she could handle it. After all, she'd nearly blown Peter's fucking head off just because of some buzzing lights.

He'd promised himself, and Chase, that he wouldn't lie to her again. But he'd chickened out.

"Stitts? You there yet?"

Stitts doubled back, swerving around a woman pushing a shopping cart full of cans and missing the rear bumper of a FedEx truck by mere inches.

"Almost, almost!"

He floored it, pulling up to within three feet of the studio before hammering on the brakes and jumping out of the car.

It was still only about six in the morning, six fifteen, maybe, and the street was completely empty. He scanned the roof first, then worked his way down. Not only did he not see anyone, but all the windows appeared to be intact and closed.

"You sure, Chase? I'm not seeing anything here."

He started to wonder if he was on the wrong side of the building when Chase suddenly shouted.

"Shit. *Shit!* It's not the studio, Stitts! It's the building across the street! Turn around! *Turn around!*"

Chapter 80

IT WAS ALL CHASE could do not to rip off the goggles and start to run.

But while she'd taken control of the drone, she'd given up control over Stitts.

Instead of taking the goggles off, she took a deep breath and started to move her head around, using the camera to find out exactly where the sniper was. She started at the bottom of the building, and then slowly raised her eyes, using the zoom feature to peek inside the windows.

The windows on the first four floors all had blinds covering them. The fifth floor was completely empty; it looked as if renovations had just begun.

Chase saw him on the sixth floor.

Not the sniper, but someone else.

"Floyd," she gasped.

The man was lying on his back, his hands and ankles bound behind him. There was a filthy T-shirt wrapped around his head and face, but she knew without doubt that it was her assistant.

"Chase? What the fuck is going on? Where is this guy?"

She'd completely forgotten that Stitts was still on the phone.

"Floyd! Floyd's on the sixth floor... he's tied up!"

"Got it! Wait—there's someone on the roof! He's—*oh shit!*"

Chase's immediate reaction was to look up, but she did this too quickly and had to close her eyes to stave off nausea.

When she opened them again, she found herself staring down the barrel of an M24 Sniper.

The video quality was so great that with the morning light shining down on the shaft, she could make out every groove, every striation in the metal.

Chase flicked the side of the goggles and zoomed out. Her perspective changed, and instead of just seeing the barrel, she saw the entire gun.

And the man with his eye behind the sight. A man with slick black hair and a grin on his face.

A man she recognized.

"Stitts!" she shouted. "Stitts, it's—"

Then the barrel of the rifle ignited in flames and less than a blink later, the video feed went dark.

Chapter 81

STITTS HEARD THE SHOT before he saw it. When he looked up, a shower of plastic and metal rained down on him.

He leaped out of the way, dropping his phone in the process. What was left of the drone smashed to the ground just feet from where he stood.

"What the hell?"

He looked up and realized that the sniper had acquired a new target, and this time, itt wasn't the drone or Senator McBain.

It was him.

"Shit!" he yelled, lunging toward the building.

Another shot rang out and chunks of sidewalk peppered Stitts's ankles. This was quickly followed by another, which shattered a concrete windowsill just above his head.

Breathing heavily, Stitts pushed his back up against the wall and made himself as flat as possible, trying to create an impossible shooting angle from the overhanging roof.

Then he pulled his gun from his belt and looked for his cell phone. It was lying in the open near the shattered drone, and he could hear Chase shouting, calling his name.

There was no way he was going to get to it without taking a round in the chest or head.

Sixth floor, he thought. *Floyd is on the sixth floor.*

Knowing that he had little time before the shooter either adjusted his position or made a run for it, Stitts strafed along the wall to the front door. He opened one of the double doors just wide enough to peek in, concerned that the shooter might have an accomplice. When he saw an empty foyer, he took a chance and slid inside.

Directly in front of him were two elevators, and there was a directory on the wall to his right. A quick glance at the latter revealed that the building was mostly empty; it appeared that it was destined to become something of a studio just like the one across the street.

Stitts moved to the elevators, both of which were open. They seemed to be the type that always returned to the lobby after dropping off their occupants, likely to facilitate the transport of supplies for the renovation. He debated taking one of them to the sixth floor but decided against it.

In the movies, the hero would just hoist himself up and out of sight of the door. When it opened, the bad guy would come and look around before the hero dropped from above.

But Stitts was no Liam Neeson, and there was no way he would be able to even get himself up that high, let alone Spiderman for the entire trip to the sixth floor. But he also didn't want the shooter to call for the elevators while he hurried up the stairs, either. Looking around, he spotted a potted plant and a doorjamb. He scooped them both up and placed one against each of the elevator doors, ensuring that they wouldn't be able to close.

Then Stitts made his way to the stairs. He pushed the door open, peeked in, then pulled back out.

There was no one there. Based on the fact that he hadn't heard a single person shout when the shots had been fired, he assumed that the building was completely empty. He listened closely again, his ear to the stairwell.

And it didn't appear as if the shooter had an accomplice, either.

Stitts quickly weighed his options. So far as he knew, the only way down and off the roof, now that the elevators were jammed, was through the stairs.

I can just wait here, see if he comes down. Chase must have called the police by now. It's only a matter of time before they arrive.

But he had to consider that there was a murderer with a high-powered sniper rifle on the roof. While, to this point, all the killings had been politically motivated, there was no way to know if the man would just start opening up on random civilians heading to work.

It seemed unlikely, but it wasn't a chance he was prepared to take.

After a deep breath, Stitts entered the stairwell. He made it to the first landing and leaned back and aimed his gun upward to the second floor. When it didn't open, he mounted the next series of steps. Stitts repeated this process on each and every landing, half expecting a psycho armed to his teeth to hop out.

But he never appeared.

Stitts made it to the sixth floor without incident. Eager to get out of the confined space of the stairwell, he quickly pulled the door open and entered.

There was dust everywhere and every step he took seemed to only stir up more of it. Swatting it away from his eyes, Stitts cautiously pressed on, searching for Floyd, while wary of the potential presence of the shooter.

Thankfully, the walls had already been torn down and it was easy to peer through the metal girders.

There was no gunman here.

But there was no Floyd, either.

As Stitts started backing toward the door again, he saw a workbench covered with a large sheet off to one side, blocking his view. On a whim, he hurried around it and then gasped.

Floyd was there, exactly how Chase had described him: the man was on his stomach, some sort of T-shirt over his face, and his arms and legs bound behind him.

Forgetting all about his own safety, Stitts ran to the man, tucking his gun into his holster as he went. And then he set about trying to untie Floyd, not even sure that he was still alive.

He somehow managed to free the man's arms, and then he flipped him over. The T-shirt was attached to his face with duct tape on his forehead and around his mouth. After ineffectively trying to find the ends of the tape, Stitts gave up and just tore a hole in the center of the shirt.

As soon as he did, Floyd sucked in a huge breath.

"Agent Stitts!" he nearly shouted.

Stitts cringed and put a hand on the man's mouth, silencing him. Then he pointed upward, to the roof, and then pressed the same finger to his lips.

The shooter is still up there; you need to be quiet.

Floyd nodded and then worked himself into a seated position. His fingers were more slender than Stitts's, and he managed to unpeel the duct tape and then pull the T-shirt off his head. Floyd winced and brought a hand to the back of his head.

Stitts took a quick glance and saw that while Floyd's hair was dark and matted with blood, the wound on his scalp seemed superficial.

Together, they untied his legs, and then Stitts helped him to his feet. Floyd wobbled slightly, but after a few seconds and several deep breaths, he got his legs under him.

Stitts leaned close and whispered in his ear.

"Go downstairs, Floyd—take the stairs. Stay close to the building when you get outside and then run. Run as fast and as hard as you can. When you're in the clear, find a phone and call 9-1-1. Then get a hold of Chase."

Floyd's eyes narrowed, and he shook his head. Stitts didn't have time for this. He grabbed the man roughly by the collar and guided him toward the stairs.

"Go!" he hissed in the man's ear.

It took another shove, but Floyd eventually gave up resisting and hurried down the stairs.

Stitts waited for a thirty count before pulling his gun out of his holster again.

And then he continued his way toward the roof.

Chapter 82

CHASE SCREAMED AND TORE the goggles from her head.

"Fuck! Stitts? You still there? *Stitts!*"

She paused, giving him a second to reply, but her partner remained mum.

"Stitts?"

A reply came in the form of two shots. They were so loud that Chase had to pull the phone away from her ear to avoid going deaf.

"No," she moaned. And then she screamed her partner's name into the phone again.

When there was no answer this time, and she heard nothing else for the next few seconds, she had no choice but to hang up and immediately dial 9-1-1.

"Nine one one, what's your emergency?" a bored-sounding operator replied.

"There's been a shooting," Chase said quickly. "There's a sniper on the roof."

"Slow down, ma'am. You said there's been a shooting? Where?"

Chase cringed at the use of the word ma'am but ignored it. She racked her brain, trying to recall exactly where the studio was located.

"Uh, it's a studio! The studio that William Woodley films his show at."

"Do you have an address?"

Chase shook her head.

"No, I can't remember."

"And are you presently at the location?"

"No, no, I saw the shooting from a drone. Listen, I'm an FBI agent... you need to get people out here fast. My partner has been shot."

"Ma'am, first responders have already been dispatched. Did you say that you're with the FBI?"

"Yes! Special Agent Adams. Please hurry!"

Chase hung up the phone and then dialed Stitts's number. There was no answer.

Please be okay, Stitts. Please be okay...

Grinding her teeth in frustration, Chase tried to think of what the best course of action was. She could run to the studio herself, but she didn't know how to get there by foot. And besides, by the time she arrived, it might be too late.

She needed a ride.

Chase dialed the only other person she thought she could trust and listened to it ring.

"Pick up, come on, pick up," she mumbled.

"Hello?"

"Peter? It's Chase. Where the fuck are you? I need a ride... shit's going down. I need a ride, quick."

"What? What time is it?"

"Wake the fuck up!" she screamed, and this seemed to snap Peter into the present.

"Chase, what's going on?"

"It's not Woodley... he's at the studio... he's already shot Stitts and he has Floyd all tied up and, and, and..."

"Calm down, Chase."

She heard the man scurrying to get dressed, and then he started breathing heavily as he began to run.

"I'm on my way. Where the fuck are you?"

"I'm—I'm—" Chase looked around quickly. She didn't really know where the hell she was; she'd just instructed Stitts to pull over to the side of the road as soon as the drone had become active.

Chase moved around, trying to find a street sign.

"Chase? I'm getting into my car now. Where are you?"

"I don't know!"

But then Chase saw a street sign and relayed the name to Peter.

"It's not far; I'll be there in five."

"Make it three," Chase snapped back. "I don't know if Stitts and Floyd have five minutes."

Chase hung up the phone and stood on the sidewalk, feeling more than helpless.

Her partner was likely shot and wounded, if he was still alive, and her friend, her driver, her FBI assistant, was tied up, likely the next victim.

I should have never given up control, she thought miserably. *I should've been the one who went to the studio, not Stitts. I should've been the one who was shot.*

Chapter 83

STITTS STAYED LOW AS he neared the metal door leading to the roof. He could see remnants of a lock scattered on the top two steps.

Thankfully, there was a window in the door, and Stitts peered out twice in an attempt to orient himself. The door to the roof jutted near the corner, and he could hear the sound of air conditioners from one side through the corrugated metal walls.

The roof itself, which was flat, was covered in gravel, and Stitts scanned the surface, looking for the shooter. His eyes first went to the front of the building, where the sniper had taken out the drone and had fired at him.

But there was no one there. In fact, he couldn't see the shooter anywhere. It dawned on him that the best place for the man to hide would be just outside the door. That way, when Stitts peeked his head out, he could just blow him away.

I should wait. I should just wait here…

The problem with that was if there was a second exit off the roof, a fire escape, perhaps, every second wasted was a second longer for the killer to make his exit.

Stitts made up his mind; he was going to go for it. There really was no other choice.

He hunkered low to the ground, and then pushed the door all the way open, waiting for a shot that never came. When the door almost closed completely, he burst through, whipping his gun to the right, where he would have hidden if their roles had been reversed.

But, again, there was no one there.

Breathing heavily, his heart racing, Stitts spotted where the sniper had been. A set of binoculars, as well as a drone remote control and set of goggles like the ones that Chase had been wearing, were resting on a patch of disturbed gravel.

Stitts snaked his way around the protruding stairwell, pressing his back against it as he moved to avoid being taken from behind. From this vantage point, he could see the entire rooftop, except for around the stairwell. He made it to the first corner and then leaned out only to immediately pull back.

There was no one there.

Stitts took the corner and then repeated the process on the next.

Again, it was empty.

This left only one side to check, the side that was pumping out heat from the mechanical equipment and air conditioners.

Stitts closed his eyes when he got to the final corner and felt a sudden surge of adrenaline.

This is it, he thought as he crouched down low.

Then he leaned out.

Stitts was about to yell *freeze*, was even prepared to shoot should he see a man standing with the gun aimed back, but he stopped himself.

Inexplicably, there was no one there, either.

"What the fuck?" he whispered, turning back around.

The roof was completely empty. The shooter *had* been here, but he wasn't anymore.

"Goddamnit!"

The shooter must have slipped down the stairs while I was on the sixth floor, Stitts thought.

He hurried to the edge of the roof and peered down, hoping to catch a glimpse of the man running.

But the street below was empty; neither Floyd nor the man with the rifle were visible.

There must be another way off this roof!

Stitts walked over to the disturbed gravel area with the binoculars and crouched. There, on the ground, were seven Lapua Magnum shell casings. He picked one up and found that it was still warm.

He couldn't believe that the bastard had gotten away.

Just as he'd resigned himself to heading back down the stairs, he heard a distinct buzzing noise. His first thought was it was his cell phone, only it couldn't be; his cell phone was still on the ground by the drone shrapnel.

Eventually, he located the source of the sound.

A cell phone was cradled in the bottom of the abandoned drone controller. Curious, he bent down and picked it up.

The phone was ringing.

With a trembling hand, Stitts pulled the phone out of the controller and answered the call.

"FBI Agent Jeremy Stitts, is it?" a male voice said.

Stitts's eyes narrowed.

"Who is this?"

"A concerned citizen—someone who doesn't want the government meddling in my business. Why don't you take a look across the street?"

Stitts looked at the front of the studio, but there was no one there. He scanned the road out front, but the only person he spotted was a man walking his dog nearly a block away. And he didn't have a phone.

"A little higher," the voice said, and Stitts could practically hear the man smiling.

With a hard swallow, Stitts looked to the roof of the studio across from the building on which he stood.

And then he found himself staring down the barrel of a gun.

Chapter 84

CHASE WAS PACING IN a tight circle when Peter pulled up in a car that she'd never seen before.

At first, she didn't even realize it was him; not that it would've mattered. At this point, she was fairly certain that she would've jumped in any car that came by and demanded that the driver take her where she needed to go.

But it was Peter, and he looked as he'd sounded on the phone: his hair was a mess and he was wearing a pair of jeans and a T-shirt that appeared to be on backward.

It took him just less than five minutes to get to her, which was entirely too long. And Chase still hadn't heard the sirens of the emergency response crew that the 9-1-1 operator had promised to send her way. She suspected that Pratt most likely commandeered them all for his parade down Massachusetts Avenue, likely passing directly below William Woodley's sign condemning the debt of the American government.

Chase literally leaped into the passenger seat and Peter was off and moving again before she'd even closed the door.

"You know where you're going?" Chase asked.

"Yeah, the studio," Peter replied, hammering on the accelerator.

Chase shook her head.

"No, the building across from the studio. On the roof."

"Got it," Peter said. "I did some research last night, seeing if I could come up with a connection between Woodley and Yablonski, any of the parties involved. Check out my phone."

Chase grabbed it from the center console and then inhaled sharply.

"Yep," Peter said. "They all did a tour together in Iraq."

Chase was staring at a photograph of three men in fatigues: William Woodley was in the center, with hair, she noted, his arm wrapped around Mark Yablonski to his right and another man with slick black hair.

"It's him," she said softly, tapping this third man's face. "It's the handler."

Peter nodded.

"I didn't put it together until just now. Woodley and this guy, Fred Browe, left after one tour. Yablonski did another tour, and, well, we know how that turned out. After they returned, Woodley and Browe started the show together. According to a whole whack of Reddit discussions, Woodley really is just a talking head; Browe is the idea man."

Chase couldn't believe her eyes. They'd walked right by the shooter without even asking him a single question about it. Shit, Stitts had been to the studio twice and never even considered Fred as a possible suspect.

"Ideas... like hating on S-89. I get it, but to kill for it? That's a stretch, isn't it?"

Chase said these words for her benefit as much as for Peter's. The man seemed to have picked up on this because he didn't reply.

What did Martinez say way back in Alaska?

You're trying to apply rational reasoning to an irrational act, Chase. There isn't a nice and neat motive for every crime out there. Sometimes bad people just do bad things.

Chase shook her head. That couldn't be the case here; she couldn't believe that. This, of any crime she'd investigated, was clearly motivated by change.

But why? To protect their show? She'd already seen Woodley's digs, and they were far from impressive. What was Browe trying to protect?

"That's it," Peter said, drawing her out of her head.

Chase nodded and pulled her gun out again. She'd promised Stitts that she would keep it holstered, but she figured, given the circumstances, that her partner would understand.

Chapter 85

"NEAT TRICK WITH THE drone, I'll give you that," the man behind the rifle said. "Hacking my hack, gotta love the irony." Stitts resisted the instinct to say that it wasn't his doing, but Chase's. He was the one who'd recklessly run up to the roof and put himself in this position. He should have checked first for a fire escape, which he now noticed dangling from the eastern edge of the roof. This was his cross to bear now.

"What do you want?" Stitts asked. In one hand he held the cell phone, in the other his gun.

He still couldn't believe that it had been Fred the Handler, Fred the Fluffer, this entire time.

Stitts cursed himself for not seeing it sooner.

"Really? You've made it this far and you still don't know what I want?"

Stitts felt like screaming at the man, cursing him for what he'd done, for the lives he'd taken but he knew better. He knew that in these situations, it was best just to give the other person an opportunity to speak.

To hang themselves with their own words.

And Fred the Fluffer didn't disappoint.

"I want to fix this country, that's what I want. I want America to be the best country on earth, not a second- or third-place finisher. I fought for that; I did a tour of Iraq and when I came back, I had a new perspective. We soldiers were handcuffed there. We had so many rules and restrictions, so much goddamn red tape that we couldn't get anything done. And it cost good people their lives. Some lost their lives, while others their legs."

Fred paused, allowing this to sink in. And sink in it did.

Mark Yablonski…

"Who is the government to tell us soldiers what to do, how to act, when bullets start flying, hmm? We're sent into these war zones but prohibited from actually warring. We're so horribly underfunded that we don't even have batteries for the archaic equipment they suit us up with. Then I come back here only to find out that the government is strapped for cash because they bailed out a bunch of private companies? Can you believe that? The fucking irony. I'm overseas fighting for the freedoms of these companies back home with shitty equipment because the government is feeding them handouts. Now that's the real Dirty Money, Stitts. What we need, is to start over; we need a period of stagflation so that private businesses can function the way they need to in order to make America great again."

It dawned on Stitts that these words were eerily similar to the ones that Woodley uttered on his show, which made sense. It was often the people behind the scenes who had the real power; they were the ones who pulled the strings.

Stitts couldn't believe that he didn't see it sooner. Especially considering Woodley had practically told him as much during their first visit.

What do I know? I just report the news, read a teleprompter filled with words that people smarter than I put together to form coherent sentences.

"We need less regulation, not more," Fred continued. "We need the government to stay the fuck out of private business. Bill S-89 was going to plummet America into the Dark Ages. Stagflation is the only cure, the only light at the end of the tunnel. A restart, if you will."

Even though Stitts was listening to the man's ramblings, he was also trying to figure a way out of this. So far, Fred had only killed those who supported the bill. Sure, he'd tied up Floyd, but he hadn't killed him.

The man was twisted, that was clear, but he wasn't a psychopath. What he was, Stitts realized, was a terrorist by definition.

Someone who uses violence to push a political aim.

It was in the FBI handbook, for Christ's sake. And this brought them full circle to Mohammed El-Saed.

"I don't support Bill S-89; I'm for free market," Stitts said, breaking his silence. "Like when you gave Tim at *Fly Right* the fifty bucks to hack Mark's drone, right? Or when you gave another fifty to Mohammed to film the President's speech, knowing full well that with a gun in the camera, he'd be the perfect distraction for you to take out Congressman Vincente."

Fred Browe laughed.

"Exactly. Now you're catching on."

"I'm with you on that one," Stitts continued. "The bloated government and redundant government agencies are the banes of my existence. Fuck, in this case alone, looking for you, I've had to run through hoops to keep everyone happy. I had to basically give hand jobs to the useless Secret Service, the DOJ, Homeland, local and state police. *Everybody*. If I had my way, if I was given free rein to do this the right way, I'd have brought you in even before you took out Vincente."

Across the roof, Stitts saw Fred pull his eye away from the sight and look at him with both eyes for the first time.

The man seemed taken aback by the comments.

"Just don't fucking shoot me. Like I said, I don't support the bill."

There was a short pause, and Stitts wondered if he'd pushed it too far.

But when the man spoke again, his tone was less aggressive, conciliatory even. This was also in the FBI handbook; the first step to talking down a jumper was to get them to stop being so angry. Any emotion, even sadness, was better than anger.

"Put the gun down now and give yourself up, and you'll be a martyr for your audience. Take out an FBI agent, particularly one who *doesn't* support the bill, and you'll just be relegated to serial killer status."

The man's eye moved behind the sight again.

"I'm not a serial killer, I'm a facilitator. How is what I'm doing here different from what I was told to do in Iraq? We were supposed to impart our way of life on them, use force to get them to accept our ideals. That's exactly what I set out to do here. It's no different than when the CIA attempted to assassinate Gadhafi, Milosevic, Castro, Hussein, and Jong-un. Oh, it's fine if it happens overseas, but here? On our soil that we are desperately trying to protect? Then we get cold feet."

"Then you can't kill me. Killing me will just put a brown stain on your agenda. Killing me will set you back."

When the man hesitated again, Stitts realized that he was onto something. Fred was no idiot, no mindless suicide bomber.

He was a dangerous individual, one who'd already proven himself capable of murder. But he was calculated, and he had a purpose, however maligned it was.

"We, as a nation, need to—"

The sound of a door opening behind Stitts caused Fred to pull out of the sniper sight again.

Stitts didn't hesitate; he immediately dropped to the ground, laying his chest flat against the gravel and shielding himself beneath the two-foot-high brick overhang.

Then he whipped his head around, leading with his gun, thinking that perhaps the man had an accomplice after all.

But it wasn't one person, but two: a man and a woman.

Stitts immediately started shouting for them to get out of here, to head back down the stairs before it was too late.

Chapter 86

CHASE BURST THROUGH THE rooftop door and saw Stitts standing with his back to her, his arms in the air. At first, the scene didn't make sense; Stitts was too close to the edge of the roof to be standing there in front of the shooter and there was nobody behind him.

But before she could figure out what was happening, Stitts dropped to the ground and actually aimed the gun at her.

Peter came through the door next, but he had had his head down and didn't see Chase stop. He bumped into her, slipped on the gravel, and both of them went down.

This probably saved her life; saved *both* their lives.

Just as Stitts shouted at them to go back downstairs, she heard a shot.

Peter cried out and his left arm was thrust backward as the bullet tore into his shoulder, causing a spray of blood to coat the stairway door.

"Run, Chase, run!" Stitts yelled at her. But Chase was still on her hands and knees; she couldn't run.

And that's when she heard another voice, one that she didn't recognize.

"Don't move—tell them not to move or I'll shoot again!"

It took Chase several moments to realize that the voice was the shooter's and that it was coming from a cell phone in Stitts's hand.

Seeing no alternative, she froze.

Beside her, Peter tried to rise, only to stagger and fall again, his back butting up against the door. His mouth was twisted in agony, and the backward T-shirt was soaked with blood from his collarbone to his triceps.

"Fuck," Stitts swore. "Don't move, Chase. The sniper's over there, on the studio roof."

Chase's eyes flicked from Peter to Stitts, then she raised them slowly.

It was like deja vu; first, she'd seen the sniper barrel through the drone camera, and now she saw it with her own eyes.

Only this time, the barrel did not ignite with a bullet. At least not yet.

"Let them go!" Stitts shouted. "They've done nothing wrong!"

Chase's eyes whipped about, trying to figure out how they could all make it off the roof alive.

"You tricked me, Stitts. I thought we were in this together," she heard the voice on the phone say. He continued to speak, but Chase turned her attention elsewhere. She was trying to listen for the sounds of sirens in the air. After all, it had been at least ten minutes since she'd called for them.

But aside from the man speaking on the phone and Peter's labored breaths to her right, she heard nothing.

Stitts glared at her, fury in his eyes, his teeth clenched, saliva dripping from his lower lip.

"I'm sorry," Chase mumbled, although she wasn't sure what she was sorry for. She'd come here to save him and, in the process, had put herself directly in the line of fire.

"Ah, the feisty Agent Adams. I thought I recognized you. What are you doing up here? Come for a fix?"

Chase's eyes narrowed. It was this man who had posted the video of her on Woodley's show.

Woodley was just a pawn. A self-righteous asshole, to be sure, but also just a pawn in Fred's deadly game.

"I want you to stand and put your hands up," Fred ordered.

Chase had no other options. She slowly started to rise, but the man stopped her.

"Leave the gun on the ground," he instructed.

Chase did as she was asked and then rose to her feet, holding her hands up high.

"I think you're right, Stitts; I don't think you deserve to die. I think we are on the same page, want the same things for our country. But this woman? Agent Adams?"

He chuckled, and Chase felt her blood run cold.

"I don't think the public will be as upset about her being taken out, especially after the bit we aired about her. About her addiction, her stint in recovery. Oh, and you can thank your buddy in the Secret Service for that."

Chase's jaw went slack, an expression that was mirrored on Stitts's face.

"Yeah, that's right. You don't make friends easily, do you, Agent Adams? See the thing is, nowadays, if you piss someone off they don't even have to confront you about it. They can anonymously ruin your life with just a few strokes of the keyboard."

Chase was fuming.

She knew that SO Pratt was a piece of shit, but he'd gone too far. Stitts had warned her about cases that involved multiple agencies, but she'd not once considered the possibility that she would personally become a target.

Chase scolded herself for being so naive.

I should've grabbed Pratt when I had the chance, she thought. *I should've choked the bastard out.*

Chase looked at Stitts and then to Peter, who was writhing in agony.

Fred seemed to have forgotten about him, but Peter was in no shape to take any sort of action.

"Stitts? You still there? What do you think? You think that they make me a serial killer if I take out just another junkie? I wonder who funded her recovery program... I looked it up, by the way. Grassroots Recovery is an expensive place. I doubt that Agent Adams could afford that on her government salary. Just another way that this socialist government spends its money."

Chase did nothing. She simply stood there with her hands in the air. The longer this took, she surmised, the more likely it was that the police arrive.

If dispatch had deployed them, that is. And if Pratt's hatred for her ran as deep as it evidently did, that was a big *if*.

"Stitts? You better answer me before I—"

Stitts looked at her again. Something in his face gave her the impression that he was going to do something stupid.

"Don't even think about it, Stitts," she warned. "Don't do it."

But when Stitts averted his eyes, she knew that it was all lost.

"No!"

Stitts ignored her and leaped to his feet, placing his body directly between Chase and the shooter.

"Leave her alone," he yelled into the cell phone. "If you want to take someone out, take me out. But leave Chase out of it."

Chapter 87

STITTS CAST A GLANCE over his shoulder just to make sure that he was covering Chase completely and then held his arms out at his sides.

"Go through me, if you have to. But I'm not moving," he declared.

Fred growled on the other end of the line.

"Get out of the way, Stitts."

Stitts shook his head and glared at the man on the opposite rooftop. He was banking on the fact that they'd formed a bond of sorts, and that Fred wouldn't just kill him and then Chase afterward.

"No-I'm not moving."

Stitts didn't want to risk looking over his shoulder again, but he hoped that the stirring he heard was Chase preparing to run to the stairs.

"I'm going to give you to the count of three, Agent Stitts. One—"

But Stitts didn't do games like he didn't do coincidences.

So instead, he took control by starting to raise his gun.

"Stitts! Don't!" Chase yelled from behind him, but he was already in the zone.

He'd made up his mind and there was nothing anybody could say to stop him.

He'd failed Chase before, long ago, and once more recently.

He wasn't about to let her die.

There was no way he'd be able to take Fred out at this range even if there wasn't a threat of his chest being blown open by a Lapua Magnum round.

This is it, Stitts thought, surprised that he didn't feel sadness. Instead, he felt remorse. It dawned on him then that he'd also let someone else down in his life: his mother.

He'd enabled the woman to use, just as he had Chase.

And his mother had died because of her addiction.

There was no way that he was going to let the same thing happen to Chase. She was finally on the road to getting better, and Stitts refused to let a domestic terrorist turn that road into a dead end.

"I'm sorry," he whispered under his breath, and then aimed his gun and waited for the bullet to tear through his chest.

Chapter 88

FLOYD MONTGOMERY MADE IT down the staircase and out of the building without incident. His plan was to do exactly as Stitts had instructed: run to safety, then call Chase.

But that was before he noticed a glint of reflected sunlight coming not from the roof that Stitts was standing on, but the one opposite.

He shielded his eyes with the blade of his hand, and then his breath caught in his throat.

The shooter was on the roof and he had his sniper rifle trained on the doorway from which Stitts was about to exit.

Floyd's first instinct was to shout, to warn Stitts, but he quickly quashed this idea. That would only serve to get him *and* Stitts shot.

But he had to do something.

Floyd was long and gangly, but he was also fast. He sprinted across the street and then pressed himself against the front door to the studio where he waited to catch his breath. He half expected shots to ring out, but the shooter was too focused on the opposite roof to have seen him.

After several heart-pounding moments, Floyd pulled the door open and stepped inside the studio.

Truth be told, he wasn't exactly sure what he was going to do. He wasn't a trained soldier; he was just a driver. A driver that Chase probably only gave the job because she took pity on him, and then placated him by referring to him as an FBI assistant.

Get out of here, Floyd. Just go call the cops, let them do their job.

But something drove Floyd onward and upward. He passed the recording studio, noting that the green screen was peppered with bullet holes, and then found the stairwell.

As quietly as possible, Floyd made his way to the second floor, then the third. It dawned on him that he had nothing to protect himself with—no gun, no weapon at all—and it wasn't like he was the smoothest of tongue, either.

There's no way he was going to be able to talk the shooter down.

He made it all the way to the door on the roof, before concluding that this was a terrible idea.

"St-st-st-stupid," he whispered to himself, shaking his head. He'd retreated down two rungs when he heard shouting and moved back to the door. Through the window, he could only see part of the shooter's back, but he knew that the man had taken aim.

A cold sweat suddenly broke out over his entire body.

You don't belong here, Floyd. His internal voice told him. *You're just a driver.*

There was no denying it; he *didn't* belong here.

But just as he was about to flee back down the stairs, he caught a flicker of movement from the other rooftop.

And then his heart stopped beating entirely.

It wasn't Stitts; Stitts was still out of sight.

It was Chase. She had somehow made her way to the roof and then had fallen on all fours.

Swallowing hard, Floyd reached for the door and slowly opened it, staying on his knees just in case the shooter turned around and took aim. But the man was yelling something at Chase, and he didn't appear to hear the door opening.

Nor did he hear Floyd as he slowly made his way across the gravel.

Floyd made sure to remain low the entire time, trying to stay out of sight. It would do him no good if Stitts saw him and suddenly cried out his name.

"I'm to give you the count of three, Agent Stitts. One—" the sniper yelled. Now that he'd closed the distance to under ten feet, Floyd could see the man start to tense, to prepare for the rifle's recoil.

When Stitts started to raise his hand with the gun, the shooter wiggled his hips to root himself in the gravel.

Knowing that he'd probably already waited too long to act, Floyd threw safety out the window, leaped to his feet, and screamed as he ran at the shooter.

Chapter 89

SOMEONE SCREAMED.

Chase thought it could've been her. She thought maybe she'd seen a flash of muzzle fire and that Stitts's chest had been ripped open by a high caliber round. And then she screamed.

But when Stitts just stared at himself in confusion, she realized that the only blood on the rooftop was from Peter.

Fred hadn't fired.

Stitts managed to bring his gun all the way up and even aim it across the roof, but Fred hadn't squeezed off a round.

Realizing that they had little time to react, she sprinted for her partner. Her shoulder connected just above his hip so hard that she almost sent them both over the roof.

Stitts landed awkwardly, his face buried in the gravel, while Chase fell on top of him.

"Stay down." She cursed. Chase didn't know why Fred hadn't still fired, or how much time they had before he came to his senses, but there was still something else she had to do.

Peter Horrowitz was exposed, and he'd already lost a lot of blood.

Chase started to raise her head when Stitts grumbled something unintelligible.

She pushed his face even deeper into the gravel.

"Stay down," she repeated.

Something was happening on the other rooftop, she realized. A struggle of some sort; she heard shouting.

Chase lifted her head quickly, then ducked back down, only to pop up again a second later.

"Floyd?" she whispered. "Floyd? What in the holy fuck are you doing?"

Chapter 90

FLOYD HAD NO IDEA what he was doing; he was no fighter.

As soon as he let loose the closest thing he could manage to a battle cry, the shooter rolled onto his back and put his feet up defensively.

Floyd's intention had been to land on top of the man, maybe bash his face on the tripod supporting his rifle, knock him out cold like in the movies.

He failed miserably, and it was a wonder that he didn't go flying over the side of the roof.

The man drove his feet into Floyd's abdomen as he jumped, but the blows landed unevenly, sending him spinning into a circle to his left.

Just as Floyd managed to scramble back to his feet, the shooter pounced on him.

The man was not particularly large, he might have even been on the slender side, but he was solid muscle. He also clearly had training.

Floyd had neither.

Before even registering what had happened, the man had mounted him, putting his knees on either side of Floyd's hips, and then pressing his weight down on his abdomen.

Desperate now, Floyd tried to shove the man off him, but he barely moved.

"Get off me!" Floyd shouted.

He swung his fists wildly at the man's face, but he simply leaned back to avoid each awkward punch.

"If I knew you'd be so much trouble, I'd have taken you out instead of tying you up," the man said.

Floyd tried punching again, but this time after parrying the blows, the man wrapped his hands around his throat.

Floyd instinctively reached for the man's arms and hands, trying everything he could think of to peel them off.

But the sniper's grip was like a vice.

By the time Floyd realized that this tactic wasn't going to work, his energy was so depleted that his options had become extremely limited.

His breath was coming out in hisses and sprays, and stars began to speckle his narrowing vision.

Floyd gave up trying to tear the man's grip from his throat and instead tried to reach for anything to brain the bastard with. But all he found was a handful of loose gravel, and even throwing it into the man's eyes did nothing to lessen his grip.

The collapsing darkness was suddenly penetrated by the sound of three gunshots.

The sniper was so enraged, so consumed with killing Floyd, that he didn't appear to hear the first shot. But when the second winged his shoulder and the third passed just inches over his head, the man ducked down and then looked across the roof.

This was the break that Floyd needed. With the man distracted, he jabbed two fingers into the crimson bullet wound on his shoulder.

The sniper cried out and protectively leaned to his left. Floyd didn't even have a rudimentary background in martial arts, but he'd seen enough fights and listened to enough Joe Rogan commentary to know what to do next. He first shifted his weight to his left hip, then immediately bucked with his right.

The sniper flipped onto his side and Floyd scrambled to his feet.

"Get up!" Floyd screamed. "F-f-f-fight like a man!"

As predicted, the man couldn't back down from a challenge. He pulled himself upward, but only managed one step before two more shots rang out.

Floyd didn't know who took the shots—whether it was Stitts or Chase—but their aim was true.

Two red cherry blossoms appeared in the center of the sniper's chest and a confused expression crossed his face.

Ever the opportunist, Floyd strode forward and planted his hands firmly on the two new bullet holes. He shoved hard, so hard, in fact, that when he pulled his hands away, they were covered in blood.

"No!" the sniper managed to shout as he backpedaled.

He almost caught his footing. *Almost.*

But just as he planted his left shoe, his right ankle clipped the ledge. His eyes went wide, his arms pinwheeled, and then he went over the side.

Floyd would never forget that expression. For as long as he lived, he would never forget the face of a man who realized that he was about to die.

In his head, Floyd counted to three before he heard a wet, organic splat as the man's body struck the pavement six stories down.

Chapter 91

"YES, FOR THE LAST fucking time, Stitts, I promise I won't take out my gun," Chase said.

Stitts made a face.

"I'd just feel more comfortable if you left it in the car."

"And I feel more comfortable with it on my hip," Chase replied quickly.

She had no intention of shooting either Pratt or Woodley, truth be told. But she would be lying if she said she hadn't at least thought about it.

"Would you two stop f-f-fighting," Floyd said as he turned the wheel to the left. He was staring out the window, evidently searching for an address that they'd somehow managed to pry out of Homeland.

"Yeah, you heard the man. Stop fighting with me, Stitts. 'Cuz we all know, Floyd doesn't need a gun to do his damage."

Chase expected a chuckle out of one of them, but it was too soon, and the car fell into an uncomfortable silence. Eventually, Floyd leaned out the window again.

"This is really it? It looks like a… like a d-d-dump."

Stitts shrugged.

"I think that's a point, Floyd. Besides, I think it's about time we stopped judging things by the way they look on the outside."

Chase made a face.

"Oh, sweet, a PSA from Daddy Stitts."

"Let's just focus, here. And no shooting, Chase. The last thing we want is your face all over TV again."

Chase shifted her head from side to side.

The man had a point. Now that the video that Woodley had played went viral, she was going to have to work hard to maintain a more 'proper' image.

The good news was, Director Hampton and the FBI couldn't deny her success. They didn't have Homeland Security, the Secret Service, or the Department of Justice to thank for saving Senator McBain's life, as well as all the other congressmen and senators who backed the recently passed Bill S-89.

No, they only had two FBI agents and an assistant to thank for that.

"Yeah, this is the place," Chase said. She spotted several unmarked black cars on either side of the street.

She hopped out of the car even before Floyd had brought it to a complete stop.

Stitts hurried after her.

"Chase, wait up."

But Chase didn't slow.

She neared the front door, which was manned by two Secret Service agents who she didn't recognize, and immediately flipped open her badge.

"FBI," she said.

The two men looked unimpressed.

"No one is allowed—"

The man didn't even manage a full sentence before the door behind him opened and two men stepped out.

"Don't worry about it," Chase said with a smile. "These were just the two I was looking for."

Hearing her voice caused Pratt to look up and over the shoulder of William Woodley whom he was leading out of the house in handcuffs. Pratt's face was a particularly dark shade of pink, a clear indication that he wasn't happy about having to release Woodley.

That he'd made a mistake parading a man around town who'd turned out to just be a pawn in Fred Browe's game of politics and murder.

"What do you want?" Pratt hissed.

Chase ignored him; she would deal with him later. But first...

"William Woodley, how are you feeling? Did they rough you up in there?"

Woodley glared at her. He had matching black eyes and a split lip. Also, some of his fake tan had been wiped off the left side of his face, making it look like he had a severe case of vitiligo.

"I'm gonna sue. I'm gonna sue you and the FBI, DEA, IRS, every person I can think of. You're gonna pay for what you did to me. And I'm going to air it all on my show. You think what I showed last time was big?" Woodley chuckled. "That's only the beginning. I've got so much dirt—"

Her hand instinctively went to her hip and she felt Stitts tense at her side, thinking that she was reaching for her gun.

"No, I don't think so," she said calmly, pulling her cell phone out of her pocket.

"Oh, yeah? Oh, *yeah*? You wait and see. I've got millions—"

Chase started to play the video, turning it around for both Woodley and Pratt to see.

"—of followers, yeah I know. You're some sort of Internet sensation. Let me ask you something, William. How would you feel if your loyal followers saw you like this?"

Woodley squinted at the phone screen. When she heard his whiny, sniffling voice out of the phone's speaker, Chase knew that they'd gotten to the part where a nude Woodley was being dragged out of the tub.

"You know what I think? I think you might change your tone a little bit on your show," Chase said with a grin. "And I think you're going to take back what you said about me. You're going to tell your followers that all that nonsense was made up, that I'm an upstanding member of society and that I not only solved this crime but that I'm a valuable asset to the FBI. Oh, you can also tell them that I'm damn good looking, too."

Woodley's face went through a series of convolutions, a process she'd seen before; it was as if he was deciding on what expression was appropriate.

In the end, he just ended up looking pathetic.

"Delete it," Woodley said, bowing his head.

"I will; I'll delete it after you air the piece about me," Chase said, slipping the cell phone back into her pocket. Then she reached out and gave him a patronizing pat on the shoulder.

He didn't look up this time.

"Okay, that's enough," Pratt barked, as he led Woodley past Chase and down the walkway towards one of the unmarked cars.

"No, I don't think it is," Chase replied.

SO Pratt turned around and glared at her.

"What?"

Chase hurried up to the man and then lowered her voice so only the three of them would be able to hear.

"You're going to make sure he says that stuff about me on the air. And you're going to make sure that it sticks."

Pratt made a face.

"Fuck you."

It was an unexpectedly harsh reply, but it didn't bother Chase. To her surprise, however, it affected Stitts, and she saw him reach for his gun out of the corner of her eye.

Chase put her hand on his and moved it away from the pistol.

"No, fuck you, Pratt," Chase shot back, no longer bothering to temper her tone now. "You are going to do it or I'm gonna tell every person I know that you leaked secret information about an FBI agent to a man who was working for a domestic terrorist."

Pratt's eyes went wide.

"Yeah, I know it was you. Fred told me before he took his swan dive. But I've also got evidence. You see, what I'm learning about this whole Internet thing is that while anybody can make any claim they want, there are ways to trace it back to the source."

Pratt opened his mouth to say something again, but when he saw the other Secret Service agents staring at him, his gaping maw slammed shut.

Then he turned around and shoved Woodley roughly in the back.

"Let's go," he grumbled.

Stitts sidled up next to her and together they watched Pratt load Woodley into one of the unmarked cars and speed away.

"Good work, Agent Adams. Do me a favor? Remind me not to fuck with you in the future, alright?"

Chapter 92

"PETER SHOULD BE OUT of surgery now," Stitts said, glancing down at his phone. "He's gonna get a Purple Heart— not bad for a lowly ATF agent."

"He deserves it," Chase said. Floyd pulled into the hospital parking lot and parked the car. The three of them got out then, and with a surprisingly somber gait, they made their way to the front desk.

"We're looking for Peter Horrowitz," Chase asked the receptionist.

The woman gave her the up down, then said, "You ain't reporters, is you? Cuz I can't be havin' no reporters in der."

Chase shook her head and produced her FBI badge.

"Friends."

"Alrighty then, third floor. He just got outta surgery."

Chase nodded and the three of them took the elevator up to the third floor.

It wasn't hard to find Peter. The outside of his hospital room door was decorated with thank you cards from the friends and families of nearly every politician in Washington.

Inside, Chase saw Peter lying in bed, his head propped up on a pillow, his left hand in some sort of cast. And yet, he still had a laptop out in front of him and he was typing away with one hand.

Chase smirked, looked over at Stitts, and then opened the door.

"Peter Horrowitz, a national hero," she joked.

Peter looked up at her and smiled broadly.

"More like a sacrificial lamb."

"No, I think you m-m-mean sacrificial l-l-limb," Floyd corrected.

They all broke out laughing.

"Touché," Peter said after catching his breath.

Chase pulled up a chair next to the hospital bed, while Floyd and Stitts decided to hover by the door.

"You're not gonna believe this," Horrowitz began, turning the laptop for them all to see. "For all that talk on the rooftop? Well, Fred Browe wasn't just a libertarian mouthpiece. He was also a very, very rich man. I dug a little deeper into his history and found out that he'd invested in some local manufacturing companies back in the early two thousands. Made a killing on it, but as manufacturing started moving overseas, his stocks plummeted. It was about that time when he started the show, that he recruited Woodley. Oh, sure he might still be pissed off about what happened overseas, and what happened to his pal Mark Yablonski, but he also lost a shit ton of money. And Bill S-89? That was gonna cost him even more."

It saddened Chase to realize that she wasn't completely surprised by this fact. The stark reality was that when the loudest people started shouting 'America First,' what they really meant was, 'Me First.'

They didn't give a flying fuck about the country. The only thing they cared about was their own personal wealth.

"Forget about that," she said. "How'd the surgery go?"

Peter glanced at his fingertips that protruded from the end of the cast and wiggled them.

"With some physio, they tell me that I should regain complete feeling and function in six months to a year. All in all, not that bad, considering."

Chase nodded.

"Coulda been a lot worse," Stitts added, a sobering thought that gave them all pause.

"No shit," Peter said, closing his laptop. "You know, they say that the recovery can be difficult, especially if you don't have someone looking after you…"

For a second, Chase didn't catch on. But when she looked to Stitts and Floyd and saw them both smirking, she started to blush.

"Unless of course, you're going steady with William Woodley. After all, I couldn't help but catch his glowing report about how beautiful and productive an FBI agent you are," Peter continued with a smirk of his own.

Chase's face continued to heat up and she looked away. If the man wasn't confined to a hospital bed, she might've punched him.

"Maybe another time, Peter. Right now, we have work to do. The FBI needs its most beautiful agent to infiltrate the evildoers," Stitts said.

Stitts, on the other hand, wasn't a patient. Chase rose to her feet and punched him hard on the shoulder.

"Ow."

Still blushing, Chase turned to Peter and leaned down and kissed him gently on the cheek.

"Thanks," she said. "You know, I was beginning to think that everyone who worked for a government agency that had a three-letter acronym was a fucking asshole, Stitts included. But you? You're okay, Peter. You're all right."

Now Peter started to blush and, taking this as her cue to leave, Chase left the room.

Eventually, the trio found themselves back at Floyd's car.

"Where to now, A-a-a-agent Adams?" Floyd asked as he got behind the wheel.

"The airport. There's somewhere I need to go, there's someone that I never got a chance to say goodbye to. Somewhere warmer than here."

Floyd put the car into drive.

"I c-c-could use some sun. Alaska's mighty c-c-cold this time of year."

Chase shook her head and stared out the window.

"No, you're not coming with us, I'm afraid."

Even though she didn't see his face, she could feel the air in the room change; Floyd was crushed.

"Oh, okay," he said softly.

"You're going somewhere else, instead. I'm afraid it's not all that warm this time of year, but I think you're going to like it, nonetheless."

Floyd raised an eyebrow.

"Where am I g-g-g-going?"

"Virginia."

The confused expression remained on Floyd's face.

"Virginia? What's in V-v-v-virginia?"

"Quantico. Quantico and the FBI training headquarters. I think you've outgrown your title as FBI Assistant, don't you think, Stitts?"

Stitts smiled broadly.

"I think it's long overdue, Chase. *Long* overdue."

Epilogue

THE MAN WATCHED CHASE as she walked up to the gravestone with the name Keith Adams engraved on it.

Her head was low, and her hands jammed deep into the pockets of her jeans.

She looked very much like the way he remembered her. Short, pretty, with dark hair tucked behind her ears.

A flash of color distracted him, and the man looked down at the plastic case in his hand. The butterflies within could sense his excitement and their sparkling wings relentlessly banged against the enclosure.

"Soon," he whispered. "We'll get your chance soon."

Chase stood in front of the grave, head bowed. He thought he could hear her speaking, whispering, but he was too far away to make out any of the words.

He'd waited a long time for this; a long, *long* time.

The man glanced down at the case in his hand again and spied the lock of hair between the fluttering wings. He wanted to take it out then; he wanted to take it out and caress his cheek with it. He wanted to smell it, he wanted to breathe Chase in.

The one who got away.

The man took a deep breath, and when Chase backed away from the grave and raised her head to the sky, he started forward. He moved quickly, knowing that time was tight, that despite her small stature, Chase was feisty and would put up a fight.

She had before.

He held the case as steady as possible as he moved so as to not disturb the butterflies within. The man was within twenty feet now, when he saw another person approach.

At first, he thought that it was just a random passerby, and he debated waiting for him to continue on before proceeding with his plan.

But when the man brought a cigarette to his lips and wrapped his arm around Chase, he knew that this was no stranger.

Biting his lip hard enough to draw blood, the man slipped back into the shadows.

He watched the two embrace then he observed them all the way back through the line of gravestones to a waiting car. Then he watched the car drive off.

As if sensing his frustration, the butterflies worked themselves into a frenzy, their blue and indigo wings fluttering like iridescent confetti.

"It's okay, our time will come," the man said to his butterflies. "We've waited this long; we can wait a little bit longer. And trust me, it'll be worth it."

END

Author's Note

WHAT A BLAST. I had so much fun writing *Dirty Money*. I even bought a drone to do some research, to figure out what it would really be like to put the goggles on and feel like you were flying without a plane. I often take real situations and spice them up before putting them in a scene in my book, but in this case, I'm not ashamed to admit that Chase's reaction was exactly my own.

If you ever get a chance to wear the goggles while someone is flying a drone, I highly recommend it. Nerd *out*.

Many of you were very upset with the ending of Amber Alert, writing me messages saying that I was cruel to kill Chase off this way. I understand that. But what you need to know is that Chase is nothing if not resilient. After all she's been through, she keeps on trucking. Sure, er truck stalls, runs out of gas, and occasionally malfunctions, but in the end, it keeps on running.

Oh, one more thing; if you're wondering about the Epilogue—and you should be—and want a hint as to who this mysterious man is, I suggest taking a look at a particular series that involves a man with alcohol dependency. A man who may or may not be a Detective in New York. Just sayin'.

Next year, 2019, is going to be a big one for Chase. She's back in early February with Devil's Den—on the hunt for a depraved serial killer—which is on pre-order now. But that's not all; she's slated to team up with an old friend in a new Super Thriller Series. I can't wait.

Well, that's it. I'm tired and my brain needs to recharge. Thanks for spending a few hours with Chase and her friends. I hope to see you again soon.

You keep reading and I'll keep writing.
Pat
Montreal, 2018

P.S. A note about Floyd: I love the guy, which is why I brought him back. And his stutter is a part of who is, too. But I hope, hope, *hope,* Chase pays for some speech therapy classes for the guy, because it truly is the most annoying thing to write. Oh, and I dictate my books now, so you can only imagine what sort of electron fart my computer has when I go full Floyd mode. Cheers.

Made in the USA
Middletown, DE
06 May 2019